The One You Cannot Have

Also by Preeti Shenoy

The Secret Wish List
It Happens For a Reason
Why We Love the Way We Do
It's All in the Planets
A Hundred Little Flames
The Rule Breakers
The Magic Mindset
A Place Called Home

The One You Cannot Have

PREETI SHENOY

HarperCollins *Publishers* India

First published in 2013

This edition published in India by HarperCollins *Publishers* in 2022

HarperCollins Publishers India, Cyber City, Building 10-A, Gurugram, Haryana-122002, India
www.harpercollins.co.in

2 4 6 8 10 9 7 5 3

P-ISBN: 978-93-5629-250-5
E-ISBN: 978-93-5629-264-2

Typeset by Ram Das Lal

Printed and bound at
MicroPrints India, New Delhi

MIX
Paper
FSC FSC™ C218906

This product is made of FSC®-certified and other controlled material.

HarperCollins Publishers, Macken House, 39/40 Mayor Street Upper, Dublin 1, D01 C9W8, Ireland

For Satish, Atul and Purvi, as always.
And for Manu too.

What happens to a dream deferred?

Does it dry up
like a raisin in the sun?
Or fester like a sore
And then run?
Does it stink like rotten meat?
Or crust and sugar over
like a syrupy sweet?

Maybe it just sags
like a heavy load.

Or does it explode?

– Langston Hughes

Chapter 1

Aman

Uprooting oneself is never easy and now that the final moment has come, I find myself unprepared.

I don't think Mark even realises the emptiness I feel inside me.

'All set, Aman? You must be looking forward to moving back to India then?' he says, as he sinks into the plush leather sofa and reaches for a can of beer.

I look at the bare walls where the Madhubhani paintings I had got from India had hung and I examine the holes left by the nails. Mark and I had hammered them into the wall, two years ago, when I had moved into this flat. The nails yanked out by Mark lie on the floor now.

'You know, in India, we don't have to do stuff like this,' I reply, avoiding his question, concentrating instead on the task at hand. I take out the tube of wall-filler bought at Thorns, the best store in Norwich for all such things. I look at it. 'Flexible filler decorator. For sealing and filling gaps and cracks before decorating,' it reads. I squeeze out the required amount of the sealant carefully and fill the two holes in the wall. I add finishing touches to my repair work and stand back to admire it. Now it only needs a coat of paint.

'That's right. I know. And in India, you lead the life of a maharaja with four servants to do your bidding,' replies Mark as he takes a swig of beer, resting his leg on the coffee table.

'Well, not four servants. But at least we can afford to hire people to do our laundry and we don't have clauses in our rental agreements which force one to fill holes like this,' I reply.

Mark chuckles. 'Filling holes ain't so bad, eh?' he drawls trying to do an Australian accent, but failing miserably and sounding very much English.

'Depends on which ones,' I retort and we both laugh, our laughter abating my feelings somewhat.

I clear up all the nails and sweep up the dust on the floor. Mark adds a second coat of paint to my patch-work on the wall.

'It looks as good as new,' I tell him. And it does.

'Hmmm. You know, Aman, I was thinking of planning a trip to India once you're settled there,' he says.

'You must, Mark. India is a fantastic place. It has beaches, mountains, hills, tons of culture—you name it,' I reply.

'If I come, will you introduce me to some nice Indian girls?'

'I do not know any "nice" Indian girls, Mark,' I say.

And then, almost immediately, I think of Anjali.

She has been emailing me a lot recently. I am not sure what she wants from me. After Shruti, I am wary of getting close to anybody. And the last thing I want is a long-distance relationship. Or any relationship for that matter. I am happy to be immersed in my work. I don't want to give Anjali any false hope.

Women are funny that way—you respond politely to them and they presume you are interested. I have tried to be as casual as possible in my erratic replies to her. It is as much of a red flag as I can wave. But Anjali refuses to back down and though it bothers me a little, it doesn't bother me enough to be overly concerned or worried about her advances, if they can be so termed.

'No? Not even one? Really?' Mark looks incredulous.

'Just wait until Eva hears this. I will tell her about your secret agenda to visit India,' I wink.

'Don't even joke about it. She will never let me visit you then,' he says, his face instantly changing its expression and his grey-green eyes narrowing. He runs his hand through his blond hair worriedly.

I don't want to mention Anjali to Mark. He would never understand.

Mark has only two goals when it comes to women.

One, to get them to bed on the first date and two; to get them to bed on any date. Mark's height is about 6' 1" and muscular to boot. He has the kind of body that can make it to the cover of a men's fitness magazine. He works out thrice a week and plays football with the boys twice a week. He is very conscious of his appearance, and with his kind of looks and charm, he is popular with women.

In the three years that I have known him (I had known him before I moved to the UK as we had worked on some projects together), he has slept with at least eight women, even while having a steady relationship with Eva. Initially, I had found it very odd, my moral compass being at variance with Mark's.

Friday nights are, by default, music night at a local pub. Mark and the others in my department (all English, I am the only Indian) have a routine they do on these pub visits. They call it 'pulling'. This basically means attracting women and charming them enough to get them to go to bed with them. When they had first mentioned to me that they would be out at the pub 'pulling', I had asked 'Pulling what?' at which they had all burst into laughter.

Later I had learnt the subtle differences between the slang used by the British and the kind used back in India. In the UK, shagging meant having sex, while in India, it meant pleasuring yourself. They had other, amusing terms for that: 'buffing the banana', 'applying the handbrake', 'teasing the weasel' and the most hilarious one—'rounding up the tadpoles'. It had taken me only a very brief while to get used to their accents, customs and usages and now, after two years, I feel right at home in Norwich with Mark and my other English friends.

'So, let us do the final recce then, eh? Do you have the list?' asks Mark.

I take out the rental agreement the real estate agent had given me when I had moved in. In the UK, unlike in India, they are very meticulous about property. The realtor had, along with me, examined each and every mark on the wall, noted each detail on the list that she had carried.

'Crack on wall in foyer, small mark on wall facing the garden in the hall, dent on boiler,' the list went on, making a precise note on the shape and condition of the property. At the time of handing back a property, the agent would compare it against this list. Any deviations would have to be taken care of by me. This was why I was so careful about repairing the holes left by nails. I do not want to shell out my hard-earned pounds towards damage to property. In the two years that I have worked here, I have saved up quite a bit and have a comfortable nest egg with which I intend buying an apartment in India. I don't want anything, especially the cost of repair, to make a dent in my plans.

Mark and I compare everything that is on the list.

'So, all done then. I think we are handing it back to them in a better shape than it was in when we rented it,' comments Mark. And I realise it is true.

Habits formed in childhood die hard and I have been meticulous about housekeeping from an early age. Baba passed away when I was seven and since then my mother raised me singlehandedly. As a child, I would feel miserable seeing her struggle to make both ends meet, and to help her out, I would tidy up the home before she came back from work. I wanted to make her life a little easier. Ever since I have told her I am moving back, she is over the moon even though I am relocating to Bangalore, not Gwalior where she lives.

Mark carries my suitcases to his car and puts them in the boot. There are a few formalities to be taken care of at work before I move to India and I will be spending the last two days of my stay in the UK at a hotel close to office.

'Let me shut down the heating and then we shall lock up and hand over the keys,' I say, as I dash upstairs to the boiler room. All homes in the UK have a central heating system which comprises a huge metallic boiler housed in a 'boiler room'. One can control the temperature, the settings and other things here. One would freeze to death without the heating.

When I turn off the boiler switch, I notice that the latch to the attic has come loose. The door, which is on the roof, has swung downwards and is open.

I am not tall enough to reach it without a ladder, so I call out to Mark.

'Hey, Mark, just come and shut this attic door for me, will you?' I peep out of the window on the first floor and call out to him.

Mark bounds up the stairs.

He reaches the door easily and pushes it back against the roof but finds something obstructing it.

He tries once more with the same result.

'Get me something I can stand on. There seems to be something up there,' he says.

'I called you because I felt too lazy to go to the garage and get the ladder and now you want me to get it,' I grumble.

'It is up to you. Shall we just leave it then?'

'No, wait, I'll get it,' I say. I rush downstairs to the garage, unlock it and carry the ladder up the stairs.

Mark climbs up and I hold the ladder steady.

From up there he says, 'Hey, there seems to be a suitcase up here.' As he takes it down, its clasp opens and the contents tumble out.

I freeze. I had forgotten all about this suitcase. I had shoved it up in the attic when I had first moved here.

It feels as though someone has punched me in the gut. I try to open my mouth but no words come out. My heart beats frantically. My hands go cold.

It is funny what memories can do to you. How they can grip you by the throat, choke you, strangle you. And just when you thought you had it all sorted, too.

Mark looks at me questioningly.

And finally I say, 'Fuck,' as I look at the contents of the suitcase now scattered on the floor.

Chapter 2

Shruti

'It would be nice to spend Diwali with my folks, like last year,' declares Rishabh as he enters the flat and throws down his laptop bag in the drawing room, on the carpet, like he always does.

It irks me today though, how casually he does it. I have told him several times that I don't want that bag in the middle of the drawing room. Can't he see how house-proud I am, for God's sake? And how well I have done up the apartment? Our apartment is tiny (all of 900 square feet), which is supposedly 'okay' by Mumbai standards. For a person who has spent all her life in Bangalore and has grown up in a large bungalow, this 900-square-foot matchbox is hard to get used to. Whenever I complain that we do not have enough space, Rishabh never fails to remind me that we live in Lokhandwala Complex in Andheri, which supposedly is one of the nicer suburbs.

'Rishabh—please don't throw your bag down on the carpet. How can you just leave it in the middle of the room like that? How many times do I have to remind you?' I am annoyed now. His bag is such an eyesore. But he is oblivious to how out-of-place it looks.

'Sorry, baby. I forgot. I will take it inside later,' he says as he switches on the TV and flips channels.

I sit beside him, my eyes still on the bag. I wait for him to pick it up, my irritation growing with each minute. But Rishabh shows no signs of budging.

'Do we have orange juice? Get me some, na,' he says as he slumps further into the sofa, fully engrossed in a cricket match now, which is a replay of a test match between India and Australia. What men find fascinating in a match of which you already know the results, I don't know. And now he wants me to get him orange juice too.

I grit my teeth and do not respond.

He looks at me and realises I am angry.

'*Arey*—why do you always make a fuss? I will put it away when I get up. I told you, right.'

'You never do. It always lies there till *I* put it away.'

'That is because you put it away before I get up. You never give me a chance.'

'I like the house clean. Look how well I have done it up.'

I have picked blue and white linen curtains. They contrast beautifully with the white futon and cream sofas that one can sink into. The carpet from Fab India is sea-blue and it goes well with the curtains. The whole effect is modern, plush, comfortable and luxurious, giving the room the illusion of spaciousness. And there is Rishabh's ugly bag right in the middle of it all.

I cannot bear the sight of it anymore. I jump up and carry his bag and place it inside the closet in the spare room which doubles as a guest bedroom, which is where he should have kept it in the first place.

'See? You never give me a chance. I would have taken it,' he says, amused.

I don't smile back. I go to the fridge and pour the juice and hand it over to him.

'You are such a sweetheart. I love you, baby,' he says as he pulls me towards him and motions for me to sit in his lap. I sit next to him and find my anger slowly dissipating. It is hard to be angry with Rishabh for long. He is an amiable guy, most of the time. He doesn't get ruffled like me. I tend to flare up in an instant but I also cool down very fast. Rishabh, however, is always calm.

In the time that we have been married, he has lost his temper only once. It was with his office colleague. Then, too, he had not raised his voice. Just the steel in his voice and his ice-calm manner as he expressed exactly what he felt without mincing words, had given me the jitters.

Rishabh puts his right arm over my shoulders and draws me to him, as he holds his juice in the other hand and sips it. I am bored with cricket and I want to flip channels. His mobile rings and when he mutes the television to answer it, I get the perfect opportunity to flip to my favourite music channel.

'Yeah—schedule it for tomorrow. Noon. In the morning I am meeting two others,' I hear him say on the phone. 'And is that a he or a she?' he asks. He listens to the reply. 'Oh yes, I had presumed Aman is a guy, but I had a doubt as I thought you said "she". Anyway I will see her tomorrow,' he says as he hangs up.

I have frozen on hearing the name Aman. I don't even notice when Rishabh grabs the remote from my hand and changes the channel back to the cricket match.

The name Aman still has the power to set my heart racing and give me goosebumps. I have a hundred thousand memories associated with Aman. Indelible memories. After all, four years of one's life is considerable time to spend with someone and even today, after nearly two years of my marriage to Rishabh, it takes little to trigger memories of our time together.

I think of how when I would make the morning coffee, I would text Aman nonstop. I would go on till the buzzing phone woke him and he replied to me. I think of the silly little code words we had which made sense only to both of us. I think of how I had teased him about his name. I had told him that he was just A-man. He had replied that for me he might have been just A-man, but for him, I was his whole world. I had kissed him then. He had held me that day, as it rained outside and we had sat listening to the sound of raindrops on the window panes. I think of what an impossibly wonderful relationship it was. Suddenly, without warning, I am filled with a deep sense of longing. A sense of loss. A sense of despondency and helplessness.

And even though my husband's arms are around me and I am resting my head on his shoulders, as he absently strokes my hair, his brow knitted in deep concentration watching his cricket, I realise I am a thousand miles away. I am in a different place. I am in a time when nothing mattered to me except Aman.

I continue sitting there with Rishabh till he asks me if I have made dinner or whether he should order Chinese takeaway, his favourite meal. It takes me a few minutes to comprehend his query.

Finally, I tell him to choose and we end up walking up to a restaurant nearby called Wang's Kitchen. The main road near Lokhandwala has a lot of eateries and we are spoilt for choice.

I have to force myself to concentrate on what Rishabh is saying during the meal. He tells me that he is expanding his team and is conducting interviews to hire a new person. I am glad that he loves his job at Club Happiness, a holiday and resorts company. His rise in his workplace has been meteoric, and he now has a team of six people working under him. He tells me that he has scheduled three interviews for tomorrow.

'I know, I overheard your conversation,' I say.

'Oh did you? I am interviewing someone called Aman who I presumed was a guy. Turns out it is short for Amandeep and it's a lady. Such a funny name,' he says.

'No, I like the name. It is nice,' I say, to my own surprise.

'I didn't know you liked Punju names. Next you will tell me you like Baljeet,' he teases.

I refuse to take the bait. Also I don't want to elucidate on my fascination for the name 'Aman'. I have never mentioned Aman to Rishabh and I don't intend to start now.

'So who are the others you are interviewing? Are they any good?' I ask him, cleverly changing the topic as the waiter serves us soup.

'Look promising. Let's see,' he says.

He asks me about work and how my day was.

I tell him that a commercial vehicles manufacturing company has signed a memorandum of understanding with our finance division for their new range and I have to prepare a press release for the same. I also talk about how I have to chase journalists to get them to cover it.

'You know, Club Happiness truly needs some serious PR talent like you,' he says.

'Hire me. Do you want to interview me?' I smile.

'It is definitely a possibility, Ms Shruti. Now, where do you see yourself in five years?' he asks.

'In a bigger, better bungalow in Bangalore as I plan to relocate. Who wants to stay in overcrowded Mumbai, where flats are the size of a matchbox?' I reply, smartly.

'Hmmm. That is a possibility. Club Happiness does have a branch in Bangalore. If we offer you a position there, would you join us?' he asks.

'Shut up and make it happen instead of showing me some dreams. I am not your woolly-eyed client whom you can sell a travel package as a holiday of a lifetime,' I tease him back.

'Ouch. That is below the belt. We don't fool our clients.'

'Yeah, you only fool your wife.'

'The customer is not an idiot, she is your wife,' he says, quoting David Ogilvy, the ad-man I admire immensely. I had written a paper on him in the final year of my PR and Advertising course. Naturally, I have studied all the books he has written.

'Ogilvy also said, "The best ideas come as jokes. Make your thinking as funny as possible" and right now you aren't being funny Mr Rishabh Prasad, just annoying,' I say. Rishabh smiles.

'See, this is why I love you. You speak your mind and are so clever,' he says.

I sit in silence and sip the soup. He does not know that I don't always speak my mind and I am happy to let it be this way. There are some things best left buried. Like past memories that creep up on you.

When we have sex that night, I am slightly more aggressive than usual. I kiss Rishabh with ferocity. I can see he is taken aback by this slight shift in my style but he quickly recovers and kisses me back with equal passion.

Later as I fall asleep, I can't help thinking that it is the best sex we have had in a long, long time. And all through it I had only been thinking of Aman.

Chapter 3

Aman

Preserving keepsakes and memories when a relationship is over is a bad idea. But the sentimental fool that I am, I just couldn't bear to throw them out. Perhaps I have held on to them in the hope that it isn't over. Perhaps a small part of me has a tiny bit of hope that Shruti and I *might* get back together someday. Now, strewn all across the floor, these symbols of our love stir emotions that are hard to bear.

Mark looks at me questioningly as if to say, 'Uh-oh', and then looks at the scattered contents. He probably guesses their significance, but he is too English and too polite to show any emotion. I pick up a handmade book which lies open at a photograph of Shruti and me smiling into the camera. I am hugging her from behind and my face nestles in her shoulder. Shruti had made a book of memories for me which was a record of every single date we had gone on. She had made this scrapbook painstakingly, by hand, filled it with photos, the bus-tickets of the rides we had taken together, especially that weekend trip to Mysore, the restaurant bills and tickets to even the house of horrors we had visited, which had scared her witless. Shruti was such a romantic—every little detail mattered to her. She had taken almost a year to put this book together and had given it to me on my birthday. Perhaps her sentimentalism had rubbed off on me. I don't know why it is, but I cherish this book. This was the first time ever that someone had created something so beautiful, exclusively for me. It was like a precious phase of our lives was captured in these pages. And it is so painful now to even look at it.

I gather it up hurriedly and close it.

There is also a beautiful wooden statue of a cat that she had got for me. I had once told her I liked cats but had never had one as a child as my mother was working and there simply wasn't time for luxuries like a pet. There is a gold-plated ring studded with zircon stones which I had given her. She had returned it when she left me. What could I do with it? I couldn't take it back to the store. There is a bottle of Versace cologne. I just couldn't bear to use it after she had walked out. And then there are at least about eighty cards. Shruti was artistic and her hobby was card-making. She would make these cards for the smallest occasion and 'surprise' me. She would spray it with the perfume she used—Eternity by Calvin Klein. Even now, I get a whiff of it as I pick up each card. The smell used to drive me insane. I have carefully kept every single one. As I gather them one by one and put them back into the box, each one feels like a cold sharp knife plunged into my heart. There is a blue and white striped T-shirt which she had bought for me. It was a size too small and I could neither wear it nor bear to give it away. There is a Calvin and Hobbes book which she gave me when I had told her Calvin was my favourite character. There is a wallet—an expensive one from Hidesign which she had bought for me with her first salary, a mobile phone cover which I had used for a while (the inner flap still has her picture in it), and a Sheaffer pen.

These are what is left of the four happiest years of my life.

The pain in seeing the physical evidence of something that no longer exists except in my memories, is excruciating.

There is a lump in my throat as I pick up everything hurriedly and shove it back into the suitcase.

'Are you okay, mate?' asks Mark, his eyes full of concern.

I nod.

But I am not okay.

'Do you need a drink?' he asks and I nod again.

I am unable to speak. I carry the suitcase to Mark's car and place it with the rest of my luggage. We sit in silence as Mark drives us both to Coach and Horses, one of our regular haunts.

Mark orders a beer for himself and, without asking, a whisky for me. I don't protest. Just by looking at my ashen face, he has figured it all out.

I am still trying to compose myself. But the truth of all that Shruti and I meant to each other has returned to haunt me. I had shut out all the memories of our love in a box. Literally. But today the illusion that I have healed and moved on has been shattered. After two years, the wounds have opened up again and made me realise that what has healed was just the surface. Underneath it is still raw, it is still painful. Lacerating. Unbearable.

'I gather it was hard then, eh?' says Mark.

Before I can reply, my phone rings. When I see the caller's name flashing, I excuse myself and step outside the pub to take the call. The cold English air hits my face and I slide the sleeve of my jacket over my hand.

'Hey, Vikram, how are you? And the kids and Dipika?' I greet him, trying to make my voice as normal as I can. This call from him is a welcome distraction.

'Hey, Aman, all of us are waiting eagerly. You arrive on Saturday morning, right?'

'Yes. I land in Mumbai and take the first flight to Bangalore,' I confirm.

'Good good, we're all waiting for you. Ria and Reema keep asking how many days are left for you to arrive. I am tired of answering them,' he says and I smile.

Vikram insists I stay with them, even though we both know that my office will accommodate me in the company guesthouse. I can never say no to Vikram. He has been a pillar of strength in my worst moment. I think of the time two years ago when I was so broken. It was he who goaded me to get out of India. It would do me good, he had said. He had completely understood my situation. He had, in his quiet way, given me a much-needed push, without even mentioning her name. I was too devastated at that time to think clearly, but he had actually done me a huge favour. It helped heal, to some extent, my wounded soul. Right from the days that I had joined as a management trainee, reporting to Vikram, he seemed to know exactly what I needed and had managed, as always, to steer me towards it.

The last time I was in India, Dipika had announced very solemnly that I was to be godfather to Ria and Reema.

'Godfather? As in Mario Puzo?' I had blinked.

Dipika had given me a mock-angry stare as if to say 'stop fooling around'. I actually hadn't been. I had no idea what being godfather to two little girls aged six and four meant. Vikram had shot me a warning look to comply. I did so and pretended to understand that if anything were to ever happen to her and Vikram, I would officially be responsible for the girls. I found it all too far-fetched, but had gone along just to please Dipika.

'Here, speak to Dipika. She is clamouring to take the phone from me,' says Vikram and Dipika comes on the line.

Dipika wants to know what time I will arrive and whether

or not I will join them for breakfast. Dipika is a very attractive woman and has a perfect, sculpted body. It is hard to not notice the sensuality she exudes without even being aware of it, which all the more adds to her appeal. God, even her voice is sexy. If she weren't Vikram's wife, and if I did not have such a good equation with him, I would have hit on her for sure.

'No, no. I will arrive by mid-morning, so will join you for lunch instead,' I answer.

'Great. Looking forward then. All of us, especially the girls, are waiting to see you,' she says as she hangs up.

I step back into the warmth of the pub, glad to be out of the cold.

I join Mark and see that my whisky has arrived. I realise that I haven't spoken about Shruti to anybody. Not even to Vikram, even though he had asked me about it.

But now that Mark has seen the contents of the box and my reaction to it, I feel I owe him some kind of explanation.

'You know, she is the reason I moved to Norwich,' I tell Mark.

'Whoa, that *is* intense,' he says.

I am not sure if he even realises what a relationship actually means. After all, even though he claims Eva is his girlfriend, he has had several flings with other women. I doubt Mark will understand something so deep, so pure and so genuine. I had been madly in love with Shruti when she walked out. Of course, she was in love with me too. Undoubtedly. How can women do this—be in love with one guy and marry another? I don't know.

For me, Shruti was truly 'The One' and I do not know if I will ever meet anyone like her. No one, just no woman, matches up to Shruti.

I do not know how to convey all this to Mark and I don't think any of it will even make any sense to him.

'So what happened then? Only if you want to talk about it, that is,' says Mark.

'I don't think her parents approved of me,' I say.

'What do you mean her parents didn't approve? Why? Was it like you did something? Or weren't you rich enough for them?' Mark is genuinely puzzled.

'No, we are from different communities. She is south Indian and I am north Indian. We have a caste system, and marriages outside the community aren't approved by elders,' I try to simplify the Indian scenario to Mark. In India, it is not just two people getting married, it is two families connecting. Everybody is involved in a wedding, unlike in the UK, where the bride and groom decide and plan everything themselves and even foot the bill for their wedding, and only the closest family and friends are invited.

Mark had asked me about arranged marriages in India (all foreigners I have met have—they are fascinated by the concept) and I had explained to him that it is just like setting up a date with a prospective partner, only in this case it is set up by parents. He had found it strange and shocking that an adult should allow his or her parents or relatives to choose a life partner for him or her. But I had not gone into the dynamics of the caste system and how it worked.

'So is that a problem then? Don't people from different communities get married in India?' asks Mark, now curious to know.

'In cities they do. Urban India is very different from rural India. In the villages it is still frowned upon,' I answer.

'Oh—so was she from a village then?'

I smile in response, trying to picture Shruti as a village belle.

'Of course not. It was complicated, Mark. Her mother got breast cancer and they did not know if she would make it. Her parents had been against me from the start. She broke up with me as her parents wanted her to get married to someone of their choice. I hope she is happy,' I say as I take a large sip of whisky.

Mark nods and we sit in silence finishing our drink. It is hard for me to even think about Shruti, let alone speak to Mark about her. Mark senses it and changes the topic deftly to the upcoming football game. Norwich has a great football team and they are playing against Everton on Friday. He talks about how much he is looking forward to it. I try my best to feign interest but Shruti has exploded back into my life with the power and force of a storm and I am reeling under the impact of the resurrected memories.

Mark drops me to my hotel and the check-in formalities are completed in no time. Once I am in my room, the black suitcase with memories of Shruti calls out to me. I don't want to revisit the past. It is sheer torture to do so.

But I am powerless. It is as though an invisible force is pulling me towards it. One part of me badly wants to throw this suitcase out. It is a dead relationship. It is over and she is now married to another guy, I remind myself. But another part of me wants to relive what I had with her, which is something that nobody can snatch away from me.

I walk up and down the length of the room. The room overlooks River Wensum and today even the breathtaking view of the river and the cobbled walkway beside it, lined with weeping willow trees and flower beds, fails to distract me. I see a young woman and her child walking along the river path. The child stops to feed the ducks that swim alongside. The woman watches and smiles at the child. I wonder if she is a single mother. Then I see a man walk up to both of them and kiss the woman on the lips. He puts his arm around her shoulders and says something to the child who runs ahead in glee as they watch indulgently. The happy scene sends a fresh wave of agony through me as I recall how Shruti had laughingly talked about the children we would have, how many and what we would name them. We had sat watching the placid waters of the Kabini river, near Bangalore, on one of our dates, she leaning against me. I had laughed in response and said that I wanted two daughters, and she said she wanted a girl and a boy, a girl first preferably. We had so many plans—Shruti and I. And now all I have are memories and a boxful of painful reminders of the one that I cannot have.

I open the suitcase and gaze at the cards. I think about how her hands have created them and imagine her tucking away an errant wisp of hair as she worked. I remember the evening she had spent at my flat in Bangalore. She had lied to her parents about an overnight trip from her college and come away with me. I remember how shy she had been when we first made love. I recall how I had assured her it was fine and when we made love again, how delighted she had been. I think about my arms around her tiny waist and how she had cuddled up to me and we had slept together naked. Next morning I had made coffee for her and watched her sleep so peacefully. I smile wryly at the memory of her opening her eyes, seeing me there and shrieking in horror when she realised the bedsheet had fallen off her, exposing her breasts. She had quickly pulled it up and covered herself. How much I had laughed at her shyness. She was beautiful, my Shruti. She was amazing. She was one of a kind. My perfect woman. I would truly have moved heaven and earth for her. I would have got her the moon had she asked for it.

Instead, she had walked away.

And left a gaping void in my heart. Leaving me incapable of ever loving another woman. She had taken my soul when she left.

I wonder how she is now. I wonder if her husband is good in bed. I realise I am gritting my teeth even as I think of her with another guy, even though he is her husband.

I am overcome by an urge to know where she is right now and what she is doing. I wonder whether she is happy or sad. She is sure to be on Facebook. She had 'unfriended' and blocked me the day that she had walked out and I had no access to her profile any more. It was painful, too, at that time to even face it and I had no desire to stalk her. So I had let it be.

But today, I cannot let go. So I log in to my profile on Facebook. Usually I do not give much thought to it and am slightly derisive of those who are addicted to it. But now I am grateful for this privacy-stealing, time-draining gargantuan social monster on which most people seem to spend hours.

I type in 'Shruti Srinivasan'. There are hundreds of profiles by that name. I start checking each one. Most of the women have their own photographs as their profile pictures and so looking at their photos alone, they are easy to eliminate. When I reach the end of the page, I click on 'show more results' and it throws up more Shruti Srinivasans. One of the Shrutis has used a picture of a baby but it is easy to eliminate her as she has studied in Faizabad. This is not my Shruti. There is another Shruti who has used the picture of a rose as her profile picture and all the info that is there is that she lives in Dhanbad. My heart beats a little faster. I know my Shruti would never use the picture of a red rose as her profile picture, but I cannot just eliminate this one, as my Shruti loved red roses. I go to the profile and check out what she has liked. There are only Hindi movies there and my Shruti couldn't speak a word of Hindi. So I eliminate the red-rose Shruti too. There is another Shruti who has used the picture of a bird breaking out of its cage and flying to freedom. Could this be my Shruti? I once again go to the profile and discover that this Shruti likes R.D. Burman and Lata Mangeshkar songs. She too is eliminated. My Shruti never listened to either.

At the end of two hours I have hit a dead end and I haven't found her.

Then it occurs to me that it could be because she had blocked me. That might be the reason I am unable to find her. I create a fake id and I log in. I once again go through all the 'Shruti Srinivasans' that my search throws up. By now I am familiar with all the Shrutis on Facebook. There is one who works in a software company, another who is a teacher, another who is a team leader at an international bank, another who works at a newspaper, another who works for a finance company and so on. I think I can write a thesis on 'Shruti Srinivasans' on FB. I can even write an essay on the Shruti with the red rose as her profile picture as I have studied her profile so much. But none of them is the one I am looking for.

And then something else occurs to me. Perhaps she has changed her name after her marriage. Perhaps she is no longer Shruti Srinivasan, but Shruti something else. If that is the case, then I will never be able to find her.

I rack my brains hard to try and remember the surname of the guy she was getting married to. Heck—I don't even know the guy's name or his last name. How will I ever find her? I don't even know where she lives now. I remember how angry I was at our last meeting when she had met me to tell me it was over between us. After a lengthy meeting which mostly consisted of silences, after she announced her decision to break up and exit my life, my final parting words to her had been, 'Look, Shruti, you *know* what we mean to each other. You *know* you are my life and I cannot imagine a future without you. You know where to reach me. You have my numbers, email and everything. If you change your mind, and I am hoping you do, please come back to me. I will be waiting to welcome you with open arms. But I, on my part, will never ever contact you, or stand in your way. That is a promise.'

She had hugged me and wept, but I had been too angry to hug her back.

I bite my lip at the memory. I set my laptop aside and walk towards the black suitcase and bring it back to my bed. My ex-box, I think, and am amused at the joke I am trying to make of it. But this is no joke. This is my life.

My heart beats faster as I open the box and take out the book that Shruti had made for me. It is made of handmade paper and has a red cover. 'Red, the colour of passion. Suits us, Aman. It is our colour. Happy birthday, my love,' she had said as she had handed it to me. I had presumed she was referring to the red wrapping paper. But when I had opened it, I saw it had a red cover too. I lovingly run my hand over the cover now.

I remember how Shruti had clicked pictures of me as I had opened the cover.

'I want to remember these moments for ever. I want to see the look on your face when you discover what it is,' she had said excitedly as I smiled. Then she had put her hand on mine and stopped me from opening it.

'What do you think it could be? Guess,' she had said.

'Hmmm—seems like some kind of a diary,' I had replied.

'Ha ha… close, yes. But not a diary. Guess again,' she had said.

I had playfully nipped her hand and she had laughed and said, 'Ouch! That hurt! Wait, you dumbo—open the gift first.'

And as I had opened it, my expression had changed to complete amazement from the initial befuddlement as I discovered that she had actually *made* it all. She said it had taken her more than eight months to put it all together. And she had done it secretly, hiding from her parents, saving everything from all our dates, during that period. She said it was the grandest thing she could think of giving me. And she wanted to make something grand, something that I would cherish.

Oh, how she had succeeded. It has been two years since she went away. I am still spellbound by all the memories she has captured in vivid detail and put into the pages of this book.

I open to the first page. My heartbeats race, competing with each other. Part of me wants to close the book and throw it away, while another part wants to re-live everything that has been. I am torn, undecided. The book is sending me to a place I don't want to go. I am done with it, it is the past, it is over—my head tells me. Yet my heart tugs.

Finally, it is the heart that wins.

I open the book and begin to read Shruti's words, in her handwriting:

'For Aman, with all my love' and she has stuck a picture of us, clicked on her birthday, when we made that trip to Kabini River Lodge. I stare at the picture for a few minutes. I remember how we had asked the waiter to click it. My arms are around her waist and she is clutching me tight, as though afraid to let me go. She is smiling and so am I. It is a picture that screams 'LOVE'. It is a picture which radiates happiness. It is a picture that says, 'Oh, look at this lucky couple. These guys are going to be happy together for the rest of their lives.' I have to fight back the urge to kiss her in the photo.

I turn the page and begin to read:

My love Aman,

You must be fast asleep right now, as I work on this book. I meant to do this a long time back, when the idea first occurred to me. I wanted to give you something truly unique on your birthday. Something that would show you how much you mean to me. Something that would involve the best and most precious gift of all—TIME. (How quickly we run out of it. Before we even realise it, it has slipped away.) So I thought of creating this book, just for you, and writing in it every memorable date that we had, stick stuff in it—stuff that matters only to both of us. I hope to be doing that starting now, till your birthday, when I will present you this book.

Since your birthday is at least eight months away, I think I will have a great book. This is our baby—till we make a real one. Heh, heh. Take care of it, okay?

And I know you will love it!

Happy birthday to the greatest guy in the world.

All my love and some more.

Shruti

The next page has at least fifty photos of me, which Shruti has printed out and used to make a border.

It is like a frame. And then in the centre, this is what she has written:

Aman—
If I could paint pictures, I would have made a million portraits of you.
If I could write poetry, I would have written a million poems for you.
Instead, I write here this poem which conveys what I feel about you.

Stars in a moonless sky

What is it that you dream about she asks.
Your Smile,Your look
Your Kiss,Your hug
Your love,Your trust
Your words,Your feelings
Your warmth,Your concern
Your presence,Your eyes
He replies.
And she smiles as she understands the language of truth.

She mulls over his words
Long after he has slept
She lies awake
Weaving with them
Her security blanket
Wrapping them around herself
And then carefully squirrelling them away
On the days when there is nothing but blackness
For his words are the stars that illuminate her moonless sky.
And they are hers.

Nothing can take them away from each other now.

For words once uttered find their way into hearts
And later spill over to paper
In the form of poetry.
Immortalised forever.
Perhaps this is what they call love.

I know you aren't much into poetry but read this one please. I wrote this specially for you. Read each line. Multiply the emotions expressed in it by a million.
That MUCH is how much I love you Aman. That MUCH.

Each of her entries is like that. Overflowing with love. Swearing undying devotion. So expressive. So full of emotion. So *her.*

And for me now, so full of pain. I read each and every entry that she wrote in that book. Each one brings a lump in my throat. As I continue reading, the lump just keeps getting bigger and bigger. Each of the entries written here brings a fresh wave of agony till I am submerged in it.

I want to find her right now and wave this book in front of her and ask her, 'What happened to all this love, Shruti? What happened? Are you happy now? How the fuck did you do this to me? Don't you have a conscience? Have you forgotten all that we had been through? Am I that disposable? Do you miss me? Do you think of me? Heck—do you even care? Or is your life now all around that husband of yours?'

And then it occurs to me. I could still find her by her email id. She has (or used to have) three email ids. Surely she would still be using one of them for Facebook?

So I log in to my email account. I am temporarily distracted by a mail from Anjali. She is asking for help for a piece she is writing and she wants to know, 'What Men Really Want'. She has marked it to her friends as well as to me. Ha. What men want—it is not much. I write out a reply to her. I want to add, 'Men want a woman who will be faithful to them and not walk off with another guy'. But I refrain. I send Anjali the email and then do a search in my account. In a few seconds, I pull out all three email ids that Shruti used to have.

I once again open Facebook with my fake id, and search using the email ids.

And then it happens.

I find her.

Chapter 4

Anjali

Dipika stretches her legs and arms and squints as the morning sunlight plays hide-and-seek on her face. She smiles and asks for another cup of coffee.

'If it isn't too much trouble, that is,' she adds as an afterthought.

'Of course not. No trouble. I knew you would want more, so I just made some extra. Let me pop it in the microwave,' I say, walking towards the kitchen.

'I so love your terrace, Anjali. It is so peaceful. I think it is the best thing about the house. And lovely deck chairs too. I can never get this kind of peace at home. Ria and Rima are a handful, you know. But I think I have told you all this a million times,' she says as she leans back comfortably and closes her eyes.

'I know, but they are such moppets. Little dolls,' I reply.

'Yes, when they are asleep,' she laughs. 'God, Anjali, I so needed this break,' she says, still with her eyes closed.

'Anytime. You are most welcome here. Offer open only for my favourite cousin, though,' I reply.

I return back with the coffees and plonk down on the deck chair next to hers.

'You know, Anjali, I wait to get away like this. I am so fed up of my life. Sometimes I feel I have had enough of husband, kids, the whole marriage thing.'

'Why? Why in the world are *you* fed up?' I ask. I am curious.

Dipika has the best of everything—a wonderful husband, two lovely girls and a beautifully done-up apartment, a posh penthouse, unlike my tiny one-bedroom flat where the only good part is the terrace. And the worst, an inquisitive landlord, a distant relative, who keeps a hawk's eye on me and reports back everything to my parents. Dipika is lucky. She has a fabulous figure, she does not need to work to make a living, and has everything going for her.

She pauses now as though carefully considering how to answer my question.

'What you see on the surface isn't the whole picture. You only see the shine, the sheen, the gloss. Beneath it, there is masonry, peeling plaster, shaky foundations. It is all dressed up and you never notice it because of the veneer.' Her voice is laced with bitterness and I am surprised.

'Are we talking about constructions here? Masonry, bricks and all that?' I attempt a feeble joke, just to lighten the mood, but Dipika does not smile.

'Do you realise it is about two months since Vikram and I even had a proper conversation?' she asks.

I don't know what to say. I am insanely fond of Dipika and, more than a cousin, I look upon her as a great friend and secretly I want to have a marriage like hers. Why, even my parents praise her all the time, and one of the reasons why they are comfortable with me staying on my own is that Dipika is around. She has assured them that she will keep an eye on me, which she does. We usually go shopping together and sometimes we meet up for lunch or just hang out. When we do, it is always lighthearted banter about movies, books and my latest dating disaster. I have been on dates with at least six guys and each of them was more disastrous than the previous one. Dipika always teases me about how I haven't found Mr Right yet. And now here she is, telling me that her Mr Right is not so right, after all?

'It is the monotony that gets to me. All I do is look after Ria and Reema, send them to school, go to the gym and work out, and then come back home. Vikram is never around. My life is always the same old routine. I think men have a button which gets activated the moment they become husbands. They change so much. He was never like this before marriage,' she continues.

'Come on, Dipika. Vikram is babysitting today, isn't he? He is in fact, giving you a break,' I defend Vikram. 'I know so many people in my office whose husbands won't even lift a teacup. Vikram is so sweet, in comparison.'

'He would have been sweeter if he was around. Most of the time he is travelling. When he comes home, he hardly has time for me.'

I want to point out that it is because he works so hard that their family leads a luxurious lifestyle. They vacation abroad every year and live in one of Bangalore's most enviable residential luxury apartments. But I don't think Dipika wants to hear that. So I keep mum.

'Anyhow, forget it. You tell me—how are things with you? How are Sriram and Latika? And how is work? All good?' Dipika has taken the tone of a concerned older sister now. I don't mind. Secretly I like it that she kind of 'watches out' for me.

'Yes, all good. I met both of them yesterday. Sriram has broken up with yet another woman. And Latika's husband was out of town. So, for once, it was just three of us, instead of their respective partners tagging along. It was like old times.'

'You three have been together quite long, haven't you?' asks Dipika.

'Yes,' I reply. 'Together since class six, when my parents decided to put me in a hostel in Bangalore. Sriram and Latika are my lifelines. I don't know how I would have survived school without them.'

Dipika smiles. 'I know about some of the crazy adventures you have had. You are lucky to have such great friends. I am barely in touch with anyone I went to school with. It all changes when you have kids.'

I hope nothing changes between Sriram, Latika and me. I want nothing to come between our friendship. And, I don't know if things change after people have kids. If they want to keep in touch, they will always find a way. But I don't see any point in arguing with Dipika. She seems to be in a cynical mood today.

'By the way, it will be great to have Aman back in India. The girls are so excited,' says Dipika.

'I know. I am in touch with him on and off. He is good with children, isn't he? He was so patient with Ria and Reema. Isn't it almost a year now since we last met him?'

'Yes, I think it has been just over a year. Do you remember how they clung to him and wouldn't let him go?'

'Of course. They both took turns sitting on his back and it was sweet of him to pretend to be an elephant and give them rides. His knees must have hurt,' I say and smile at the memory.

Aman had been visiting India, and Dipika and Vikram had invited me over for dinner while he was around. Since then, we had kept in touch online. He is refreshingly different from all the men I have known so far. There is a kind of sincerity and kindness in his eyes. Also he is articulate, well-mannered, polite and has a great sense of humour. He is a good conversationalist and he listens when you speak. It isn't hard for me to see why Dipika's family is so fond of him.

Dipika and I lounge around on the deck chairs, chatting about everything. She calls it our 'hanging out' time. I rustle up some sandwiches for lunch. Finally, Dipika says that she has to leave, as it is time to take both the girls for their ballet lessons and Vikram will not be able to do their hair by himself.

After she leaves, I lie for a long time on my deck chair thinking about what she has said. I wonder if people change after marriage. She does sound down. She never used to be so cynical on her earlier visits but, of late, she has sounded increasingly negative.

I just hope that it is a phase and will pass.

My mother calls as usual. She never misses her weekly call to me.

'How are you, darling? Are you doing well?' she asks.

'Yes, all fine, Ma.'

'And what are you working on at the moment?'

My mother is quite proud of the fact that I work for a magazine. She boasts to all her friends that her daughter is a writer. My mother too writes for the Indian community magazine in Muscat, which is where she and Dad have been living for many years now. But she does not consider her writing a 'real job' as it is purely voluntary.

'I have two stories, Ma. One is on fashion trends in colleges, the other on relationships.'

'Good, good. Send me the scans when they appear.'

'Of course, I will. Don't I always?'

'Yes, you do,' she says and I can picture her smiling proudly.

'And?' she prompts.

I know this is my cue to tell her about whether or not I

have found a 'suitable' man. My mother is always pushing me to go and 'find' a man. Like it is so easy! Like there are suitable guys growing on trees and all I have to do is pick one.

'Ma, I haven't met anyone, okay? If I do, I will definitely tell you,' I say.

'I didn't even ask,' says my mother and she chuckles.

Mothers are so darn clever. They know exactly which buttons to push to get information out of you. Especially information that you don't want to share.

I laugh with her and tell her that.

'Naturally,' she says. 'After all, I am your mother.'

My phone buzzes just as my mother hangs up and it is a text from Jeena. Jeena takes her job as the chief editor of *Tiara* very seriously. She is ambitious, driven and somewhat like the boss from *The Devil Wears Prada*. I can't but help sit erect each time she passes my cubicle. She likes me though. Or rather, she likes my writing and the pieces I write. I don't think she cares for anything else.

`Change of plans. We're running the piece in this issue, not the next. Do you think you can submit it by tomorrow morning?`

I have not even started working on the piece. Since I had a good fourteen days to turn in the piece, I had not even thought about it. And now she wants it tomorrow!

I don't want to ask Jeena to extend the deadline and I definitely do not want to confess to her that I haven't even thought about the piece.

I message her back with a confidence that I am far from feeling: `Yes, No problem. I have already outlined it and will send it soon.`

Latika and Sriram will have to help me out. And I will ask Aman too to give his inputs.

From: Anjali Prabhu <anjali.prabhu@tiara.com>
To: Latika Nair <latika@fundoo.com>; Sriram Surve <sriram.surve@everest.com>;
Aman Mathur <aman.mathur@zmail.com>
Sub: Help—Urgent
Hey guys—Help!
Deadline and Bitch-boss on my ass.
What do you think a woman should do to keep a guy hooked?
Sriram, Aman: What turns you on in a woman and what will keep you hooked?
Latika: What do you think women should do to keep men interested?
Please reply ASAP. Need to submit this quick. Who else can I turn to but my closest friends in times of need? (Yeah dramatic dialogue, I know—can't help it. Writers are like that.)
Reply immediately.
Anjali

From: Sriram Surve <sriram.surve@everest.com>
To: Anjali Prabhu <anjali.prabhu@tiara.com>
Sub: Re: Help—Urgent
In answer to your query: What do you think a woman should do to keep a guy hooked?
1. Show cleavage
2. Show some more cleavage
3. Wear short skirts
4. Flirt
5. Be receptive to flirting
That's it—so simple. Men are so easy to please.
Good luck!
SS

From: Anjali Prabhu <anjali.prabhu@tiara.com>
To: Sriram Surve <sriram.surve@everest.com>
Sub: Re: Re: Help—Urgent

Big help you are.

Idiot.

A

From: Aman Mathur <aman.mathur@zmail.com>
To: Anjali Prabhu <anjali.prabhu@tiara.com>
Sub: Re: Help—Urgent

I can't speak on behalf of the entire male population, but I think by and large what I would want in a woman is companionship. She has to be a friend first. I think sex can keep the relationship going only up to a certain extent. It is important, yes, but it is not the only thing that guys look for. I would also want her to have a kind heart and be a nice person. I would like her to be open and honest and not hide her feelings. I would also like her to have a great sense of humour.

Intelligence is a big attribute for me too. I don't like women who are dumb.

I like women who are confident and who are at peace with themselves. I don't like clingy, whiny, demanding women. They come across as too needy.

A woman doesn't have to wear revealing clothes to attract a guy—and trust me, while it might get her initial attention, the relationship will continue only if the other above-mentioned aspects are being met.

I don't know how much this has helped.
Good luck with your article!
Aman

From: Latika Nair <latika@fundoo.com>
To: Anjali Prabhu <anjali.prabhu@tiara.com>
Sub: Re:Help—urgent

I think there has to be basic chemistry for the relationship to work. There has to be a certain wave-length match for it to develop and last.

I've been married three years now and, at the end of the day, we wait to talk to each other, swap stories and laugh. It is that easy sense of camaraderie we have with each other that works in our favour.

And yes—no egos. When I am wrong, I apologise. He does too.

We love each other unconditionally.

I think that is important.

Good luck with the article.

Tons of love
XX
Latika

From: Anjali Prabhu <anjali.prabhu@tiara.com>
To: Jeena Kapoor <jkapoor@tiara.com>
Sub: How to keep a guy hooked

Article attached.

Anjali

How To Keep A Guy Hooked

By Anjali Prabhu

Are you looking to find out how to keep him interested in you? Are you wondering why he hasn't asked you out for the next date yet? Do you want to keep the relationship going but don't know how? Use these tips and keep a guy hooked to you.

1. **Do not cling:** So you have texted him and he hasn't got back to you. Yes, we know you are dying to get that second text from him. But, do not, at any cost, message again and ask him if he got your earlier text. He has. And, no, he hasn't lost your number. And he isn't that busy that he forgot. If a guy wants to get back to you, he will. Do not sound desperate or whiny. Clingy and needy women are a big turn-off for men.
2. **Develop a friendship:** Allow a friendship to develop naturally first. Try to find mutual interests and take a genuine interest in what he likes. If it's basketball, look up the internet for NBA league fixtures. Watch a couple of games. Follow what is going on and be in a position to discuss the game with him. But do not fake this. If you have no interest in sports, find a common ground that you can enjoy together.
3. **Sense of humour:** 'Those who laugh together, stay together,' says Latika Nair, an HR professional who has been

married for three years. 'At the end of the day, we wait to talk to each other, swap stories and laugh. It is that easy sense of camaraderie we have with each other that works in our favour.'

4. **Treat him with respect:** Respect your guy for who he is. Do not play the 'I'm a princess'. Do not be a drama queen or a diva. A woman who is full of drama is likely to find it harder to keep a guy hooked. Men like women who are positive and understanding. Listen to him when he talks and figure out what is important to him.
5. **Be independent and have your own life:** If the guy calls at four pm and asks you for a date that evening but you already have prior plans, do not change your plans and go with him. (Yes, we know you are dying to go on that second date, but hold on!) Make him work a little harder to get you. Also, show him you have a life.

Use these simple tips and keep a guy hooked to you forever. And you thought just showing cleavage and wearing short skirts was all that men wanted, eh?

Good luck, girls—and may you be happily hooked to your man, forever.

From: Anjali Prabhu <anjali.prabhu@tiara.com>

To: Aman Mathur <aman.mathur@zmail.com>

Sub: Re: Re: Help—Urgent

Hey!

Thanks.

That was brilliant and helped. Thank you for the prompt response. Hope you have a great flight to India!

Anjali

Chapter 5

Shruti

I cannot believe how time has flown. The subtle pressure has started now from all quarters. This is inevitable if you live in India and have been married for a year or more. Everybody makes it their business. The business of procreating and raising babies. It is as if a marriage is complete only if a child is produced.

Mom calls as usual when I am on my way to work.

I speak to her every single day. If she doesn't call, I do. The routine never varies. It is as though her breast cancer was brought upon us to make us realise how very fragile life can be.

'So, Shruti, changed your mind yet?' she asks.

'About what, Ma?' I feign ignorance.

'You know, you should never delay such things, Shruti. The older you are, the harder it will become to conceive. Certain things have to be done at a certain age. You are gambling with your fertility and your baby's health.' She is armed today with arsenal that can down me.

But I am prepared too. I have my own load of ammunition ready.

'Well, Ma, do you know of Madonna, the singer? She

had her baby at thirty-eight. And Halle Berry—she became a mother at forty-one,' I retort.

'Shruti, all these are foreign celebrities. They are different. Look at the Indian film stars. Most of them quit movies when they get married. You should have a child, it is what makes a family complete.'

There is no point arguing with my mother. We will only go around in circles. I certainly do not want to quit my career and raise children, just because some Indian movie stars have done so.

'Look Ma—I cannot, and do not, want to emulate a Bollywood star. I just want to go to work and come home and lead my life. Why do you keep talking to me about this?' I ask, now a little irritated.

She is quiet for a few seconds and I immediately feel contrite.

'Okay, you know best. I won't bring this up again,' she says in a quiet voice and I know she is hurt.

'Oh, Ma—I didn't mean it that way. Look, I am sorry. Let's not talk about this, okay? When we decide to have a baby, you will be the first to know, okay?

I am glad that there is no one I know in the bus to overhear my conversation as I am one of the first to get on. Asha, my colleague from the finance department, travels in the same bus but she gets on only after about five stops. Till then I usually sit alone. Today, I am thankful that we all have our 'fixed places' in the bus, much like school, and nobody changes them. So till Asha gets in, I have a lot of time (and privacy) to contemplate. And that is just what I do after I hang up.

I think about how my mother's breast cancer has changed her life and thrown mine on a path I never planned or envisaged. I cannot blame her though, for subtly pressuring me to have a child. After all, I have been quite a handful for them and I still recall the relief on their faces when I finally agreed to marry Rishabh.

I still have mixed feelings about all of it and have dealt with it by not dwelling too much on it. My mother's cancer was a rude jolt that catapulted all of us into unfamiliar territory. After all, cancer isn't easy to fight. My mother is a very brave woman. She had gone for a routine check-up and the doctors found a lump and advised a lumpectomy. But when they operated on her, they discovered a tumour which was twice the size that the scans had detected. So instead of taking out just one affected lymph node, they had to take out eight infected ones. Then there were rounds of chemo, radiation and further investigations. A shudder passes through my body as I recall that period of my life.

I do not know if my relationship with Aman fell apart because of my mother's cancer or not. All I know is that I was in no frame of mind to fight my parents then.

My mother had to finally go in for a mastectomy. The doctors had said it was absolutely essential to eliminate all risks and to ensure its total eradication. I remember the relief washing over me when she had finally come home. She had hugged me and we had both wept and wept. My mother never saw mastectomy as an inconvenience. If there was any sadness, she hid it well. I think it was I who had cried. My tears were because of my helplessness in the whole matter. My tears were also for an end of a relationship that had meant the world to me. My tears were for my mother's maimed body—the body that had given birth to me, nurtured me, taken care of me. My tears were also tears of relief—that the monster that we had all been fighting was finally vanquished and my mother was cancer-free. She has beaten it and is a survivor now.

Throughout those years, I have been her biggest support after Papa. Being a single child, the onus on me was that much more. Perhaps if I had siblings, they might have been there for Ma. Sometimes I wonder if it had not been for my mother's cancer, I might have been married to Aman, not Rishabh. Even though it is too late now to contemplate what could have been, my thoughts find their way to Aman, a cruel reminder of how it would have been, had things panned out differently. Thoughts of him still cause a storm inside me, though outwardly I appear calm. Four years with him and I could not imagine a future without him. How can I forget the time I had with him? There is nobody who can make me laugh like he did. There is nobody who has cherished me as much as he did. We were so right for each other.

Aman is history—you had a chance with him but you were too cowardly to take it. You are married now and Rishabh is a great guy. Get over him.

Rishabh dotes on me. He is nice-looking, earns well (he also has the coveted IIM tag which automatically elevates him in the 'good catch' category when it comes to matchmaking), is helpful around the house and is a great guy.

But he is not Aman.

I wince at my own thoughts. I feel like a traitor to be even thinking of Aman nearly two years into my marriage. Everybody says that things change after marriage. Everybody says that you forget the life you had before you got married. But they lie. How can you forget who you were? In many ways, still are. Marriage does not change your memories. Marriage does not take away your past. At best, it paints a rosy picture of a 'new life'. But can a new life be built on the foundations of a past soaked in unforgettable memories?

I think about my conversation with my mother and her questions about having a child. Isn't it enough that I got married to someone they chose? Now they want me to produce a baby too? Why does Indian society put this huge pressure on couples to produce children soon after marriage? I wonder what joy elders get in seeing their adult married child pregnant. How can they interfere so shamelessly?

Even the lady living in the flat opposite mine (who I barely even speak to but for the cursory greeting when we run into each other in the lobby while waiting for the elevator) had asked me the other day, '*Beti*—any good news?' The 'good news' being a euphemism for being pregnant.

'Yes, Aunty, I am getting a promotion at work,' I had replied, pretending to not understand what she had hinted at.

'*Uffo*—I didn't mean that,' she had said.

'I know,' I had answered with a smile and rushed off.

My mother-in-law is not so easily fobbed off, though. She has started dropping not-so-subtle hints on the phone. She talks about longing to hold a grandchild, she talks about how much a baby will cement a marriage, she talks about how a family is complete only when it has two children. It is annoying to listen to her. I nod politely whenever she calls and respond in monosyllables. I just cannot be rude, even though I want to bang down the phone and tell her to keep her nose out of my business and that Rishabh and I will decide when it is time to have a child.

The problem is Rishabh too is very keen. But I just don't feel ready. Heck—I am only twenty-six. I want to wait a few more years. I do not want to have a child now. I want to have a child when I am ready—not because my parents and my in-laws and my husband want it. I may not be certain about too many things in my life, but this is something I am certain about.

Asha gets into the bus and is, as usual, in a chirpy mood. I wonder how she manages it all. She seems so nonchalant about her weight. She is grossly overweight and she does not even diet.

'I am the mother of a seven-year-old now. How does it matter? It is not that I have to model on the cover of *Playboy*,' is her favourite line when it comes to her weight.

Asha's mother-in-law lives with her. When I tell Asha about my in-laws and my mother pressuring me to have a child, she laughs.

'They tell you on the phone only, right? It is not as though your mother-in-law is living with you, like mine. Then why do you get so affected? Just let it go,' she says.

'You know how it is for me. I am so close to my mother. I just can't let it go. Rishabh also wants to have a baby,' I say.

'So what do you want to do? Have a baby to please them? Look, I know how it is. Everything goes for a toss once a child arrives. It is horrible if you aren't ready for it. Ask me—I speak from experience. You know how it was for me—I conceived by accident and by the time I realised it, it was too late. So I had no choice. It is our life, we have to make our choices,' she states in a very matter-of-fact way.

She is right, of course.

I have made my choices. Walking away from Aman, the one true love of my life, and marrying Rishabh, my parents' choice. It was hard but I have done it. My mother is free of cancer. I have a career which has just taken off and I am doing reasonably well in my job.

I have everything going for me.

Yet why am I unhappy? What is this strange sense of discontentment I feel? Why can't I just be happy-go-lucky like Asha, who has so many more problems than me?

For the rest of the journey to the workplace I force myself to listen to Asha's chatter about her mother-in-law and also about a party that she is organising which she wants Rishabh and me to attend. Asha has decided to wear an Indian dress with a very low plunging neckline. She says her mother-in-law will hate it but she has made up her mind that it is exactly what she will wear.

I wish I could be as defiant as Asha. I wish I could be so certain.

But more than anything I just wish I could exorcise Aman from my thoughts.

Chapter 6

Anjali

On Monday morning, when I go to work, there is a big surprise for me. Jeena calls me in and asks if I would like to write a regular column on relationships for *Tiara*. I cannot believe that I am actually being offered this. That I have managed to win Jeena over. The tough-as-nails, hard-to-please Jeena.

The first thing I do is message my mother. My mother is overjoyed.

'I am so proud of you, baby, this is no mean feat,' she says and a few minutes later I get a call from my father who congratulates me too. My mother must have immediately relayed the news to him.

After we finish talking, I call up both Sriram and Latika and tell them.

'Paaarty. So happy for you!' says Sriram and I can feel the joy in his voice.

Latika and he both insist that we celebrate and that is how we end up at *Zero G* on a Wednesday night, a Bollywood night. The place has a fabulous view of the city and the city lights twinkling like stars add to the atmosphere of our celebration.

Latika has brought her husband Manish along. Manish

hates to dance, but Sriram, Latika and I rock the floor. We even have a little co-ordinated number from school and we do the steps in perfect rhythm, synchronised, much to Manish's amusement.

Looking at Latika and Manish, I feel a small pang of loneliness. They seem so happy together, so content and so much in love.

It is late by the time we are done and Sriram says he will drop me home. We bid goodbye to each other and as I get into Sriram's car I ask him, 'Hey, Sriram, do you miss being in a relationship? Don't you ever feel like settling down with somebody? Look at Latika and Manish—they seem so happy.'

Sriram looks thoughtful. 'To be honest, I don't want to, at this point of time. I am too busy having fun,' he says.

'What is the fun in changing girlfriends every two months?' I ask.

'Ever done it?'

'Of course not.'

'Then how will you know what fun it is?'

'Hmm, you have a point. But the thing is, I haven't even found a single suitable guy. How will I ever change boyfriends every two months.'

'You are so darn finicky, Anjali. You have gone on six dates. And each time you have phoned me to rescue you. I must admit I do a rather good job of acting like a jealous ex. Every one of the guys who you have dated has fallen for it.'

'That is because all the guys I dated so far were dumb,' I giggle.

Secretly of course, I am happy that I can always count on Sriram, to rescue me from bad dates.

'Tell me, is there no one you like? Even a little bit?'

'There is someone I like. He is relocating to India from the UK soon. Hopefully, I will get to see him more often then.'

'Wow. A UK-returned boyfriend and all that. Somebody's going places.'

'Shut up, Sriram. He isn't my boyfriend. We have just exchanged a few mails. That is it. We're just friends.'

'Yes, yes, that is what they all say. "We're just friends",' and he does a perfect imitation of a Bollywood starlet. I burst out laughing.

'You are such a riot, Sriram,' I say.

'Thank you, my lady. I can apply for the position of your boyfriend. Do you think I qualify?' he says solemnly and that makes me chuckle even harder.

'Yeah, and you will dump me in two months. No, thanks,' I say.

Sriram is just kidding. He and I can never be anything more than friends. While he is a fantastic friend to have around, there is no sexual attraction between us whatsoever.

I hug him goodbye and thank him for dropping me home.

My mother calls me up the next day.

'So, who were you out with last night? Met anyone interesting?' she asks.

I know immediately that Mr Joshi, my landlord, has informed them that I was dropped home late last night by a guy.

'Ma, what is this? Some live-relay centre, which tells you even if I sneeze? Stop spying on me! And, God, does he actually wait up and convey to you who I went out with?'

'He is just keeping an eye on you because Papa asked him to. Come on. No need to take offence. Met anyone interesting?' persists my mother.

'Uff, Ma. Sriram, Latika and I had gone out to celebrate

my getting a column. And it was Sriram who dropped me back last night.'

'Oh,' says my mother sounding disappointed.

'Don't worry, Ma, if there is a guy in my life, you will be the first to know,' I say.

'I better be,' she says as she hangs up.

I can only smile at my mother's repartees.

The next day I ping Latika from work.

Me: Hey there. Busy?

Latika: Hello *Tiara* columnist. Never too busy for you.

Me: You know what? Between you and me, we should have postponed yesterday's celebrations.

Latika: Why?! We had a great time, didn't we?

Me: Yeah, but if we had gone out on Saturday instead, I could have asked Aman to join us. He gets back to India on Saturday morning.

Latika: Oooh. So plotting to get time with Aman, eh?

Me: Not like that. Just thought it would be nice if he was there.

Latika: Nice for whom?

Me: Heh heh. How is work?

Latika: I haven't had time to even breathe since morning. We have a team from the US arriving next week. Going crazy with all the work. What *is* it with you and Aman? Tell the truth.

Me: We exchange emails now and then. I have chatted online with him a few times. But, I somehow get this feeling that Dipika knows something about him that she isn't telling me.

Latika: Why?

Me: Because any time I ask about Aman, his background, his girlfriends, she gives some vague replies and changes the topic. I've asked twice and both times she did that. After that I stopped. I wonder why.

Latika: Hmmm. I can see your journo mind dying to investigate. Do you think there's something going on between Dipika and Aman?

Me: OMG. I hadn't even thought of that. She is very fond of him. But, hey, come on, I don't think so. She is too loyal to Vikram.

Latika: Ha ha. That's what it seems like on the outside. I have been married three years and have friends who have been married much longer. Three years and that is when the cracks appear in a marriage. You cement them, fix them, seal the cracks and it lasts. Else they grow bigger over time and poof! One day, it falls apart. Sometimes couples deliberately choose to ignore the cracks. They hope they will go away on their own. But they never do. Trust me on this.

Me: Wow. Profound. I think you ought to be a writer.

Latika: You can quote me on this. Wink.

Me: Ha ha ha. No, this one is too good. I will pass it off as my own. I will use it in some article and pretend I wrote it.

Latika: Feel free!

Me: Do you think I should ask Aman out?

Latika: Do you like him?

Me: Well. Sort of. He is interesting.

Latika: Then what are you waiting for? Go for it!

Me: Don't know. Somehow I feel odd to make this move.

Latika: Then what will you do? Keep waiting till he asks you? Life is short! Go for it. You keep saying that in your writings. Practise what you preach.

From: Anjali Prabhu <anjali.prabhu@tiara.com>

To: Aman Mathur <aman.mathur@zmail.com>

Sub: Free on Monday?

Hey Aman,

Welcome to India! Dipika told me that you arrive on Saturday and that you are staying with them for the weekend.

When do you join work?

And hey—free on Monday evening? If so, let's catch up.

Anjali

Chapter 7

Shruti

'Look Rishabh, I do not feel ready yet. We have already discussed this. And is this why you brought me out for dinner and why you're plying me with wine, hoping I will soften my stand? Mr Rishabh Prasad, it just isn't working.' I am annoyed now as he seems hell-bent on bringing up the dreaded C topic again—the topic of Children.

That too in this very upmarket Italian restaurant. I had been so pleased about this 'surprise date'. Rishabh isn't a romantic guy. In the time that we have been married, it is always me who has made all the plans—for an outing, a movie at the multiplex, for the only vacation we have taken. Rishabh is laid-back and happy for me to co-ordinate every detail. Therefore, his taking the initiative to book us a table in this place had impressed me—until now.

I glare at him, willing him to shut up. I definitely do not want to discuss this issue now. But Rishabh is relentless.

'See, sweety, it is easier if you have a child now than later. Anyway it is not like you don't want to have kids ever right? The sooner, the better.'

'Says who?'

'Say all the websites. I have been reading up on the

advantages of having children before you hit thirty. This way, when the child is twenty-four, I will still not have retired. We will still not be too old to enjoy life.'

'God—how crazy is that argument? If we plan our finances properly, it is going to be fine. Which era do you live in? And, yes, I can show you ten other websites which tell you it is better to have a child after thirty.' I try hard to be patient, but my voice betrays me. Though I try to keep it normal, I notice it rises a few decibel levels higher than usual.

'Shhh… Look, be calm. Even your mom agrees it is a good idea. My parents are also both in their sixties. It is not unreasonable to want a child after almost two years of marriage, surely? And think of how happy your parents will be.' His tone is gentle, persuasive. As though speaking to an errant child.

That does it. What does he mean by 'Be calm'. How patronising is that statement. Like I am the unreasonable one here. I am fuming now. How can he not think from my point of view? Understand how I feel about it? About my not being ready. After all, it will be my body inside which this baby will grow. I feel like throwing up at the very thought. Pregnancy terrifies me. I don't feel ready to have a child. I am only twenty-six. I don't want to be a mother now. Heck, I don't even want to think about it now.

Yet here is Rishabh looking at me like he expects me to say yes, and we go home, do the deed and produce a baby in nine months. What the hell?

I am very upset now.

So I grit my teeth and say nothing.

Rishabh takes this as a sign of giving in. He takes my silence as acquiescence.

'Shruti—I promise, I will do everything for the baby. I will change the diapers, I will wake up at night, I will sing lullabies. Seriously I will. I will be a very involved father,' he says earnestly, his eyes shining and hopeful.

I am so upset at how he goes on and on about it. How can he not see how strongly I feel about this? I do NOT want a baby. Not now. I don't want to have a baby just because his parents are in their sixties. To have a baby, one must be ready to give unconditional love. A baby must happen because two people want the same thing. Not because one feels forced. Also, one must be selfless enough to put another human being first. I know from my friends how demanding children can be. I certainly am not prepared for motherhood.

'Do one thing then,' I say.

'Yes, darling, anything you say,' he replies as he reaches across the table and takes my hand.

'Grow a pair of breasts, get a uterus, fuck yourself and go produce your own goddamn baby,' I reply coldly as I yank my hand back and stand up, pushing back my chair which makes a grating sound against the stone floor. People have turned towards our table and are looking at me now.

I pick up my handbag and quietly walk out even as a stunned Rishabh stares at me, not knowing what to do.

He recovers in a few seconds and is beside me as I reach the door.

'Shruti, don't be silly and please don't create a scene. Wait for me outside. I will pay the bill and join you,' he hisses, his earlier shock having been replaced by embarrassment and anger now.

But I am angry too. Too angry to care. Too angry to give a fuck about what people think and what people will say. Too angry with Rishabh, his parents, my mother and the great Indian society. Like a woman is worth something only if she gets married and produces a baby. Like her thoughts and her wishes don't matter. Like it is this whole damn concept of motherhood which makes a woman complete.

I march outside and walk. I am shaking with rage. I just want to get away from Rishabh. I look for a cab or an auto and I don't see any. I have no idea what I am doing. I am too angry to think. This topic of 'have a child, have a child' has been going on for so long now and today I have reached breaking point. I had been relieved when he hadn't mentioned it for the past two weeks. I was sure he had started seeing my point of view. But no. This was his gameplan all along. To lie low till I 'cooled off' so he could bring it up again.

I remember the last time after we had had sex, he had said, 'You know what I should do, I should throw away your birth control pills. Then you will have no choice.'

I was stunned at the callousness of his remark. For a few seconds I had been unable to speak. I had been so hurt. The look on my face perhaps betrayed me and Rishabh had made a joke of it. 'Hey, relax. Just kidding,' he had said.

But it wasn't a joke to me. He knew very well that it was an issue I felt strongly about. How could he make a casual remark like that? *Throw away the birth control pills*. I had chosen to keep quiet and did not mention it. Rishabh sensed my irritation and he was extra nice to me the next morning. He even made coffee and breakfast for me. I knew it was his way of making up. And then he hadn't brought up the topic of having children at all, until today.

I start walking along the road, hoping to find cab or an auto. The Italian Bistro is not too far from Juhu beach. Before I realise it, I find myself walking in the direction of the beach.

The cool breeze hits me and I feel the saltiness of the ocean in it. I keep walking along the path. This seems to be some kind of a lane that reaches the beach. I am so immersed in my thoughts that all the food stalls, the crowd, the couples strolling hand in hand, families, vendors and the general mass of humanity that throngs the beach are a blur to me. A little boy walks up to me selling some kind of a snack, wrapped in paper cones.

'*Didi—channa*?' he asks, imploring me to buy.

I ignore him and continue walking towards the water. I find it difficult to walk in my heels now and so pause to remove them and carry them in my hand, rolling up my formal trousers.

My phone rings and I see it is Rishabh. I am too angry to answer and so I put it on silent and continue walking towards the water.

I walk till I reach the water. It is low tide and the sea has receded leaving behind a vast expanse of sand. I keep walking and my feet leave a trail of footprints in the moist sand. The solitude is comforting. I spot a couple, a few metres away from me. The guy holds her tightly and she has her arms around him. Her *salwar* is rolled up to her knees and the wind carries the sound of her delighted laughter to me.

The waves lap at my feet and soothe me. I stand for a long time in shallow water, my feet sinking into the sand a little deeper each time a wave comes and recedes. Soon my feet are buried in the wet mud and are not visible anymore. I cannot help thinking that a marriage is just like this. You get into it without planning too much. It grows and grows, ever so slowly and before you realise it you are deep into it, your identity submerged. You are now so-and-so's spouse. There are compromises. You have to take joint decisions. Your decisions are not yours alone. You have to be considerate towards what your spouse wants.

What if you want something completely different from what your spouse does? No marriage considers that. I have no answers to that question as I stare at the dark waters of the ocean and the glint of the waves as the moonlight falls on them. The sound of the ocean is comforting. I stand there for a long time.

Then I turn and start walking back. I have no idea how long I have stood in the water but it has cooled my anger. I now feel that perhaps it was a bit immature of me to have walked out of the restaurant like that. So I take out my phone and see twelve missed calls. Ten are from Rishabh and two are from Asha.

I am sheepish now.

I call up Rishabh and he picks up instantly.

'Where are you? ' he says. He sounds cold, curt, unfriendly.

'Sorry,' I reply in a tiny voice, ashamed now.

'Where are you? Let me come and pick you up.'

'I am at Juhu beach.'

'Hold on. I am coming right now. Don't take public transport at this time.'

I glance at my watch and realise it is 11.30 pm. Mumbai is a city that never sleeps. I am certain that I will not have a problem taking a cab home but I don't want to argue with him. 'Okay. Did you call up Asha? There were two missed calls from her. How did you get her number?'

'We need to talk, ' he says and hangs up.

I rack my brains to figure out how he could have got hold of Asha's number. I have only mentioned her name a few times. Maybe he got it from my office. But the security guards would not have her number. After all, we have several office blocks spread over fifteen acres of land and even though the central board (which is where his call would have gone, presuming he had called up my office) would have Asha's number in their data base, they wouldn't give it out to anyone who called. Or would they? I have no idea.

Rishabh pulls up and I get in silently.

'Okay, I am sorry. Look, I lost it. I agree I shouldn't have walked out like that,' I say.

He does not answer. His expression is one that I have never seen before. A kind of silent rage. I get a sinking feeling. Something does not feel right.

'Hey baby—I am sorry, okay?' I apologise further.

Yet he is quiet.

So I am silent till we reach home. In the elevator, I try to hold his hand but he pulls it away. There is nothing left for me to do except follow him meekly.

It is only after we enter our apartment and he closes the door behind him, that he speaks.

And what he says sends a chill down my spine and tautness in the pit of my stomach.

'Who the fuck is Aman?' he asks as he looks at me accusingly.

A million thoughts run through my mind. How does he know about Aman? Why is he asking this now? I haven't had any contact with Aman for the last two years. Heck, I don't even know where he is. Who has told Rishabh about Aman? And why is he angry?

Rishabh is looking at me accusingly now. He is waiting for answers.

And I have no idea what to say.

Chapter 8

Aman

The first thing I feel as soon as I see her picture is utter shock and a strange sense of disbelief. I stare at the picture that has popped up with her name. She has changed her name. She calls herself Shruti Prasad now. I stare for a few more seconds to see if my slightly drunken mind is making a mistake. It isn't. It is her all right. She has cut her hair short now. Very short. When I used to know her, she had long tresses. I loved burying my face in her hair. It was straight and silky and the memories pelt me like a sudden downpour. I remember the familiar smell of her hair—she always smelt so good. I loved running my fingers through her hair. But now it is so short, almost like a boy's. She is looking into the camera and smiling. She seems happy and carefree.

And he is there right next to her, with his arms around her. In the exact same pose of my treasured picture with her which she had stuck in the scrapbook she made for me.

It rips me apart. Shreds my heart to bits. It is as though someone has smashed my face with a large mallet. The pain mingled with a sinking feeling now spreads all over me. It is hard to bear. So darn hard. And here I was, thinking I had got over her. She has obviously moved on. It is only me, the sentimental fool, who is still holding on to the book she made for me, and it is only me who is still mooning around for her. I feel like the biggest idiot in the world to have wasted the last two hours looking her up.

What did you expect? For her to be single and looking for you?

I do not know what I expected, but I certainly did not expect to feel like this. And what I did not expect is this sudden rush of emptiness and excruciating agony that hit on seeing her picture.

I want to scream and shout. I want to yell at her. And yet I do not want to feel this way. I want to be free of her. I want to move on. I *have* to.

I call up Mark and ask him what he is up to.

'We're going to be at Jamo's tonight. Want to join in?' he asks.

I accept without a moment's hesitation. I ask him if he can pick me up and he says he is happy to. I think Mark senses my loneliness. Whatever it is, I sure am glad to be getting out. Sitting alone and thinking of her is becoming unbearable. I need distraction and I need it big time.

Jamo's, a bar and nightclub with a dance floor and some electrifying music, is spread over two floors, and is one of the nicer places in Norwich to have a 'wild night'. They mostly play hip-hop and R&B both of which I do not particularly enjoy, but I don't care. I just want to forget.

Andy who is our colleague also joins in and tonight it seems like almost all the best-looking Norwich girls have made their way to Jamo's. We are a little early and manage to get seating—a low leather couch not too far from the bar or the dance floor. It is a nice place to sit—and we can get a great view of the dancers from here. I down three tequilas straightaway.

Three hours later, I am too drunk to care. I feel happy

and light. Mark has worked his charm and a group of three girls have joined us now. It is funny how we have 'paired off'. We can hardly hear each other (or even see each other clearly as the lighting is very low) over the sound of the music, but the girl who is sitting next to me (I cannot make out if her name is Tracy or Gracy) has her hand on my thigh and is stroking it, giving a clear indication of what she wants. She tells me that she wants to smoke and we go to the smoking area.

Thankfully this is quieter and we can have a conversation. Tracy (or Gracy) is wearing a strapless shoulder dress and she has a nice pair. I have to make an effort to not stare at her cleavage. As she sits down to smoke, her already short dress rides a couple of inches up her thigh and it is tantalising. She is so darn attractive.

'Tell me about In-di-yah, yes?' she drawls. I do not know how much she has had to drink.

I find her question funny and I am drunk myself.

'Great country. You must come with me,' I say and laugh.

'Really? I just might take you up on that,' she says.

'Sure. I would love it,' I reply.

'You would love what?' she asks as she narrows her eyes and licks her lips and looks straight at me.

'You taking me,' I reply.

She laughs.

'So let's go?' she asks.

It is that simple. I have never done this before. Mark and the gang are professionals at it. Usually, I just go along with them and leave before I get too drunk and before things start 'heating up', which basically means pairing off with women looking for some fun. This is the first time I have gone the whole length. I am just a beginner but I am learning fast. I tell her that we can go to my hotel.

'That is great. As I share a home with three girls, unless you don't mind them watching,' she giggles.

'Oh no. I wouldn't want that!' I say quickly.

'I was only kidding,' she says and winks, like she does not mean it at all.

We decide to leave. I tell Mark that I am leaving with her and he winks and gives me a smile as though to say, 'Enjoy the night, mate.'

We take a cab to the hotel and she giggles incessantly. She tells me about how she finds In-di-yah fascinating. My hands are stroking her thighs now and she parts her legs, inviting me to explore further. We can't wait to get to my hotel room and tear off each other's clothes.

It has been two years since I last had sex. This feels so good. No wonder Mark and the others do their 'pulling' act so often.

As soon as we are inside the hotel room, we have wild, unrestrained sex. I am overcome with desire and she kisses me aggressively. I am surprised when she even pulls out a condom from her purse. She is unabashed, insatiable, unstoppable—so darn different from Shruti.

Fuck. I am having drunken sex with another woman and she is still somewhere at the back of my mind. But Tracy (or Gracy) is begging me to do it harder now and I oblige, shutting out everything else, just indulging in pure physical passion and immersing myself in it totally. This feels amazing.

And at last we are done. The last thing I think of before falling asleep is that I should have done this a long time back.

The next morning I wake up with a massive hangover. I only vaguely remember the happenings of the previous night. I remember calling up Mark and heading over to Jamo's and I remember the three girls, particularly the one with the strapless dress.

Gradually the events of the night come back to me. I

vaguely remember having sex with her and feeling terrific about it. I get out of bed and there is a discarded condom lying on the floor. I pick it up, wrap it in a piece of toilet paper and throw it in the bin. I switch on the kettle for some coffee.

Then I see the note that she has left for me.

There is her number and she has scribbled, *'U were awesome. Call me. xo xo'*

I smile and realise that I still do not know if her name is Gracy or Tracy. But the sex sure has helped ease the pain I was feeling last night.

Perhaps I would have saved the number had I intended continuing to live in Norwich. But I have a flight to catch in a few hours from now. I have no intentions of seeing her again. So I crumple it up and toss it in the bin, thinking that I must be the only guy on planet Earth to toss away a girl's number, which she has so willingly given me.

I log in to my laptop and clear a few pending things. There is a report which has to be sent out before noon today. There are a few mails to be replied to. I also have to go to office and hand over the security key tags and clear my desk.

I reach office and as I walk along the cobbled streets of Norwich in my heavy overcoat, I pass all the familiar landmarks—the Norwich Millenium Library, the marketplace, Jarrolds where I have spent many afternoons, Pret a Manger where I have had lunch so many times, the buskers who sing at street corners, the artists who display their paintings on the fence of St Peter Mancroft Cathedral and the flower shops that have the loveliest of flowers—my thoughts instantly go to Shruti. She loved flowers. Each time I pass the flower shops in Norwich, I think about how she would have loved it and almost instantly I push it out of my mind. I realise that a part of me will definitely miss this town which gave me such a lot, these last two years.

But another part of me also longs to be back in my own country. I will not need these heavy coats there. I long for street food like *chaat* and piping hot *ragda pattice* which you do not get in Norwich at all.

Finally, I reach office and when I log in, there is a mail from Anjali. She has actually asked me out on a date.

I smile. Maybe that is just what I need. A nice distraction from all these thoughts of Shruti which are clinging to me stubbornly, refusing to leave me in peace.

I draft a reply to her telling her that I would love to join her on Monday evening and I hit send.

I get her reply almost instantly.

'Oh, lovely! Looking forward to it!' it reads and I smile at her enthusiasm and bubbly nature.

Later, Mark drops me off at the bus station. There are coaches that drop you off at Terminal Five at Heathrow airport, which is where I will take my flight to India. I prefer the bus to the train, as taking a train will mean changing trains at Liverpool and I do not want to lug my rather large suitcase and my shoulder bag.

Finally I board the plane to India and I have got a seat right in front, just behind the business class section. I peep in and it looks so comfortable and cozy compared to the economy class where we seem to be packed like sardines. I look longingly at the people who travel business class and think to myself that I will some day get there.

I finally settle down for the eight-hour flight. I realise that I need to fully exorcise Shruti from my system. There cannot be any more mooning around for her.

She has moved on and so should I.

The more I think about it, the more my head tells me that Anjali is exactly what I need right now. But my heart still refuses to listen.

Shut up heart. I have had enough of you.

Of course, I have no idea about what lies in store. I think about how badly I am looking forward to finally being in India. I have no idea that the saying, 'The road to hell is paved with good intentions', is about to come true. I have no idea what I am setting myself up for. And so I drift off into a peaceful sleep, presuming that I am starting a new chapter in my life, not knowing that at times, the unfinished ones come back and haunt you, dance on your head and suck every darn thing out of you, till you are reduced to a jumbled mess of nothingness.

Chapter 9

Shruti

I do not know what to say and so I remain silent.

'There is something you are hiding from me, Shruti. I asked you a simple question. Who is Aman and why haven't you told me about him all this time?' Rishabh's tone is low and controlled. As though he is holding himself back.

I do not know why I feel guilty. After all, it is not as though I have cheated on Rishabh. Rishabh's tone has made my throat go dry. My hands have gone cold. I am acting as though he has caught me having sex with Aman. I am nervous and I do not know why I feel so.

'Look, I can explain,' I say, my brain furiously searching for explanations. How do I tell him about the four years that I have spent with Aman? How can I tell him that I never thought about a future without him? That every waking moment during those four years were spent in thoughts of each other. That he loved me more than life itself and I loved him back. And that I never expected my parents to take such a hard stand and, worse, I never expected to not have the strength to oppose them. My mother was in such a state. Things were so different then. There was also that scene between Aman's mother and my parents too. There is just too much history for me to tell Rishabh.

Besides, I also wanted to start life over on a clean slate. I wanted to leave all that behind. And I have indeed not contacted Aman, even though I have thought often about him, worried about him and even secretly said prayers for him, almost every day.

How in the world can I confess all of this to Rishabh?

'Aman is history. I haven't been in touch with him for the past two years,' I finally manage to say.

'What I meant is, why didn't you speak about him till now? Haven't I told you about all my past relationships, all my ex-girlfriends? Have I ever hidden anything from you?' he accuses.

Have you ever considered that it might be because I am open enough to listen to you and not judge you, but you might not do the same?

'You have. You haven't hidden anything.'

'Then? Don't you think you owe me an explanation?'

'Why do you want to know, Rishabh? I told you, it is history. And how did you find out about Aman? Who told you?'

'If there is nothing, why are you hesitating so much?'

'Why are you insisting so much? And you still haven't told me how you came to know.'

He looks at me with an expression that is hard to comprehend. Then he looks at the dining table which has my laptop on it. My email account is open. That is when it sinks in.

Rishabh has gone through my emails.

Which means he has read all those private messages between Aman and me. Shit. There must have been hundreds. I feel like sinking into the earth. There is such a lot Aman and I have shared. I quickly try and remember if there were any mails that were explicit. I do not recall. There probably were. We were so madly in love.

It is horrifying to know that Rishabh has had access to all of this. Nobody, no one other than Aman and I were meant to read any of that. It was highly personal, very private and so darn intimate. And now here is Rishabh questioning something that I shared with a guy before he even came into my life.

I am hurt now. He has no business going through my personal stuff. How dare he. And how can he question me like this now. Like I am some criminal. I feel wrecked. I feel angry. I am a vortex of emotions.

'Why did you go through my mails? And how the fuck did you log into my account?' I ask.

'Because you fucking left it open. I did not even know it was open. I logged in to find your office board numbers to contact Asha. Then I saw you hadn't logged out of your account. So I thought, I would find Asha's email id as that would be faster as she might be on Blackberry and would see the mail instantly, which she did by the way. I was bloody worried about you. Is that a crime?' he asks and his voice has lost that controlled calm.

I don't know what to say.

'So after you contacted her, you decided to go through my mails, is it? You pervert. You... you creep.' I am upset now and so angry that I am unable to speak.

'Watch your words, Shruti. I was not thinking as I was worried. I was desperately trying to reach Asha, and while searching for Asha, Aman popped up. It caught my attention because you said you liked the name. And I wondered who this Aman was whom you have never mentioned before.'

'And so you decided to find out. And read all the mails.

How could you, Rishabh? How the hell could you? Don't you have any concept of privacy? Do I ever go through all your personal stuff? Have I ever once logged into your email account?'

'I too hadn't, till now. But I want to know who this Aman is and what your relationship with him was.'

'How will that matter? It is over. It was in the past.'

'Have you slept with him?'

'So is this all about that? Why the hell should I answer that?'

'Because it matters to me.'

'What do you want me to do? Give you a performance scorecard? Aman versus Rishabh? Grow up. I told you it was in the past and it is over. I haven't contacted him since.'

'No? Are you sure? I am not so sure now, after reading all those mails. How do I know you aren't texting him?'

'God, Rishabh. I cannot believe this. Are you suspecting me? Are you seriously thinking that I am hiding something from you?'

'Heck yes. Till now I didn't. But now I feel I do not know you any more, Shruti. If you could hide such a huge thing all this while, God knows what else you have been hiding.'

I do not know what to say to that. In a marriage, trust is the biggest thing between partners. If the trust is gone, the relationship stands on fragile legs. Right now the legs have taken a huge beating. I haven't yet recovered from the shock that Rishabh has gone through something so darn private, something that he had no right to, and even before I have recovered from that, he has unleashed another arsenal on me—that he suspects my fidelity. I don't even know how to react. On the one hand, is the hurt. On the other is the guilt of hiding such a big part of my life from him (even though it was over two years back—or am I feeling guilty because deep down I haven't yet got the closure?). Added to that is anger at his having snooped through my mail. In hindsight, I should have deleted them. Then there would have been 'no evidence'. But it is too late for that now. Besides I never even thought in my wildest dreams that Rishabh would sink so low.

'Look, Rishabh, firstly, you had no right to snoop. You had no right to read those mails. Secondly, even if you did, how can you suspect me like that?'

He is silent for a while. I am silent too. I pour myself a glass of water to calm down.

Then he delivers another blow. 'I want to read all your text messages right now,' he says.

I can scarcely believe what I am hearing.

'My text messages?' I ask as though I haven't comprehended.

'Right now, before you get a chance to delete them,' he says as he stretches out his hand for my phone.

'No,' I say. This is the limit. How can he even ask to see my phone? How can he not *believe* me?

'Then you are having an affair. Tell me the truth—didn't you march out just now and call him?'

'What rubbish are you talking, Rishabh. This is utter nonsense.' I am angry now and I hurl the phone at him. 'Here go through my messages, check for yourself,' I say.

The phone lands with a soft thud on the futon and I am furious at Rishabh's attitude. He calmly walks towards the futon and picks up the phone. And before my very eyes, he goes through each and every text message of mine.

I feel naked. I feel stripped. I feel robbed. I feel violated. I feel like a criminal being paraded to be identified. I cannot believe that the guy I married is treating me like this. He doesn't believe me and he is checking my phone. I clench my fists as he continues to scroll through each and every message on the Instant Messenger app.

Rishabh is oblivious to all that I am going through.

'Who is Dev? And why is he sending you jokes?' he asks.

Dev is the nerdy guy in accounts who I don't give a damn about. I get irked with these jokes he sends me every now and then. But I do not want to explain to Rishabh. I am aghast at his behaviour. I am hurt. I am shocked.

I don't reply and I continue sitting there as Rishabh continues to scroll and read all my messages.

'Look, Rishabh,' I finally say, 'I think there has to be some trust in a marriage. If you snoop like this and you are so suspicious, it is going to be very hard for me.'

'Ha! Rich that is—coming from you. You were the one who had an affair behind my back.'

I can't believe that the reasonable, sweet Rishabh is even saying all of this. It seems so absurd to me.

'That was before I met you, dammit. I have never ever contacted him after I split up. Why don't you believe me?'

'Maybe because those mails tell a different story, Shruti. Tell me something—if roles were reversed and if you had discovered mails like the ones you have written from my id, would you trust me?'

'If you told me that it was in the past and it was over, I would. I wouldn't ask to see your messages. Snooping is horrible, Rishabh. It is a violation of trust.'

'That is easy for you to say. You aren't the one affected. Tell me what happened between Aman and you. I want to know.'

'It is a long story, Rishabh. And it is over. I don't want to talk about it.'

'Why not? That shows you have some feelings left. If it is past and over, you should have no issues talking about it.'

Rishabh has inadvertently hit the nail on the head. He is right. I still haven't closed the Aman chapter. But I am emotionally too battered by the turn of events to reopen it.

Please not now, I want to plead.

But the way Rishabh looks at me, daring me to open up, accusing me with his eyes of something I never did, does me in.

'Very well. I will tell you if you want to know,' I say.

'Yes. I want to know what happened. The whole story.'

'I was madly in love with him and he with me. We had never forseen a future without each other. I had taken it for granted that it is him I would marry. I even went with him to Gwalior to meet his mother. I lied to my parents about a project I had to do. His mother liked me. His mother was all for us. Then I spoke to my parents. My parents were dead against this match as he is a north Indian. They wanted someone from our community. But Aman convinced us that if his mother met my parents, they would be okay. I too believed that. So he flew his mother down to Bangalore. We sprung a surprise on my parents, hoping that if his mother spoke, they would be more open and see for themselves how nice his mother was, and how keen we are on marriage. But we couldn't have been more wrong. Aman's mother mentioned how wonderful she felt when I had walked into her home. My parents hit the roof when they knew that I had lied and gone with Aman to his house and that his mother had been a party to it. My father insulted her. She is a widow and has raised Aman all by herself. He made allegations about her moral character. I have never been so ashamed of my father. He questioned her about her property, her caste, her family. Then he went on to elaborate about our wealth and reach and prestige. I cringed hearing all this. He then threatened that if she dared set foot again into our compound, he would have her thrown out. I was shell-shocked to see my father speak this way. I apologised profusely to his mother and they left. My parents berated me and gave me a solid dressing-down. They said Aman was not suitable at all. When I asked why, my dad said that it was obvious that he wanted to marry me for money. God! I still cannot believe he said that. They wanted me to have nothing to do with Aman anymore. Of course, I refused. I told them I would walk out and they couldn't stop me. But a week later, my mother was diagnosed with breast cancer. I couldn't walk out. They needed me. By now, Aman's mother too was against the match. She said that if that was the culture I came from, she had second thoughts about me. She couldn't believe that my parents were so narrow-minded. Also, I was spending less and less time with Aman. He wanted me to walk out and get married. How could I? I couldn't desert my mother. I began having fights with him. It was too much for me to handle. I didn't know if my mother was going to live or die. Only the first round of chemo was over. I broke off contact with Aman. In between one of the numerous hospital visits, my parents reiterated the importance of family background, of same caste and community in marriage. They said love would grow over a period of time. They said everyone has crushes like the ones I had on Aman, but they don't last in the long run. They emphasised the difference we would have in language, custom, economic background and how much all of it mattered. Day in and day out, my mother would get teary-eyed and emotional. Finally, I had no strength to stick up for Aman anymore. He wasn't making it any easier for me either. By then, communication between us had dwindled. I told him I had to break up with him. My parents were delighted. I was happy to see my mother finally relieved. And later, when my mom's sister brought your alliance, my parents felt it was the perfect fit. When I met you, I liked you. And the rest you know.'

I have explained everything to Rishabh now. He knows the whole story. There is nothing to hide anymore.

Aman was history and a part of my past. But now he is a part of my present too. By telling Rishabh about Aman, I have now actually added him to *our* lives. Mine and Rishabh's.

Rishabh is silent for a very long time. He reflects on all that I have said.

And then he says, 'Tell me the truth, Shruti. Did you marry me as a consolation prize? Do you even love me?'

And I stand dumbfounded, unable to meet his eyes or answer the question he has so simply asked.

Chapter 10

Aman

When I emerge from the plane at Mumbai, the first thing that hits me is the noise. It is funny how quickly one adapts to a new country and integrates so well with it, that the once familiar feels strange again. I have grown up and spent all my life in India and yet, after two years out of the country, I find it extremely noisy in comparison to the UK, where the decibel levels are probably one tenth of the decibel levels in India, by default.

I have about an hour and a half before my flight to Bangalore and the first thing I do upon landing is call my mother. She is elated to hear my voice.

'*Achha, beta*. You just landed? How are you? When are you coming to Gwalior?' asks my mother even before I have a chance to answer her first question.

'*Haanji, Ma*. Just landed. I will come the first chance I get. It hasn't even been five minutes since I landed,' I smile at her eagerness and typical 'mummy-enthusiasm'. You cannot beat Indian mothers when it comes to asking questions about your life. They want to know every single detail.

'How was the flight? You slept well? And what time is your flight to Bangalore?' she asks.

'In an hour and a half. Yes, the flight wasn't too bad. When will you visit me?' I ask her, giving her a taste of her own medicine.

'Look, *beta*,' she sighs. And I know immediately what is coming next. Sure enough, she says, 'Get married soon. Then I will consider moving base. More proposals have come. Shall I send you the photos?'

'Ma, we have been through this so many times. When I am ready, I will tell you. What can you make out from a photo anyway?'

'As though you can make out anything without a photo. I am only telling you to meet these girls, not marry them. In fact, one of them is Bangalore-based. She is an MBA and she is working in some software company. Very good family.' My mother does not give up so easily. Ever since that fiasco with Shruti's parents happened, her one-point objective in life is to see me married. It is almost as though it will be redemption for the insults she suffered at their hands, and her ghosts will finally be laid to rest when I am married. While I was in the UK, she couldn't do much except mention it every time I called her and email me pictures of the girls, which I never opened. The thing is, I just am not interested in marriage. How many times do I have to explain that to my mother? I am doing well in my career and marriage is the last thing on my mind. I can see her point of view, but it is my life, and I do not want to mess it up by adding marriage to it, till I am ready. When I marry, it has to be for the right reasons.

'Look, Ma, we have had this conversation many times. I will tell you when I want to get married and you can start the bride-hunt then okay?'

'All boys your age are getting married. Everyone in the community asks about you. I don't know what to say at social gatherings anymore.'

I smile at her choice of words. At twenty-seven, I am still a 'boy' in India. I imagine explaining this to Mark and the others. They would never get it.

'Ma, we cannot live our lives to please society. You, yourself have told me that so many times. And now what happened?'

'Maybe I am getting old, son. I so miss your father,' she says.

I do not know what to say to comfort her. She has started feeling insecure about her age. She was never like this earlier. She was always a strong-willed woman and after my father's death, she has been very brave. Never once has she talked about how unfair my father's sudden death was, about missing my father or any such thing. I have never seen my mother's vulnerable side and today her voice sounds forlorn and defeated. I wish I could just say yes and meet the girls that she keeps lining up, just so that she is pleased. But, honestly, I know I have no inclination to. I do not want to simply cheat my mother and give her false hope. So I change the topic.

I ask about her garden. That is a topic she loves talking about. My mother started gardening ever since she retired and even won some prizes at the local horticultural fair for her produce of bitter gourds and bottle gourds. She tends to the garden almost every waking hour, and our terrace has been turned into a small little farm by her. She grows several vegetables in crates and her hibiscus collection is enviable. People come to visit her garden and she has been featured on local television channels for her gardening skills. She even conducts workshops for a local gardening chapter. My mother now describes all her latest projects and I am happy that I have deftly managed to change the topic.

Finally, I tell her to take care and that I will see her soon, and I hang up.

When I browse through a bookshop at the airport, just before boarding my flight, my eyes fall on *Tiara* and I remember Anjali. I buy the copy on a whim and go through the contents. I am happy to see a relationship column with her picture in it and the article that I gave inputs for. 'Five Things to Keep a Guy Hooked to You' reads the title. Anjali looks fantastic in the picture. It is perhaps professionally clicked or she has got an image makeover since the last time I saw her, which was at Vikram and Dipika's place, when I visited India last year.

I briefly consider calling her up. If I do, she will probably read too much into it. Women always presume that if a guy calls them, he is 'interested'. I definitely am not into her in *that* way, even though I have agreed to go on a 'date' with her. Finally I decide not to call her and instead I drop her a mail.

From: Aman Mathur <aman.mathur@zmail.com>

To: Anjali Prabhu <anjali.prabhu@tiara.com>

Sub: Just read your piece

Hey Anjali,

Am mailing you from Mumbai airport. I just landed and am on my way to Bangalore. Picked up a copy of *Tiara*—and I must say 'Congratulations'! It feels good to think that a columnist is my friend.

Will see you Monday evening.

Aman

I get her reply within seconds. She says she is delighted to hear from me and thrilled that I saw her column in print and that she is looking forward to meeting me on Monday.

When I land in Bangalore, I call up Vikram. He informs me that Dipika has cooked biryani and jokes that because of me, he too will get some nice food. Dipika comes on line almost at once and asks me not to believe him and that she makes it often.

'Yeah, yeah, the last time you made it was when your brother came and that was more than eight months ago,' says Vikram.

'What is this? Am I on speaker phone?' I ask

'Yeeeeeees' yell a unison of voices—Dipika, Vikram and both the girls.

I smile. I know I am home.

Their apartment, a penthouse on the fifteenth floor, is in one of the premium residential properties on Sarjapur Road in Bangalore. It has a lovely terrace garden with a well-landscaped lawn and all their parties are hosted here. The security guards at the gate check with Vikram on the intercom and then make me sign a register and wave me in. I dismiss my cab driver and my rather heavy suitcase glides smoothly across the Italian marble in their spacious lobby. I wonder at what point in my career I would be able to afford a place like this.

As soon as I ring the bell, Ria and Reema tumble out and then, suddenly, stand there, shyly smiling at me. They look adorable, dressed prettily in white sleeveless frilly frocks and polka-dotted large hair bows. I have bought tons of chocolate for them from Heathrow airport and a pair of Moxie dolls which the store assistant at Hamleys assured me the girls will love. I can't help thinking that Ria and Reema look exactly like the dolls I have. I give them a big warm smile. Then I say a hello to them and ask if I may hug them. Reema shakes her head from side to side which I guess indicates a no and Ria nods a yes. I laugh and hug Ria and extend my hand to Reema who then decides that a handshake is a good idea.

It is then that Vikram emerges.

'Oh hello. I can see the welcome party has already greeted you warmly,' he says as he shakes my hand and thumps me on the back and then proceeds to give me a 'man-hug' as well.

Then I see Dipika. Her hair is still damp from the shower and the shoulders of her white *kurti* are slightly wet where her hair touches it. Her *kurti* is semi-transparent and I can make out the outline of her bra clearly. She looks so stunning I draw in a sharp breath. I had forgotten how very sexy she is. She smiles at me and hugs me lightly.

'Welcome back,' she says softly and I get a whiff of her perfume. Her breasts brush against my arm as she steps back from her hug and I feel a flush of embarrassment at the sudden erection in my trousers.

Fuck. It has been a long time since that has happened.

'Thank you,' I say and turn away quickly towards my suitcase and call out to Reema and Ria, 'hey girls, I've got something for you,' and I sit down and unlock it.

'What is it?' asks Reema half curious and her sister follows suit and chimes, 'What is it?', in her baby voice.

'Oh, that is sweet of you, Aman, but at least have something to drink first. Give it to them later,' says Dipika.

'No no, let me give it to them. It is right on top. I hope they like it.'

Besides, let me calm myself down. You look too darn hot.

Ria is unable to hide her curiosity. 'What is it? What is it?' she asks, dancing around. Her sister copies her and they chant, 'What is it' like a war-cry.

'*Chup*! Wait and see and if you don't stop that right now, I will tell Aman to take it right back,' says Vikram.

That makes them silent for a second. Then Ria says, 'No you won't. You cannot do that. Gifts cannot be taken back.'

Dipika and I burst out laughing and a second later Vikram joins in too.

'Ha ha, yes, they cannot be. Here you go,' I say handing them their Moxie dolls.

The girls squeal in delight.

Dipika looks at them and is stunned too. 'Wow, they look so gorgeous. Aman, you shouldn't have. But thanks,' she smiles.

I smile and I try hard to not look at her breasts but I steal a glance anyway. It is hard not to, the way she looks right then.

'Girls, say a thank you. Remember your manners,' says Dipika.

'Thank you, thank you,' they chime and then vanish into their rooms, delighted with their new toy.

Vikram asks if I will have a beer and I gladly accept. After the cold in the UK, India feels warm, although by Indian standards, Bangalore has one of the most pleasant climatic conditions in the country.

Vikram talks about how the new Chairman Steve Bagshaw is taking over and how sharp he is. He talks about a leadership forum that he recently attended and how forthright Steve was. He says he is a total go-getter unlike some of the older ones he has had in the past. He talks about the changes he has made in the reporting structure and Dipika joins in.

'So you guys are having beer, eh? And nothing for me?' she looks questioningly at her husband as she flops down next to him.

'Sorry, darling. I forgot to ask you what you will have. What can I get you, my lady?' asks Vikram with exaggerated politeness.

'Some red wine will be nice, my lord,' replies Dipika without missing a beat and she winks at me.

I am not sure what to make of that wink. Is she flirting with me?! I am a little taken aback and I shift uncomfortably in the plush leather sofa.

Vikram goes to get the wine and Dipika suddenly bends down and fiddles with the strap of the sandals that she is wearing.

Good Lord. Is she doing this on purpose? I can get a full view of her lacy bra which is some sort of purplish-pink and her breasts spill out invitingly. The erection in my pants is now like a tent-pole. I am so turned on and I cannot tear my eyes away from her.

She slips off the sandals and straightens up and, for a millisecond, catches me staring. She narrows her eyes and smiles and then tucks her leg in underneath her and undoes the first button of her *kurti*, looking at me all the while.

God! I cannot believe it. She is definitely flirting now. And I am finding it increasingly hard to not stare.

Vikram returns with her wine and I busy myself listening intently to all that he has to say. I nod at appropriate intervals but all the while I can feel Dipika's eyes boring into me. Her movements seem slow, sensual, like a cat on the prowl and I feel like a prey being hunted.

Perhaps it is the long journey and the beer that is playing tricks on my mind. How can Dipika flirt with me? I am probably imagining it, after that wild encounter with Tracy/Gracy. My brain has probably gone into sexual overdrive, I tell myself.

I try harder to pay attention to what Vikram is saying about how the audit report that the team submitted shook up the top management and made them take notice, how the board has, in all probability, decided to stop outsourcing to third parties and how they feel it is imperative to set up their own internal resources. He talks about a role for me in it, perhaps spearheading the whole thing and now he has got my attention. That would be exciting and it would mean a huge leap in my career, from my current role to being involved in setting up this new division. It would be a big challenge and opportunity. Vikram says he is confident that I will deliver and also that it would be good for me, as a career move.

'Hey guys, I am bored. This is not polite. No talking shop,' interrupts Dipika and she stretches her arms above her head which again thrusts out her breasts. I quickly look away again and tell Vikram that she is right and it isn't polite to talk shop.

'So how was your stay in the UK? Met any nice *firang* babes?' asks Vikram, taking the suggestion and changing the topic.

'*Haan,* women there are something else but, honestly, I prefer Indian women,' I say and Dipika smiles at me.

She says she will set the table and I offer to help.

'No, no, it is all done. I am just heating it up in the microwave,' she says as she unravels her legs and then once again bends down to fasten the straps of her sandals and I get a good view of her breasts spilling out, yet again.

Fuck. At this rate, I will probably come in my pants.

Is she doing this deliberately? Is she making a pass at me? Or is my imagination actually working overtime? I am not able to decide. Dipika has never done anything like this in the past. What is this new thing she is trying with me? Perhaps I am just thinking too much about it.

Later we sit down for the meal. Ria and Reema, whose mealtime is a lot earlier, have already eaten. Dipika sits opposite me, and Vikram sits next to her.

The biryani she has made tastes heavenly. I am eating proper Indian food after very long and relish it.

Helping myself to the *raita*, I nearly spill it, when I find Dipika's bare foot, on mine, under the table, making slow circles on my leg.

I freeze and stiffen up and the only thing that I can think is, '*Fuck, I am dead now. Really dead.*'

Chapter 11

Shruti

Jealousy is a strange monster. It gobbles up relationships without leaving a trace, only a vileness so foul the stench permeates forever, staining the very soul.

Ever since the time Rishabh has read those mails exchanged between Aman and me, he has definitely changed towards me.

Gone is the easy camaraderie that used to be the hallmark of our relationship. It is now replaced by a terse coldness and measured responses to everything he says to me.

I do not know what to do to make him feel better. I feel miserable about it. Is it so important for him to have known all my relationships before marriage? (Actually I have had only Aman.) Or is the fact that I slept with Aman that is haunting him? I wish he would open up and rave and rant about whatever is bothering him. I wish he would just express his anger instead of bottling it up inside. It would help if he got it out of his system.

He comes now from office and he places his laptop bag inside the cupboard and settles down in front of the television.

'You remembered to keep the bag inside today,' I say, trying to lighten the atmosphere, even though I am dying inside at how he is treating me.

'Yes. I don't want to inconvenience you in any way,' he says coldly.

I wish he would go back to being the old Rishabh. I ignore what he has said as I want to make peace.

'Can I get you orange juice?' I ask.

'No thanks. I am okay,' he says.

I sit next to him and put his arm over my shoulder. He yanks it back like my touch has given him an electric shock and says, 'Just leave me alone, Shruti.'

'Please, Rishabh. Don't be like this. Come on. It isn't that I did something behind your back. Please let it go. It was two years back,' I plead.

'How do I know?' he says and each of those words stings like a sharp slap.

The trust is gone now.

Is he going to look at me through eyes clouded with suspicion from now on? It isn't as though he never had relationships before we got married. He too has slept with at least two women. I haven't crucified him for that. Why then can't he accept the same for me? Why is he so upset?

There is only one way to find out and so I decide to ask him.

'Look, Rishabh. You also had your share of flings before marriage, didn't you? It isn't like you were a virgin, right? Then why in the world are you making such a big deal of this?'

'Shruti. It was different for me. I was never involved with them *emotionally*. I did not *love* them. They meant nothing to me,' he spits out the words in contempt.

I do not know what to say. Is loving someone a crime? Is getting emotionally involved with someone so wrong? Would he have been okay if I had had multiple one-night stands and not gotten emotionally involved? I am unable to understand his logic. But I do not want to argue with him right now. I just want to make peace.

'Shall we go out for dinner?' I ask

'No. Not in the mood,' he replies.

'I haven't cooked.'

It is an unspoken understanding between us that dinner is usually fixed by whoever gets home first. And on days that both of us are too tired to cook, we eat out. On a normal day, if I had told him that I hadn't cooked, he would have either suggested that we go out or he would have offered to fix something. But I think the 'normal days' are gone. It has been a week since he read those mails and he still shows no signs of forgiving. It is almost as if the old Rishabh has been thrown out and in his place is this angry, grouchy person who feels wronged. I want to shake him and tell him to quit being so silly. But I guess he is entitled to his anger. After all, he has been completely open and transparent with me about his past relationships but I haven't been the same. I have wished a hundred times that I had at least told him in passing—casually, like it was no big deal. We had talked about our relationships many times, and when he had asked me I had said that I only had silly schoolgirl crushes and since I went to a women's college, he too had presumed that I probably hadn't met a whole lot of guys, which was the truth. I had no one in my life except Aman.

I recall the first time that I met Aman. Our respective colleges were participating at a cultural festival in his engineering college and it was one of Bangalore's best intercollegiate fests. What caught my eye was that he was wearing the same shirt as I. I had represented my college in the personality contest. I had shopped for a Van Huesen shirt (a huge luxury in my student days) and picked a dark-blue one with white pin-stripes. Aman had been chosen to represent his college for the personality contest and had worn the same shirt as mine. When the participants met backstage, I had immediately spotted this. He hadn't noticed it and saw me smiling at him. He approached me and introduced himself and asked if I knew him. I replied that I did not know him but his shirt sure looked familiar. That was when he had noticed the coincidence and we had burst out laughing. Even now that memory brings a smile to my face. Aman had won the personality contest. We had gone out for coffee afterwards and that was how it had all started.

We had hit it off and had exchanged numbers. He was living in a hostel and had a lot more freedom than me. But I was good at making excuses and I lied blatantly to my parents to meet him. Soon our dates had increased and before we realised it, we were in a relationship. Aman was so easy to be with. He made me feel light-headed and special. The time I spent with him left me with an all-time high. He was intoxicating. His company was pure dynamite—I had never felt so alive in my entire life. He made me feel cherished, and how he made me laugh. I recall how much we had roamed the streets of Bangalore together. I remember how we had even visited the Visvesvaraya science museum once, as we had run out of ideas for dates, and surprisingly we had enjoyed it.

'Let's have Maggi,' says Rishabh, interrupting my thoughts and I am startled out of my reverie. God, I am still thinking of Aman and actually enjoying thinking of him, while my husband is mad at me.

'Okay, I will make it,' I say and jump up eagerly to camouflage my guilt.

I hope that Rishabh will eventually come round. I go about my business as usual. I am polite and nice to him. He is curt and cold.

Three days later, things continue to be tense between us. Rishabh hasn't thawed even a tiny bit. I am frustrated and angry now. I have a huge workload at office, as I am handling the work of a colleague who has gone on vacation. And when I come home, the last thing I want is to confront an irritable spouse.

I try my best to not let my irritation show but it is getting increasingly hard. Rishabh has got home earlier than me today but shows no signs of budging from the television.

'Hey, when did you get back?' I greet him as I plonk down my handbag on the dining table and sink into a chair and kick off my heels.

He does not respond.

'Hello, I asked you something. At least reply,' I say.

'Shhh... Can't you see I am watching TV?' he snaps at me.

That does it. This has gone on for long enough now.

I jump up and grab the remote from him and switch off the television.

He tries to grab it back but I am too quick. I dodge him and thrust it behind my back and I stand defiantly looking at him, challenging him to have a physical brawl with me if he wants it.

'Shruti—stop acting childish and give me the remote,' he says, his eyes blazing.

'Look, Rishabh, we need to talk. This has gone on for many days now. Do you realise we haven't had a proper conversation about it? Enough is enough. I explained everything to you. I told you I have buried the past long back. But yet you insist on acting like you have the whole world's burden on your shoulders,' I say.

'Just shut up, Shruti,'

'No. I will not shut up.'

'Your handbag is on the table and your heels are lying next to it. You are making the house untidy. Go and put them away.'

'Don't try and change the topic, Rishabh. I told you I want to settle this once and for all. This has gone on long enough.'

He is silent for a while. I am not willing to let him go so easily. So I continue standing there and look at him till he has no choice but to speak.

'Very well. Then listen. I am very upset about this discovery. We have been together for almost two years and today I feel I don't know you at all. You aren't the person I thought you were and I was such a naïve fool to have been taken in by all that you said. What else have you been lying to me about?'

'Rishabh—I never lied, okay?'

'I wasn't the one who hid things from the person I am married to. That is honestly the worst thing anyone can do. So you married me on the rebound, is it? Or did you marry me to please your parents?'

'Look, Rishabh, we have been through this and I don't want to discuss it. I have had a tough day at office.'

'You were the one who brought it up, Shruti. I didn't. I was watching TV quietly.'

'Rishabh, I am tired of fighting like this. Can we just forget this whole thing, please?' I ask him.

I want him to just give me a hug, and I want all of this to be forgotten.

'Shruti,' he says and there is a kind of finality in his voice. A kind of acceptance and defeat, a kind of quiet resignation. 'I will forget about it. After all, I have grown to love you. But the question here is not whether I will forget. Will you ever be able to forget him?' he asks.

And his question breaks my heart.

Chapter 12

Aman

Dipika's playing footsie is freaking me out. There is no doubt now that it wasn't my overactive imagination. What she is doing is deliberate. I shift my chair back a little and move my legs away very subtly.

She is smiling coyly at me now and Vikram is saying something about catching a movie the next day. I am only half able to focus on what he says.

'Sure, I don't mind,' I hear myself saying.

'What about you, Dipika? Do you want to come?' asks Vikram.

I am certain that Dipika hasn't heard a single word of what Vikram is saying. Or perhaps she has.

'Yeah, of course. I wouldn't want to miss it,' she says.

'Since when did you start liking action movies? It is all gore and blood, you know,' says Vikram.

'Hmmm, it has been so long since I saw a movie that I wouldn't mind watching even a black and white documentary as long as I get to go to the multiplex,' she says.

I hurriedly finish the rest of the meal and push my chair back without making it obvious, so that Dipika cannot reach my foot.

'You have hardly eaten, Aman! What happened? Didn't you like Dipika's cooking?' asks Vikram.

'Of course, it is lovely. It's just that I am feeling a bit queasy. Maybe the long travel and difference in time zones,' I reply.

'Oh yes. You must be tired. Go and rest, Aman. Let me show you to the guest bedroom,' says Dipika.

'Yeah, you do that. I want to catch this NBA game and we'll all go out for dinner in the evening,' says Vikram, as he proceeds upstairs to the AV room to watch his match. I recall the room from my visit here last time. Their house has a nice den with an entire wall lined with bookshelves, on which rest an enviable collection of books. They also have their home theatre and collection of movies there.

'Shall I help you clear this?' I ask Dipika, trying to keep a straight face. Two years of living in the UK and I cannot for the life of me, not clear up a table when I finish a meal. In the UK, when friends invite you over for a meal, you always help clear up. You even help them do the dishes.

'No, leave it. The maid will do it. Get your suitcase and bags to the room,' she says.

She marches ahead and I pick up my stuff from the floor of the living room and follow her.

As soon as we're inside, I glance outside and make sure that Vikram is out of earshot. I can hear the TV upstairs and I am certain that he must be fully engrossed in it. I whisper to her, 'Hey, listen. What was that all about?'

She giggles and says, 'Come on, Aman. I was just having some fun. No need to get so serious about it.'

'Fun? I nearly had a heart attack,' I say.

'Oh really? Why? Am I that irresistible?' she asks as she moves closer and I hold my breath. I am hard now and I hope she hasn't noticed it.

I take two steps back.

'Dipika, please. You're my friend's wife. Not even my friend—my mentor, guide, everything, I look up to Vikram and, honestly, you are putting me in a spot here.'

'Come on, Aman. Don't tell me you don't want me. Vikram doesn't have to know everything, you know, and it is not that I intend leaving him or anything,' she says and smiles.

I am shocked. Here she is, blatantly suggesting a 'no-strings-attached' affair. For a brief few seconds I am tempted. But then I consider Vikram—all that he has done for me, how he has helped me, what he means to me and most importantly his position in the organisation. You don't mess with guys like Vikram.

It takes me only a few seconds to decide. Thanks, but no thanks. I would rather be safe than sorry.

'Dipika, you're a married woman and a mother to two lovely girls. How can you say things like that?' I ask her, trying to kind of make her feel a little guilty. After all, it is not me who has made a pass at her.

But she is unfazed. 'Don't be such a holier-than-thou. And don't act like you have never done anything like this before.'

'If you are talking about messing around with married women and that too mothers, no I haven't,' I answer truthfully.

'What's it with "motherhood"? Mothers are women too you know. Women do like to feel attractive. And, trust me, after becoming a mother, you need validation all the more. But heck, why am I explaining all this to you? I don't know. Maybe it is because you are acting all ideal and great.'

I am honestly not acting 'ideal or great' as she has put it. Any other guy in place of Vikram and I would have grabbed the chance, probably. But I cannot do it to Vikram. I do not tell her that though.

'Look, I find you very attractive, okay? But this thing you have in mind, I can't do it.'

'I didn't have anything in mind. God, how can you presume anything like that? I was only having some fun. And I never expected you to take it all seriously. Please,' she says and forces a laugh.

I do not know what to say.

'Anyway, I guess you're tired. Rest and we'll have a good time in the evening,' she says as she leaves the room and closes the door.

I go to the door and bolt it, just to be sure that she won't come back in. I feel strangely restless. It is evident that Dipika wanted more and she did offer it to me on a platter—a no-strings-attached relationship if it can be called that. I do not know what it is. But I don't think she expected me to be open about it and refuse. And by pretending that I am making a big deal out of nothing, she has, I suppose, found a way out of an embarrassing situation.

I am now increasingly uncomfortable at the thought of going out with them in the evening. But there is no way to wriggle out of it. Also, I would have thought that with Vikram around, Dipika might be careful. But her suddenly playing footsie has convinced me that she is capable of anything. I decide that I will move out of their place as soon as I can. It will be difficult to explain it to Vikram and I wrack my brains for a valid reason.

Then I hit upon the perfect idea. Anjali. She will have to come to my rescue.

I cannot tell her what just happened between Dipika and me. But what I *can* do is shift our date.

I call her up. She sounds overjoyed to hear my voice.

'Heyyyyy, Aman! When did you arrive?' she greets me like a long-lost friend and I can feel the warmth in that greeting even over the phone.

'This morning. How have you been?'

'Terrific. How does it feel to be back in India?'

'Oh, it's good. Home is home.'

'Not missing UK?'

'Well, a little bit. And hey—I was just thinking about our date on Monday. Do you think we can change it?'

'Oh. But why?' she asks and I can sense her disappointment. Then I realise that she probably presumes I am shifting it to a later date. So I hasten to clarify.

'What I meant is, can we change it to tonight instead of Monday?'

'Oh, okay. But I have already agreed to go out with my friends.'

'Oh—that's okay then.'

'No no, wait. It is just a shopping trip. We were planning to go in a group. It is with some colleagues from work. In fact, I was just dragged into it. Give me ten minutes and I will call you back,' she says.

She calls back in three.

'Yeah, Aman. Super. It is all taken care of. But why a sudden change of plans? I thought you were staying with Vikram and Dipika for the weekend?' she asks.

'Well—I just remembered that I have something on Monday. And so I thought meeting you tonight would be better,' I quickly improvise and lie.

'Hmmm. I think that's sweet of you, Aman. But we could have gone out on another day too,' she says.

'Well, let's just say I couldn't wait to congratulate you on getting your own column,' I reply and as soon as I say it I realise it didn't sound the way I intended it to. 'I mean—I had put it off long enough,' I quickly add.

She laughs.

'So where do we meet? What time?' I ask.

'Plan B? It's a nice new place which has just opened. They play some great music and have a nice dance floor too.'

'Okay—will look it up. I'll see you there at say seven pm?'

'Yes. Great. Looking forward to it,' she says.

I look around the room and discover a copy of *Love in the Time of Cholera*. I spend about fifteen minutes trying to read it, but I am unable to concentrate. Dipika has managed to rattle me by her behaviour.

Then I see the Instant Messenger indicator of my phone light up. I can never resist checking immediately. It is Mark.

'You okay, mate? How was your journey? And how is India?' he asks.

'Yeah. Fine. But feels like an oven after UK,' I type back.

'Planning to visit,' he replies.

'Great! I will show you around. There is so much to see and do in India. Are you coming with Eva?'

'No. She can't make it. Will be coming alone. Will send you the tentative dates. Can you help me plan a good itinerary?' he asks.

'Of course, leave it to me,' I reply.

I can't help thinking about how methodical and organised the Brits are when it comes to planning holidays. Most of the Brits I know make a plan at least six months in advance and they pencil it in their diaries. They also don't work at all on weekends, unlike Indians. Most of them use weekends to 'do something'. They either have a game that they play or they go somewhere or get together with friends. I had found it very hard to get used to when I had initially moved to the UK. Mark had mentioned that he would like to visit India once I returned, but I hadn't expected him to actually follow through.

There is a knock on my door and I almost jump out of my skin, startled. I hope to God it isn't Dipika, as I open the door. It is Vikram.

'Rested well? Want a cup of tea?' he asks.

'Couldn't really sleep. Yes, would love some,' I reply.

Dipika doesn't seem to be around.The maid serves us tea and Vikram speaks about the new division which the company is starting. He tells me how excellent an opportunity it will be for me. I am glad to have him as my mentor. His vision is clear and his goals are focused. He is also quick in decision-making and it is no wonder that he has risen so rapidly in the organisation.

I absorb everything he says and I am quite happy that I will soon get an opportunity to work with him, just like the early years, when I had first joined the organisation as a management trainee. I ask him about the others involved, the time-frame and other relevant details and Vikram is happy to answer me. I learn that I will be reporting to Rao (whom I have worked with earlier) and not directly to Vikram.

I listen in rapt attention and that is when Dipika makes an entry again. She is now wearing a skirt that ends just above her knees and her red heels make a clickety-clackety noise as her legs slowly come into view. The sight of her descending the stairs makes my heart beat faster even as I try hard to concentrate on what Vikram is saying.

She walks towards us, wearing some sort of a lacy top that seems to hug her curves and shows some cleavage. She is stunning. She is irresistible. She looks hot. I guess she knows it too.

She hugs Vikram and then looks at me.

'You never mentioned about the date with Anjali. So aren't you going to join us for dinner? I thought you were staying here,' she says.

'Oh, that is news. A sudden date?' asks Vikram.

God—that was quick. Anjali had immediately relayed the information to Dipika. I had not anticipated that.

I squirm uncomfortably in my chair and I do not know what to say.

Dipika and Vikram are both very surprised by my sudden change of plans. I wriggle out of it by lying.

'So sorry. I seem to have muddled up the dates,' I finally say and that is the best I can come up with.

Vikram of course believes me. There is no reason not to. I am certain Dipika knows the real reason. But I am confident that there is no way she can tell Vikram about it.

I then say that since I will be out late and it is a working day the next day, it is best if I shift into the company guesthouse straight away.

'You can still come back here after your date and come with me to office on Monday,' Vikram offers.

But I say that I do not want to disturb them late at night and I will be at ease if I stay in the guesthouse.

'Yes, yes. After all, when you are out on a date with a pretty girl, anything can happen, right?' Vikram guffaws and winks at me. I look away, unable to meet his eyes.

Vikram offers to drop me at the company guesthouse, but I refuse, saying that I will take an autorickshaw as I didn't want him to drive all the way to Indiranagar from Sarjapur Road.

At the guesthouse, I bump into an old batchmate from my engineering college days whom I have completely lost touch with. It takes me a few moments to recognise him.

'*Yaar*, you have forgotten me,' he says.

I blink for a couple of seconds.

Then the penny drops.

'Oooh yes. Omi Shukla! How have you been? Oh my God. You have changed quite a bit.'

'Yes, say it directly. I have put on weight and lost my hair,' he says.

He indeed has and he looks about ten years older than me now. Had I seen him on the street, I wouldn't have recognised him. We had both joined as management trainees, after our engineering stint. During our engineering college days, we had organised many events together. We weren't very close, but Shukla was one of the guys I had got along very well with. Later when we joined the company, we had been given our postings in different cities and we had drifted apart. We chatted about work. Shukla too was moving to Bangalore after a stint in Jaipur.

'Glad to be back to civilisation, man. The last stint was truly lousy. You got to work Saturdays too,' he says as he shakes my hand and makes himself comfortable on the sofa.

'But you must have got a chance to learn so much, right?' I ask plonking down, as the guesthouse attendant takes my luggage to the room.

'*Kyaa learning-verning. Goli maar* learning *ko*, I just want to chill a bit, man. There is absolutely no night life in Jaipur.'

I laugh at that statement and he wants to know what I have been upto all these years and then he asks about Shruti. I wince. Shruti and I were a well-known item those days. We were the envy of all our batchmates and we were considered to be a 'solid-sure-shot-will-get-married' couple. In fact, we had roped in Shukla once, as a proxy attendance for me, at a seminar, when I had spent the whole day with Shruti.

'We broke up,' I say simply, not offering any details. I know that he is dying to know. But I certainly do not want to talk about Shruti.

He looks at me questioningly as though expecting me to tell him the whole story.

I just tell him that things changed and I have moved on. I also say that I have a date for the evening, just to throw him off-track. He grabs the bait and perks up. But now he quizzes me about Anjali and I deliberately give him only the briefest of details, just mentioning that she writes for a magazine and I have met her only once. I myself am not sure what this 'thing' with Anjali is and I don't want Shukla to presume she is my girlfriend.

When Shukla figures out that it is a first date, he asks if I have transport and how we would be going. Then he surprises me by saying that I can borrow his bike for the evening if I like.

'Oh, that is very kind of you,' I say, floored by his gesture.

'*Arey*, no problem, bro. It isn't mine,' he laughs.

He goes on to explain that a friend of his had left the bike in Bangalore, and was on a project in the US. The project had got extended. So he had wanted someone to use the bike, as it had been lying neglected for very long now. When Shukla had said he was moving to Bangalore, his friend had been glad to have him use it.

I get an even bigger surprise when Shukla shows me the bike. It is a Ducati Monster.

'Holy cow! He lets you have this?!' I ask in disbelief.

Shukla nods as though it's nothing.

'Does he know you are lending it to me?' I ask.

'You want to use it, take it. How many questions you ask! It must be your journalist girlfriend's influence,' comments Shukla.

I let his comment stay. I am too besotted with the bike. Besides, even if I correct him and tell him that Anjali isn't my girlfriend Shukla will not believe it.

It is a long time since I rode a bike. After I moved to the UK, I haven't driven a vehicle at all. In Norwich, my office was just a five-minute walk from my home. I did not see any need to get a car, as during the weekends, I was always with Mark and the others and they had their cars. After I had moved, I had decided to buy a car 'at some point', but the 'some point' never came and before I realised it, my stint in the UK was up. I feel excited at the prospect of having a bike all to myself after so long.

I take a small test ride down the road, just to get familiar with the controls. She roars to life under me. I am riding a bike after years and I feel a rush of adrenaline as I accelerate and the machine leaps to life. 'Woo hoo!' I want to scream. The bike is indeed smooth and the controls are awesome. The ride is a ballet of grace and for a brief moment I feel invincible, victorious and strangely peaceful.

'I owe you one for letting me borrow this beauty,' I tell Shukla as I park it and glance at my watch.

'Yeah, just buy me a drink and ask your girlfriend if she knows some nice single girls,' he says as he vanishes into his room.

I smile at Shukla's comments. I don't know whether his friend would be happy if he knew that he lent his bike to someone he barely knows. But then Shukla is like that. He is the kind who will let you have the shirt off his back and think nothing of it.

I shower leisurely and get ready for my date with Anjali, all the while willing Dipika to just get out of my head. My phone buzzes and I almost jump out of my skin when I see that it is a message from Dipika.

`Hey—sorry about today. It must have been the wine. I don't know what came over me. All cool, I hope?` it reads.

Cool? She must be kidding. I am terrified. I don't want to

meet her again. I don't want to get into any kind of relationship with her. I am running as fast as I can.

`Let's just forget it. My lips are sealed,` I message back.

`Take care, Aman, and have a nice evening,` she texts back.

I do not reply to her. I know she wants to chat. It is funny how I am running away from her. I guess any red-blooded male would have jumped at a chance like this. I think of Mark and how he would have said I was a total fool to pass this up. Whatever Dipika's reasons are for making a pass at me, I do not want to encourage her in any way. I have made my stand clear on this and decide that I will stick to it.

I find myself looking forward to meeting Anjali. She would be a welcome distraction from events, since I landed in India.

Chapter 13

Anjali

I can hardly believe this. Latika always talks about the law of attraction—that if you want something badly enough, the entire universe will conspire to give it to you. I tell her that it comes true only in Hindi movies or in Paulo Coelho books. I am a sceptic. But today, I have dropped my apprehensions. Maybe this thing works after all. All I wanted was a date with Aman so darn badly that I was even willing to go out on a Monday evening with him, despite Mondays mostly being bad days for me, as the deadline for my column is Tuesday. I usually work last minute and hand it over just before the deadline.

And now out of the blue, Aman has shifted our date to tonight instead of Monday. I have already picked out what I will wear (an off-white sleeveless Vero Moda dress that ends just below the knee, and have co-ordinated the jewellery, footwear, everything). I think about my 'thing' with Aman. I have given enough hints to him that I would like to be a little more than friends, but either he is incredibly daft and cannot read the signs I am sending out or he is not interested in me *that* way. If he isn't, why then is he responding to my messages, and why did he sound so eager to advance our date? I don't know.

Now I am eager to see him and take this a little bit forward. Who knows, maybe Aman is one of those guys who needs a nudge?

Sriram calls me up and asks if I want to meet, as he isn't doing anything.

'Sorry, I have a date,' I say and I cannot keep the joy or excitement out of my voice.

Of course, Sriram catches it immediately.

'Who are you going out with? Tell!' he demands.

'Why do you want to know?'

'Because I am your friend and I have a right to look out for you. And I need to give the seal of approval to this guy you are going out with.'

'Do *you* choose *your* friends on the basis of *my* approval or disapproval?! Then why should I tell you anything at all, Sriram Surve?' I question him with mock anger.

'Because if you don't like the guy you are going out with, it is me you will call in fifteen minutes and I will be forced to bail you out. And honestly, now I have become so used to it, I kind of look forward to pretending to be your ex and barging in and terrifying the bewildered souls you date by picking up a fight with them. You should pay me for all this.'

'Rubbish! You should pay *me*. After all, I am giving you free practice for real-life acting. Not like the studied stuff you do in your theatre plays. And hey, I can't help it if the guys turn out to be boring or jerks. In any case, I can assure you this one is different,' I say.

Sriram is part of an amateur theatre group and I think he secretly dreams of acting in TV serials, although he will never admit it.

'Oh I see. And how have you concluded that?' he asks.

'On the basis of his intelligent replies to my mails, his

demeanour and general attitude. Besides this isn't like an unknown guy like the others were. I have met him once before.'

'Ah-ha! Oh yes. You mentioned him. Your UK-returned *boyfriend*!'

'Not my *boyfriend*, Sriram. We hardly know each other, except for a few emails. He is a good friend of Vikram and Dipika. I met him at their place. I mentioned him to you—Aman, remember?'

I am a little exasperated with him now and want him to get off the phone. I have to yet put on my face pack for this date, and leave it on at least thirty minutes. Talking to Sriram is holding me up.

'Okay okay. If you need me, just call me. Ain't no mountain high enough,' says Sriram, singing the popular classic song quite tunelessly and distorting it so completely that I burst into laughter.

'Okay, I will. I have to go,' I say and I am still smiling when I hang up.

When I reach the guesthouse, I spot Aman waiting for me outside. I find that rather sweet of him. He is wearing a crisp white cotton shirt with broad light blue stripes, classic faded blue jeans and Caterpillar shoes. He looks great.

'Hey,' he greets me with a semi-hug and I am enveloped in an all-male woody scent that I instantly like. Then he says, 'Let me get this,' and before I can protest, he has paid off the auto guy.

'Hey, Aman. Come on! There was no need to do that!' I say.

'Too bad, it is done now and good to see you,' he smiles.

God, he has become even more attractive since I last saw him.

'Great to see you, Aman. Nice shirt!'

'Oh, thanks. Bought it in the UK,' he says absently as

though he has just noticed it. 'Do you want to come in? Or do we leave right now?' he asks.

I glance at my watch. It is only seven pm.

'We will be too early if we leave now.'

'Right then. Let's hang around here for some time,' he says as he escorts me in.

The guesthouse is wonderfully done up. With Italian marble flooring, luxurious sofas that you can sink into, a large chandelier dominating the room, muted pastel modern art on the walls, carpets your feet disappear into, it is as good as the lobby of a five-star hotel.

'What an awesome place!' I can't help exclaiming. 'Your organisation sure knows how to take care of you! And here I am, stuck as a writer living in a little room, that passes off as a one BHK apartment!' I say.

'Oh, this is just for two months, till I get my place. I am looking, by the way. Looking to rent a place close to office.'

'Okay, get a copy of the *Ad-mag*. It is this weekly paper that has ads and ninety per cent of them are property listings. It's very useful. I also know a few real estate agents. If you want, I can put you in touch with them,' I offer.

'That's very kind of you. But our company has their brokers and their standard properties. They will help me find a suitable one,' says Aman.

I notice the slightly British manner of speaking that he seems to have picked up and it endears him to me all the more.

'See what I mean? Your company pampers you so much!' I smile in what I hope is a coquettish way. But I don't think Aman even notices.

'Yeah, as long as you perform. Else you get the axe. They are very clear about that,' he says, shaking his head and pursing his lips.

Aman asks me if I will have a fresh lime soda or juice or anything aerated. I am watching my weight. I still need to get rid of four kilos. I weigh 64 kg at a height of 5'6". I will look awesome if I weigh 60 kg. I watch my calories like a hawk but I don't want to tell Aman about it. So I settle for fresh lime with just salt, no sugar or ice. Aman asks the staff for an iced tea.

'So what was it like living in the UK?' I ask.

'Very good in some ways and bad in others,' he says.

The writer in me is curious to know more. Being inquisitive and knowing what makes people tick is an intrinsic part of my job and is deeply ingrained in me. I prod him for more.

'Well the bad in the usual sense—you miss your country, you miss being near your parents, my mom in my case, and you feel like an outsider sometimes. But the good thing is the kind of facilities they have. There is a gigantic difference between a developed country and a developing one. There is no comparison,' he says as he sips his iced tea and I nod in agreement, as though I know exactly what he is saying.

We make small talk. He tells me about how he had to slightly modify his accent and slow down how he spoke in order to be understood better. He asks me about what I am working on at the moment. The conversation flows smoothly and I secretly congratulate myself on it. By about eight, I tell him that we ought to leave. And as we leave his company guesthouse, he smiles impishly and takes me towards a bike, a splendid one, parked in the garage. Even though I am not a biking enthusiast, I am impressed by this one.

'Guess what, we don't have to take an auto,' he says as he turns the key in the ignition.

'Wow! How did you manage this? This is lovely!' I say.

Aman handles the bike expertly. I thoroughly enjoy the

ride with him. I hold on to his shoulders politely without crossing the 'you're-a-friend' border. What I want to do is stick to him like cling-film. But I don't want to scare him off.

The date turns out to be the best I have ever had. The atmosphere inside is electric. I absolutely love the music that this place plays. The dim dance-floor lights, the DJ playing just the right tracks, great ambience, good crowd and most of all, Aman by my side. He is the perfect gentleman, very attentive, and gets me my daiquiri. I stop after three and in between we dance. Aman is not a great dancer, but he copies my moves and we make a good pair on the dance floor.

Aman doesn't touch a drop of alcohol though. I am amazed at how responsible he is.

'Come on. Have at least one drink. It must be hard for you, to come to a place like this and not drink,' I speak in his ear as the music is too loud. He bends down to hear me.

'Oh no. I have to drop you back safely. I cannot risk it. Another time we will take a cab and then we both can totally let go and have fun,' he says.

We leave just before midnight and Aman drops me back. Since the next day is a working day, both of us don't want to stay too long. The streets of Bangalore are empty now and I feel great sitting behind Aman and my hair flying in the wind.

When we reach my place, he says a polite goodbye and shakes my hand.

'Aww, come on! What's with the formal hand-shake. I had a super time. Thank you!' I say as I stand on tiptoe and plant a kiss on his cheek.

He smiles and says, 'Bye and take care', and then zooms off into the night.

Later as I lie in bed and replay the events of the evening,

I realise that Aman, by saying, 'We will take a cab next time', has already made up his mind that there is indeed going to be a second date.

'Yes!' I think as I do a mental air-fist punch and the smile on my face refuses to go away even as I fall asleep.

Chapter 14

Shruti

I don't know what to do with Rishabh anymore. How much more patience must I show? It is almost a month since he spoke to me like the old times. The new Rishabh is excessively polite. At least if he yelled at me, I could yell right back and we could sort it out. His passive-aggressive anger is now getting to me, wearing me down. I have been trying my best to get things back to normal. But his 'silent-treatment-and-talk-only-when-needed' policy is now grating on my nerves. After office stress, this tense atmosphere at home makes me want to scream. I do not know when I will snap. I cannot handle it anymore. I detest the new Rishabh. I want the old one back.

Of course, I mention nothing of this to my mother when she calls. I pretend everything is happy-go-lucky. I pretend I am having a great time. I tell her about work and we chat about the latest movie. My mother every now and then hints about a baby and I deflect the topic time and again.

If I go by Asha's words, having your in-laws with you is even worse. I comfort myself saying that at least I don't have to deal with that. Rishabh's parents hate Mumbai. They have lived in Hubli all their lives and are comfortable in the huge palatial house that they have built. His business is very successful and there is no way they will wind up all that and move in with us. So to that extent, I am glad I will not have 'in-law problems' like Asha or some of the other women at work who share horror stories about their in-laws during lunch-breaks.

On Monday morning I wake up feeling like my stomach is on fire. When I sit up in bed, everything spins round and I lie back, unable to focus on anything. I turn towards Rishabh and he is still asleep stretched out on his stomach like he always is.

'Rishabh...' I call out to him.

He stirs in his sleep but does not wake up.

'Rishabh, I feel horrible. Please wake up,' I say again and nudge him a little harder this time.

'What?' he sits up.

'I feel sick, Rishabh. Something is wrong,' I tell him.

'What happened?' he asks, fully awake now.

'I don't know. If I sit up I feel dizzy,' I say as I prop myself up in a half-sitting posture on the bed with the help of pillows.

'Lie down, let me get you something to drink. Maybe you will feel better then,' he says as he gets out of bed and heads towards the kitchen.

He emerges ten minutes later with a cup of tea.

This is the first kind act he has done for me ever since the reading the emails fiasco. Even though I feel sick, his act of kindness registers and I am grateful for the tea and I gulp it down. Ten seconds later, I feel bile rising to my throat and I rush to the bathroom and throw up in the toilet bowl. I am unable to even stand and I half-squat and half-sit, clutching the closet.

A worried Rishabh emerges behind me.

'Are you okay?' he asks.

I am not even able to reply with the awful taste of puke in my mouth.

But the retching has now stopped and I feel slightly better as I rinse my mouth and flush. Rishabh holds me as I make my way to the bed.

'Shall I call the doctor?' he asks.

'No, let's wait. I don't know what this is,' I say.

'Let's just go. Why wait?' he asks.

'It's probably nothing, Rishabh. Maybe last night's dinner didn't agree with me. Let's wait and see,' I insist. Somehow I detest hospitals after spending so much time in them when my mother was undergoing treatment for her cancer. The smell of hospitals depresses me. I will do anything I can to avoid going.

Rishabh fetches me a bottle of cold water from the fridge.

'Are you sure?' he asks.

'Positive,' I say. I am feeling better already but I don't want to say that to Rishabh just yet. I am enjoying his attention and concern after being deprived of it for nearly a month.

'I will call in sick today and rest. I will be fine,' I say.

'Should I stay at home too? Are you sure you will be okay?' he asks.

'Yeah. Don't worry. You go to work. If I feel worse I will call you up.'

'Hmmm… okay,' he says and then he hesitates a bit and looks at me. I am unable to make out his expression despite knowing him so well. 'Do you… you know… do you…?' he says.

'What?' I ask him, puzzled.

'Do you think you could be pregnant?' he blurts out.

I almost laugh. 'Ha. We haven't had sex for the past one and a half months at least. It is more than a month since you even spoke to me. How will I conceive? Divine intervention?' I snap at him though I don't mean to.

He looks crushed. Then gets up and walks out without a word.

I should have remained silent. This was the perfect chance for a truce and I have ruined it.

I hear him pottering about in the kitchen and I do not budge from bed. I just feel exhausted and tired.

Before leaving, Rishabh comes to the doorway of the bedroom and says, 'See you,' and walks off. The unfriendly, sullen, angry Rishabh is back once more.

'Aaaaaargh,' I scream after I hear the door shut. I fling a cushion off the bed and it lands a few feet away. I am so angry with him.There is a limit to punishing me for something I did—or rather didn't do (which is to not have told him about Aman before marriage). Honestly—what was there to say about a relationship that was over?

But why then were you unable to answer him when he asked you if you still loved Aman?

Do I? Is it possible to love two people at the same time? I do have a special place in my heart for Aman. But I love Rishabh. Or is that what I have conditioned myself to believe? What is love? These questions go round and round in my head.

Scenes from my wedding with Rishabh flash before my eyes. I think of the time with him. Though we have got along well, I have never felt as alive with Rishabh as I have done with Aman. The time spent with Aman was simply magic. We used to laugh so much. With Rishabh, it has always been polite ribbing and teasing. Not the kind of easy familiarity and wild abandon that Aman and I shared. Aman understood me perfectly and I, him. There was nothing in the world that was too trivial to share with Aman. We even told each other what we ate, how long we slept and what we were doing throughout the day. We used to speak to each other on the phone for hours, whereas, with Rishabh, even during the time we were engaged to each other, conversations never lasted more than a few minutes. Rishabh is indeed a nice guy but it is Aman who made me feel that the whole world is mine for the asking.

With Aman, once we talked to each other over the phone the whole night. Finally at five am, we had said goodnight and fallen asleep. I couldn't of course, wake up in time for college. My parents had been worried and my mother had presumed that I was ill, and had let me sleep. Aman on the other hand, had been woken up by his hostel-mates and had promptly fallen asleep in class and been sent out. I smile at the memory.

Being in bed the whole day with nothing to do but rest gives me a lot of time to think and my thoughts keep rushing back to Aman. God, I miss him so much now.

I wonder how he is and if he is happy. I wonder if he thinks of me as much as I think of him. I wonder if he is single or has a girlfriend now. The very thought of a girlfriend causes a sinking feeling in my stomach. It is ridiculous to feel this way, because I am already married and I was the one who walked away from him.

How could I ever make him understand that it has broken my heart as much as it had broken his? I did what had to be done at that time. My mother's health was most important. Heck—we did not know if she would even live and I wanted to do everything to make her happy. One crazy illogical part of me even believed that if I perhaps sacrificed my love and did what she wanted me to, perhaps her cancer would go away.

And strangely, after her breast had been removed, it had. I knew logically that it was supremely foolish of me to think that way—that my action had somewhat played a part in curing her. But the illogical part of me still felt maybe there is something like a 'pay-off'. And when the person who is closest to you, your parent, is fighting for their life, what choice do you have other than make it as easy as possible for them? That is what I had done.

Aman was a single child too, just like me. He should have understood. Perhaps if he was in my place, and it was his mother who had been battling for her life, he would have done all that she wanted, who knows.

I am overcome by a sudden urge to know what Aman is doing right now and how he looks and what is happening in his life. My laptop is right beside me on the chest-of-drawers next to my bed. I sit up and reach out for it and I log in to Facebook. I had blocked him on the day that we had broken up. I go to my profile and see my blocked contacts. Then I unblock him. Instantly I have access to his profile but he isn't on my friend list anymore.

I look at his profile picture. A sharp pain passes through me. A deep sense of loss. A dull aching longing. A desire. Memories. A million emotions.

My Aman.

Except that he isn't mine anymore.

His profile picture is one of him alone. It is one which I have never seen which means it must have been clicked after we broke up. I look at his cover picture which is different from the profile photo. He seems to be in some foreign country now, judging by his cover picture which shows him and four of his friends, all foreigners.

I am surprised. They seem like good friends too as one of the foreigners has his arm around him and he is laughing, looking straight into the camera. There is a girl in the picture too, right next to Aman. She has jet black hair, she is wearing a strapless dress and looks like a super-model. She is gorgeous. I burn with jealousy. I wonder who she is.

This is ridiculous, I tell myself. You can't expect him to *not* move on with his life. You were the one who got married and stomped all over his heart and now you deserve it. Burn!

And burn I do.

How can a person still live on inside you for two years?

I wish now I hadn't opened his profile and looked at his pictures. I wish I had just let it be. God knows what came over me.

I feel even more miserable than I did when I was sick. And then once again without warning bile rises to my throat and I run to the toilet and throw up violently.

I wish now Rishabh had stayed back home to look after me. I wish Rishabh had at least spoken to me and been there for me. Who knows, then, I would not have even bothered to look at Aman's profile.

But now I have and the ghosts of the past are back. They are dancing all over my brain. They have overtaken my very soul. Jealousy, longing and desire are very potent to handle even one at a time.

And now all three are attacking me simultaneously and I have no place to hide.

In desperation I call up Asha.

She is in the bus, on the way to work and has all the time in the world to talk. I hear myself pouring out my whole story to her. I tell her every single detail about me and Aman. I tell her about how close we were. I tell her about the four inseparable years. I tell her about how we never envisaged this twist of fate. I tell her how much I miss him and how I long for him. I tell her about how Rishabh has been treating me for the past month ever since he read those mails. I tell her about how I am burning with jealousy ever since I saw the foreigner chick with him in the snap. I am dying to know who she is. I just want someone to understand what I am going through. I just want Asha to tell me it is fine and to hang in there.

Instead Asha does something that adds fuel to the already blazing fire.

'Hey, babes, there is only one way to get over him,' she says.

'How?' I ask.

'Meet him,' she says.

'What nonsense. How can I meet him? And why should I? And even if I do, how will that help me get over him?'

'You will see for yourself that he has moved on. He will perhaps tell you about his life in whatever country he is in. Right now you are holding on to a chimera. A memory which belongs in the past. He is a different person now and so are you. Once you realise that, you will let him go and be at peace.'

Maybe she is right, I think when I finally hang up.

Maybe I should contact him and make a final closure.

Or at least that is what I tell myself—that I am contacting him, so I can move on.

But deep down I am not sure at all.

All I know is that the thought of being in touch once more with him is making my heart soar.

Chapter 15

Anjali

From: Anjali Prabhu <anjali.prabhu@tiara.com>

To: Aman Mathur <aman.mathur@zmail.com>

Sub: Oh no! Another mail from Anjali!

Hey!

Yeah, me again. On mail.

Could not resist even though I fought with myself. The fight I lost, but I am grinning as I get to write to *you*. I love it, you know—writing. After all, I make a living out of it.

How *is* work? Is India treating you well or do you want to run back to UK?

The 'date' (permit me to delude myself by calling it a date please) was awesome. The best I have had in ages. The bike ride was great too. Do thank your friend for it. (The friend who was so scared of me that he hid in his room. Was I that intimidating?)

Noticed one thing—you were so elusive at the guesthouse when I asked about Vikram and Dipika. Why?! And hey—between you and me, the reason I asked you about it was that she seemed a bit annoyed that I hadn't mentioned we were going out. Struck me as a bit odd, and hence I asked you as you were the one right there, face to face with her! Hope you didn't mind. If you did—too bad, it's done now! I do tend to shoot off sometimes without thinking. I blame it on my zodiac sign even though I don't believe in it, despite the fact that Praneeta Menon who writes the 'Your Fortnight' swears that astrology is a science and it is true. She is also into tarot reading, energy healing and all such stuff. Do you believe in it? Personally I think they are all placebos for the weak-hearted but who knows! Maybe it is true too.

So are you asking me out for our 'next time that you won't take the bike' or should I?

Take care!

Luv

Anjali

From: Aman Mathur <aman.mathur@zmail.com>

To: Anjali Prabhu <anjali.prabhu@tiara.com>

Sub: Oh! Look! Aman has replied super-fast!

Hey Hey

This must be the fastest reply I have typed. I have never emailed someone back this quick. Not even at work. And for the record, I have tons of work as I am now in a new division, after my UK stint which was laid-back and easy in comparison to now. The work-culture is so different in both places. My mental and physical faculties are taking a bit of time adjusting to the new regime. I quite like it though. Am not complaining.

'Date' *was* a date. No delusions there. And yes, I enjoyed it too. No—you weren't intimidating at all—just that you looked so good the other day that most people would want to tidy up, just a little bit even to just appear before you. That's why Shukla disappeared the other day. (For a shave and shower, but we were gone by the time he emerged. And don't tell him I told you, he will kill me, as I have just broken the bro-code.)

About Dipika and Vikram—no comments. They were both okay with me.

About astrology—yes, I do believe in it. (Surprised?) My maternal uncle practises it and he learnt it from my grandfather. My uncle works in the US, in a multinational and had started doing it as a hobby for close friends. His predictions were accurate and now on weekends and holidays he is flooded with requests. So perhaps your Praneeta Menon may be right after all.

Yes, let's meet again.

Soon. This weekend? Where?

Until then, take care.

Aman

I am so pleased to get such a prompt, warm and lengthy response from him that I read it thrice. I find myself smiling. Aman does like me and he too had a great time. Besides, he has asked me out again. It is only when I feel my phone vibrate that I am jolted out of my dreamy reverie. It is Sriram. He asks if I can talk.

'I work for a magazine. Talking to people, quoting them, getting their stories is a part of my work, my dear,' I say with a smirk.

'Yeah yeah. We all know Anjali, the writer-journo. No need to boast or rub it in. How did your date go?' he asks.

'Why do you want to know? Give reasons in fifty words,' I say and smile even wider. It's an old joke between three of us—Latika, him and me. We used to have a science teacher, back at school, whose favourite question would be to state a science principle and then ask: 'Why. Give reasons in fifty words.'

'Reason number one, I am your good friend. Reason number two, I watch out for you. Reason three, you always tell me all that happens to you. And final reason, because I want to know,' he says.

'Ha ha, but if I tell you now, I will have to repeat the whole story to Latika too. After all, she too will want to know,' I tease him, prolonging the moment a little more. Actually I am dying to rave about Aman. But I also enjoy teasing Sriram, as I know he is just as keen to know. This is probably the first date where I haven't called him up to 'rescue me' like I usually have done in the past. So he must be curious.

'So what if you have to repeat it? You can charge me money for it, okay? Tell!' he commands.

So I rave to my heart's content about Aman. I tell him what a gentleman he was, how he paid for the auto, how he got a bike and that he also dropped me home.

'And?' asks Sriram.

'What do you mean by "and"?'

'Didn't you invite him in? Didn't anything happen?'

'Are you crazy? It's just a first date!'

'So?'

'So I am content, okay? It's not that I am dying to get into bed with him. Sriram, you have such a one-track mind.'

'Okay,' he says and he bursts into laughter.

'What is so funny?' I am indignant.

'You think only you can tease me? Can't I give it back to you?' he is still chuckling.

'Hmmmph,' I say and hang up but I am smiling.

In a few minutes, I am on the phone again, this time to Latika, repeating all that I said to Sriram, giving her a blow-by-blow account of my date with Aman.

'I am very happy for you, babes. Finally, you seem to have successfully completed a date without calling Sriram up to rescue you. Finally, you like a guy. Congratulations!' she says and I smile.

She is right. I *am* so hard to please. Actually that is not true. All the 'decent' guys are already taken or married. There is seriously a shortage of good guys these days. And Aman fits my 'requirements'. At least from what I know of him.

The rest of the day I am too distracted to concentrate on my work. The piece that I have to turn in is on 'How to Get Over an Ex'. To be honest, I have never had an ex. I have just had a one-sided crush in school on my senior and he never even knew about it. But I know some of my hostel mates who were in relationships for two and three years and who have broken up. I have been witness to so many of them. And I have always ended up comforting either the 'dumper' or the 'dumpee'. I have seen how ugly break-ups can get and how real and deep the grief can be.

I decide that I will speak to a few of the girls and take some 'tips' from them for my article even though I know that back then, I had dragged them out, distracted them, made them feel loved, and not allowed them to think about that person at all. In the end that was all that had helped.

I can't wait for Friday to arrive. I ask Aman what kind of place he has in mind. Does he want to go to a pub? He says that even though he enjoyed himself immensely the last time, why don't we try something quieter and more peaceful now? Somewhere where we do not have to shout to be heard. So I suggest this lovely place at Koramangala which serves some authentic north-eastern cusine. Aman is okay with that and he says he is a non-fussy eater and isn't much of a foodie either.

'That makes two of us. For me even a packet of instant noodles and a fruit is fine,' I say.

We don't exchange anymore emails after that even though I am dying to mail him about my day. I follow my own 'Rule No.1' of the article that I had written, the one which was on 'How to Hook a Guy and Keep Him'. I haven't heard from Aman—no instant message, no mail and no text and I have to use every bit of my will-power to resist casually messaging him.

I hear from Aman promptly on Friday morning.

`We're on for this evening, right?` reads his Instant Message on my phone.

I type, `Yes, of course,` but then delete it and instead type, `Oh. I had almost forgotten. Since I didn't hear from you at all, I wasn't sure.`

`Aman: So sorry for dropping off the radar like that. It's been crazy. I have been working till almost eleven pm every day. It is this new project that is being set up and I am in` charge of a lot of things. Looking forward to today.

Me: Great. Will meet you there at seven?

Aman: Super. See you soon!

I am elated to have heard from him. I was beginning to worry that he had forgotten about the date. Rule No.1 *was* hard to follow.

This time, I make an effort to look my best. I wear a pale cream flowing dress, a designer one, which fits me flatteringly. I had spent a fortune on this. I make an effort with the mascara and eye-liner. As a final touch I splash on some Chanel. When I finish I realise that I do not want to take an auto as it will mess with my hair which I have left free. So I dial for a taxi.

When I arrive Aman is already waiting and this time I am ready with the cab-fare and I pay it as I alight, giving him no chance to grab it, like he did the last time we met.

Aman looks at me appreciatively.

'Anjali, you look stunning!' he says and I find myself blushing a bit.

'Thank you,' I smile and for the first time in my life I am actually a bit tongue-tied.

The terrace restaraunt we have chosen is done up in the earthy tones of terracotta tiles. Candles and tiny lanterns illuminate the space instead of electric lights. From here, we have a bird's-eye view of the city. The atmosphere is romantic, warm and cozy. A cool night breeze adds to the charm and Aman draws a sharp breath as soon as we walk in.

'This is very nice, Anjali,' he says and I nod in agreement.

Aman asks me what I will drink and I choose Shiraz, a wine which I have recently developed a taste for, and he surprises me by saying that he will have the same.

'Oh! You drink wine?! I would have thought you were a whisky kind of a guy,' I say.

'I like whisky too, but the one you have chosen looked interesting. I have never tried a local wine before,' he says, his eyes twinkling.

As the evening lapses into night, we finish a bottle of wine between ourselves. The food is delicious and the conversation flows smoothly. Aman is easy to talk to and we do not run out of conversation.

He is also a good listener. He asks me about what I am working on, how I got into journalism and why I studied in Bangalore while my parents were based in Muscat. I tell him that my parents wanted me to be independent, hence chose to send me to a school in Bangalore which they felt was better than the schools there. He teases me by saying that had I remained in Muscat, I would probably be the fourth or fifth wife of a rich sheikh. I tease him right back by asking what is wrong with that and I know he harbours a secret fetish for a sheikh's wife. He throws back his head and laughs at that suggestion. He looks so good when he laughs. We get chatting about ourselves and he tells me about how his mother raised him after his father passed away. He talks about his childhood, about his life in the UK, the new project he is working on, and I notice that he does not mention anything about his relationships. So I ask him whether there is parental pressure on him to find a girl to marry, and tell him that my parents sure have started making noises in that direction.

He is quiet for a while and there is an awkward pause. I know I have touched a raw nerve.

'Hey, you don't have to tell me if you don't want to, you know,' I quickly say, trying to put him at ease.

He looks straight into my eyes.

'No, I want to. Somehow it is important that you know,' he says. 'It's important that I talk about it and get it out of my system. It will help me let go as well.' Then he goes on to tell me about the one and only relationship he has had. He tells me how they were inseparable for four years, how he had never seen anyone but her as his life-partner, how close they were and how madly in love. He says he wonders sometimes if he will completely get over her ever.

I am surprised that he has suddenly opened up like this. I could never have imagined that he would have been so deeply involved with someone. But then, Aman is that kind of a guy.

'So where is she now? Any idea? Did you ever try to contact her?' I ask.

'Funny you ask that. For two years I didn't bother. I tried to put the past behind me. But before moving from the UK, I did manage to track her down. I looked up her Facebook profile and God, it still hurts, Anjali. It's crazy. But I have vowed never to contact her. She is married now and is hopefully happy. As far as I am concerned, she is a closed chapter.'

I don't know why, but I feel hugely relieved to hear that. I know I find Aman attractive and nice. But I didn't realise that I cared this much.

Finally when we leave, Aman calls for a cab. He says he will drop me home first and then would go back to his guesthouse. As it is quite late and it would not be safe for me to go alone, I gladly agree.

As the cab makes its way through the darkness of the city lights, I sit close to Aman, my leg touching his and my shoulder brushing against his. He makes no attempt to move away. It feels good to be this close to him physically. I desperately want to take his hand in mine, but don't. I sit very still. He doesn't talk and neither do I. We're comfortable in the silence.

And when the cab reaches my place, I say 'bye' and quickly squeeze his hand and kiss him on the lips. A tiny peck. He smiles.

And as soon as I enter my room, there is a message from him.

'You're amazing, Anjali. I had a great time. Thank you for a fabulous evening,' it reads.

I want to sing and shout and dance with joy.

Instead I type back that it was the same for me and go to bed insanely happy, happier than I have felt in years.

Chapter 16

Aman

Anjali is definitely a livewire. It is hard to have a dull moment with the girl. And yet she is perceptive and sympathetic too. Maybe it is all the analysing she does for writing her pieces! I am surprised that I have told her all about Shruti. I have never opened up like that to anyone but Anjali *is* so easy to talk to. Or perhaps after seeing Shruti's profile on Facebook, I needed to somehow get it out of the system because I have bottled it up long enough. Or maybe it was the way she asked. Or maybe it was just the wine. Who knows!

Whatever it is, I am glad I did it. Shruti is a closed chapter now (forcefully shut I must admit, but closed nevertheless) and even though it hurts when I think about her, I think Anjali might inadvertently have given me a push in the right direction—a push towards moving on. She did surprise me with that peck on the lips last night. I know she is ready to take this relationship to its next level. But I do not want to 'get involved' with a woman unless I am very sure about her. Till then it is best I keep Anjali in the 'friend zone'.

I am neck-deep in work. I report to Vikram only indirectly. But I am one of the 'star players' as Rao puts it. All of that is good, but it just means that I don't get breathing space.

Our company has made an acquisition of a shared service centre, which is a part of the strategy to access a new business segment, dealing with financial services. As large global firms look to reduce their costs, they are turning to companies such as ours to become more efficient. My jump to this division gives me exposure to a completely new function. Vikram has the overall responsibility for the financial services vertical. He wants nothing to go wrong, and this in turn translates to micro-managing by Rao. Most of the time, Rao gets on my nerves. Honestly, I feel like telling him to sod off, but I control my irritation and get down to work. Anjali's mails come as a welcome respite. They make me smile.

These days, I have got into the habit of checking my mail every now and then and quickly scanning through the deluge in the inbox to see if there is a mail from her. Today, sure enough, there is yet another mail from her.

From: Anjali Prabhu <anjali.prabhu@tiara.com>

To: Aman Mathur <aman.mathur@zmail.com>

Sub: Your forecast for this fortnight

Double hey!

You know I have a confession to make. After your last mail (the one where you told me about your uncle and his astrology), I actually went and checked the column by Praneeta.

This is what it said for my zodiac sign: You will realize early this fortnight that progress depends upon your willingness to work diligently and remain focused on details. It is definitely time to get down to business, to focus on work, and finish anything that has been left undone. You are laying a foundation for the future, proving to yourself and others that you are worthy of the responsibilities and challenges.The temptation to shirk will be strong, but do not give in. 'Focus' should be the mantra.

And this is what it said for *your* zodiac sign:

Your energy is strong and focused. You can concentrate even when work becomes routine and boring. You are in a crucial stage in your life, but you have got the energy and a take-no-prisoners attitude that will lead you to success. The best way to balance such determination is to get in touch with nature: take a walk in the woods; sit at the edge of the lake; feel the earth and her connection with it.

Looks like Praneeta Menon can read my mind!

I had half a mind to take sick leave (a massive hangover and inability to focus on work counts as an ailment, right?) but I am trying to do what she advises and I am trying to 'Focus'.

What about you? Is your day any better? Are you that focused?

Luv

Anjali

I smile as I read her mail. Judging from her earlier mails, this is vintage Anjali. She just dashes off what's on her mind in a mail without pausing to think. And she doesn't mind if you do not reply. In the early days, I used to find it puzzling how someone could write so many mails. But I had soon got used to it. Anjali was born to write. Today I am happy about it.

I see at least thirty 'Urgent' mails in my official inbox, all work-related and yet this one mail from Anjali in my personal one, I decide, needs to be replied to immediately.

From: Aman Mathur <aman.mathur@zmail.com>
To: Anjali Prabhu <anjali.prabhu@tiara.com>
Re: Your forecast for this fortnight
Hey hey!
Praneeta Menon is right. I *am* focused. Slogging my butt off. The works (literally and metaphorically).
And I so need that walk in the woods, the edge of the lake and I need to feel connected to the earth.
Any options?
Aman

The rest of the day I have meetings and video conference calls and so I don't get time to check mails.

However, when I reach the guesthouse and retire to my room after a sumptuous meal which the staff has kept ready (they are so efficient and sweet and pamper the residents), the first thing I do is check my mail.

Sure enough, there is not one but two mails from Anjali, one from Vikram and there is one from Mark. I want to savour Anjali's mails, so like a child, who saves a chocolate for later, I read Vikram's mail first. It is crisp, friendly and yet to the point, much like the man himself.

Aman,
Trust all fine with you.
Good progress on the work front. Am travelling from tomorrow and if all goes well, we ought

to acquire Core-Cubo ACS, which will be fantastic.
About your acco, I think there are some fully furnished options. Dipika can help you look if you want. Both the girls say hi and want to know when you will join us for dinner next. Let me know.
Vik

I am surprised at how cleverly Dipika is playing her cards, even after what has happened between us, and even after I have clearly told her I can't give her whatever it is that she wants from me. I wonder if Dipika planned it and told Vikram to mail me or whether it is his own idea. Whatever it is, I certainly do not want to go house-hunting with her. About Vikram's dinner-invite, I can always make excuses and keep putting it off. I don't want to have another 'episode' with Dipika. I am clear about that.

Then I read Mark's mail. Mark has gone ahead and booked his tickets to travel to India. He arrives in about a month and a half from now and he is taking a three-week break. He is travelling to Delhi first. He is then doing white water rafting at Rishikesh and after a week, he flies to Bangalore. He says that he wants me to help plan his itinerary and asks me to join him.

Then I read the mails sent by Anjali. I read the one sent earlier first.

From: Anjali Prabhu <anjali.prabhu@tiara.com>
To: Aman Mathur <aman.mathur@zmail.com>
Sub: Options
1. Coorg (nice walks)
2. Sakleshpur (coffee estates—you can substitute it for woods)

```
3. Bandipur (wildlife, nature—connection
   with earth)
All three can be reached from Bangalore, in
three-four hours.
But if you do not have time for any of them,
my terrace is a great option. I have deck
chairs and greenery all around, and it makes
you feel like you are in the midst of woods.
See—you ask for options and I give you so
many!
Got an article to write. Jeena on my ass to
submit.
Later!
Anjali
```

I smile reading her options and for a few seconds, I actually consider a quick holiday. A weekend getaway. Honestly, a break like that, would be a terrific idea. But there is such a lot of work, and also I have to find a home soon and shift out of the guesthouse. While the company guesthouse hospitality is welcoming and everything is taken care of, I will not be able to stay for more than three months as per company norms. I make a mental note to call up the company brokers and go house-hunting. I wonder if Anjali would like to accompany me. I find it boring to see homes on my own and it would indeed be nice if she does.

The second mail from Anjali is an article she wrote. She says that she felt moved by what I shared with her, about my relationship with Shruti. She says that while she hasn't been in such a situation herself, she has hand-held countless friends who have broken up. She wants me to read what she has written and give her a honest feedback as to how I find it, whether it is useful and whether she has covered all the points. She says she partly used what I shared with her too, and that is what gave her an impetus to write this piece. I find her request hugely flattering. I open the attachment and begin to read:

How to Get Over the One You Cannot Have

By Anjali Prabhu

If you are in your mid-twenties or older, chances are you have definitely been in a relationship before. Perhaps two or three or may be even several. They have ended for whatever reasons, but sometimes, there is that one person, no matter how hard one tries, that one cannot get over.

The harder one tries to get over that person, the deeper they seem to fall for them. Loving somebody who does not reciprocate your feelings or who cannot be in a relationship with you, can be one of the most painful experiences of life. It can be heartbreaking and can completely shatter one. More so, if you encounter that person every single day at the work-place or at college.

How does one get over that one person, who will never be yours (for whatever reasons), and then move on?

Here is a five step plan which if followed is very likely to help.

1. Acceptance

The first would be to ask oneself if one really wants to move on. Have you accepted that this person and you are never going to have a relationship and you cannot even be friends? Have you decided that you truly want to get over them and move on with your life?

2. Axe the sentimentalism

If so, then one has to be ruthless, hard hearted and determined. Remember, you are trying to reclaim your life. You do not want to keep checking out their photos on social networking sites. So block that person and delete all the old mails, chats, texts and any reminders of the past. The more you hold on to them, the harder it will be to get over the person.

3. Distract yourself

The moment you find your mind wandering to their thoughts and what they used to say, do, look and sound like, distract yourself quickly. Show a red light to your mind and ask it to STOP. Hit the gym, go for a walk, do something, but don't think about that person.

4. Remind yourself that you are loved

Just because that person does not love you, it does not mean you are worthless and your life is going nowhere. Remind yourself of the people who love you—your best friends, your family. Spend more time with them and surround yourself with them. If you have had relationships before, then think of how you overcame them. If you did it once, you can surely do it again. Also remember that there are new people waiting to enter your life. Just like we need to get rid of clutter to make space for something on a shelf, so too we need to clean up our mental space.

5. Drown yourself in a hobby or a passion

One is spoilt for choices when it comes to recreation these days. Take up your once forgotten hobby. Join a dance class. Go para-sailing if that is what makes you happy. Do not wallow trying to figure out why that person does not want you. Remind yourself that you are truly worth more than clinging to somebody who does not care in the same manner you do.

It may be hard to follow the above initially. But steel yourself and do not waver. Before you know it, you would have reclaimed your life.

I read the piece once and I read it again. This seems to have been written exactly with me in mind. It seems to be speaking to me. I feel as though Anjali is begging me, pleading with me to move on and let the past lie. Of course, that is what I intend to do. What she has written is excellent. I feel an overpowering urge to speak to her right then and so I dial her number. I am disappointed when she doesn't answer the phone.

I get busy typing out a reply to Mark, telling him that by the time he arrives, I would probably be in my own house, and hence he could stay with me. I tell him that I will plan out an itinerary for him soon.

Just as I am concluding the mail, Anjali returns my call.

'Hey, sorry I missed your call. I was in the shower,' she says.

'Shower at this time in the night?' I smile.

'Yeah, at this time and I am wearing a bathrobe and speaking to you,' she says and giggles.

I smile at how candid and unself-conscious she is.

'Your piece, it is brilliant. It is so well-written, I had to call you and tell you,' I say.

'Yay!' she says. 'I am so glad you like it. You know, I wrote that with you in mind.'

'I know. That's why I called. You seem to know me so well, Anjali.'

She is quiet for a while. I wonder if the connection in the phone line dropped.

'Hello, are you there?' I ask.

'Yeah, very much. You know what, Aman, I feel the same way too. I feel I have known you forever. All my life,' she says.

We talk for a long time after that. I tell her about Mark and his visit to India. She says she has never interacted with people from a different country and she finds it fascinating that I have English friends. I tell her they aren't that different, and that no matter what the colour of your skin, human emotions are the same everywhere. Then I tell her about how I have to find a fully-furnished home soon. She offers to go with me and I gladly accept.

I realise that I am slowly but surely getting emotionally entangled with Anjali even though I have no intention to move her to the 'relationship zone' from 'the good friend' zone. My logical mind tells me to stay away from relationships and to focus on my career instead. It reminds me of what a wonderful thing I had with Shruti and how it all ended, and how two years later it still hurts, although I have learnt to cope with it better. The logical part of me remembers the pain and hurt and disappointments that relationships come with. How even the best ones die out and all that remains is the embers that still burn.

And yet, despite all of that, Anjali seems to be a balm to my wounds, and despite not wanting to get involved with her, I am unable to stop myself.

Chapter 17

Shruti

My illness turns out to be nothing at all. Just a day of rest and I feel fine. I was probably right—it must have been indigestion. I am glad that I didn't go rushing to the doctor who would have in all likeliness ordered a battery of tests. Even though I am very tempted by Asha's suggestion—to contact Aman once more, and try and meet him, if only to get some sort of a closure—I don't do anything about it.

Asha, of course, confronts me the next day in the bus on the way to work.

'So, are you okay now?' she asks as she sits down beside me.

When I reply that I am indeed okay, she straightaway asks me, 'Did you write to him? Find out how he is? Where he is?'

'No Asha, I didn't.'

'But why? You want to know, na,' she persists.

'I do, but what good will it do me? I am married now. It's been almost two years.'

'Come on. Just because you are married, it doesn't mean you don't have a right to know!'

'It isn't about rights, Asha, it is about duties and responsibilities.'

'Stop talking like a sixty-year-old! What duties and

responsibilities? Has Rishabh even spoken to you for the last one month? Is he even bothered about what you might be feeling?'

'He is hurt, Asha. He feels he has been wronged. I guess he will come around, eventually.'

'*Haan*, so let him. There is nothing wrong in contacting Aman. I am telling this to you, as a friend. You know, I had this relationship with a senior from my college. But we broke up, much like you and your Aman. I wondered how he was and what he is doing. I contacted him after about six years. He too is married like me and he has a daughter. He has settled down in New Zealand and is happy. We still keep in touch through mails and phone-calls. We're good friends now and we are happy with our respective families. Had I not made that effort in contacting him, I would have probably always wondered and maybe even felt guilty. But now I gained a good friend and so did he. That is why I am urging you to contact him. You have nothing to lose.'

I think about what Asha has just said. Perhaps she has a point there. But we don't get a chance to speak further as another colleague joins us and this is something which is just between Asha and me. So we change the topic and talk about inane stuff.

Once we reach office, we get busy in our work, but we catch up again during lunch hour, at the cafeteria. We always have lunch together and today we take a table which can seat just two people. Asha senses I want to talk. We continue exactly where we left off. I am very curious now about this double-life that Asha seems to be leading. Okay—not exactly a double life but a secret that she has so carefully tucked away.

'But what about your spouses? Do they know you are both still in touch? Do they know about your relationship and are they okay with that?' I ask.

'He hasn't told his wife. But I have told Gaurav and have kept him in the picture. I downplayed the relationship part of course. I told him it was just a crush, which it probably was. All these college romances are just that. They don't last,' says Asha as she twirls her fork around the noodles that she is having.

How do I make Asha understand that it was never that casual between Aman and me? We were *serious* about each other. I don't think Asha will get the intensity and depth of what I shared with Aman. Aman and I were *meant* to be together. Forever. Or so we had thought. Neither he nor I, ever had envisaged a life without the other. It was simply unthinkable in both our books.

'I don't know, it just doesn't seem right, being in touch with your ex without your spouse knowing,' I say.

'*Arey!* I am telling you Gaurav knows. It is just that he doesn't know how close a friend he is. About his wife, I can't do anything but I can understand where he is coming from. Come on, Shruti. You have been married what— nearly two years? I have been married eleven. And trust me, it is hard to stay "confined" to only your spouse. Marriages are strange things. They are all shiny and glossy when they start out, but become jaded with time. I know how it is. Maybe it's just early days for you and that's why you talk about "right" and "wrong" in marriage. There aren't any absolute rights or wrongs,' says Asha.

I know there is some truth in what Asha has just said. I have been married nearly two years and I have already begun to feel stifled. The newness of the relationship has indeed worn out. I cannot imagine how Rishabh and I will be in eleven years' time. I can't even think of the next five years to be honest. I know I cannot put off having a child forever. But will I ever feel ready? Right now, I certainly don't and talking to Asha who is in a particularly pontificating mood today, is making me consider my options.

'I guess so,' I say lamely to her little speech, not knowing what to add.

'Yeah, babe. Being married—it's a bitch. At least we can make it comfortable by having good friends who are supportive and, as far as I am concerned, I am glad I have Navin. That is his name by the way,' she says. And when she says it, her eyes light up. She looks happy. Light. Different. As though she has no more worries in the world.

It takes me a moment to figure out that she is talking about the guy she broke up with, but who is a 'good friend' now. It is amazing how she transforms before my very eyes, when she mentions his name.

'So Navin is the one you cannot have, eh?' I tease her.

'No, I already have him. Only his wife doesn't know,' she says and smiles.

I do not know what to say to her 'relationship' with Navin. But I am nobody to pass judgement on the way she has chosen to lead her life.

'Don't look at me like that, Shruti, it is okay. After all, I do everything for my husband as well as my son. I also look after his mother, to boot. I deserve some happiness, something exclusively for myself. Navin and I are very discreet about it. We will never have a physical relationship. But emotionally we feel the connect with each other. In fact, I often tell him that he is the glue in my marriage. But for him, my marriage would have fallen apart long back. He gives me a man's perspective and because of Navin, I am able to understand Gaurav better. I wouldn't have normally shared all this, but I do feel kind of bad to see you stuck in a rut like this and so I told you my views,' she says.

'I appreciate it, Asha. Thanks and you can be sure whatever we spoke now will never go out from me,' I say.

'It better not!' she warns.

That evening Rishabh drops a bombshell on me.

'My parents are coming to stay over,' he says.

'Oh! How suddenly?' I ask.

During the time that we have been married, Rishabh has invited his parents many times, but they have never visited us. His dad always protests saying it will be difficult to leave Hubli as there is no one to manage the business on a day-to-day basis.

'I have been asking dad to take a break. He has finally agreed. His younger brother will go daily and do the stock-taking and tally accounts. It will be a nice change for them,' says Rishabh.

I am glad that he is excited about it. More than that I am glad he is talking to me. Saying more than his curt and to-the-point, one-liners. His indifference of the last one month has been unbearable.

'Let's prepare the guest room. We need to buy a new bed and mattresses. I want my parents to be comfortable,' he says.

'You mean a kingsize bed? But that will leave us with no space at all. The second bedroom is tiny,' I point out. I don't see any point in buying furniture when we have guests only for ten-fifteen days in a year. The rest of the time the bed would just lie there, occupying space. And our apartment isn't exactly spacious. Besides, when my parents had come, they had managed perfectly well on the futon which doubles up as a bed. I am tempted to add all this as well, but I wisely don't.

Rishabh thinks over what I have said. Then he finds the perfect solution.

'Hmm, okay—in that case we can give them our bedroom. We can sleep on the futon in the spare bedroom,' he declares.

God. That was not what I had in mind.

'How can you give our bedroom to them, Rishabh? What about our privacy? All my clothes are in that room. All our stuff is there,' I protest. I find the whole concept of surrendering *our* bedroom to anyone else, even if it is his parents, very invasive.

'It's just for a few days. We can adjust. Come on, Shruti. This is the first time my parents are visiting. I want their stay to be comfortable,' he says.

I don't see how giving our bedroom to them will make their stay 'comfortable'. It will, in fact, cause more awkwardness as I will have to keep intruding on them to take out any stuff that I may need. I detest this idea of 'giving our bedroom' to them. But I keep quiet as I don't want to start another fight.

I can see the change in Rishabh because of his parents' visit and he runs around like he has got a bee in his bonnet. He stocks the house with fruits. 'My dad always has a fruit after each meal,' he says. He tells the house-help to clean all the fans and the window grills. He goes into the kitchen and checks the shelves and tells me that it is very untidy and it needs to be fixed.

'You know what, I shall take an off from work, and stay home and tidy everything for you,' I say sarcastically.

But he doesn't get the sarcasm at all.

'Will you? That will be good,' he says and I am so irked, I want to slap him.

'I was just kidding. You know my workload is too much these days,' I say.

He doesn't ask me why my workload is so heavy. He doesn't

even want to know how my day was and what I did. In fact, most of what he communicates is something that has to do with his parents' visit.

All that Rishabh does these days is to potter around the house once he comes back from work. He has even gone shopping (without me) and got new bedsheets and bedcovers. I have never seen him take this much interest in the house in the time that we have been married.

Finally I can't stand it anymore. When I come back from work and when I see that he has shopped for a cutting board and some kitchen knives (of all things!) I decide I have to speak up.

'Rishabh, do you realise you are acting like someone possessed. Why in the world did you go and buy a cutting board and knives? We already have all that,' I say.

'They were old. So I threw them out. How does it matter? Is that such a crime? Can't I buy stuff for my own home?' he retorts.

'Look Rishabh, the issue is not about the cutting board and knives and we both know that. This lack of communication, ever since that day, is killing me.'

I cannot bring myself to say Aman's name. I don't know why.

He is silent for a while.

'I am trying to get over it, Shruti. I truly am. But it is not so easy to forget. How could you hide such a huge thing from me?'

I have nothing to say then. So I just say a 'sorry' and I ask him if he has made dinner, which he has, since he got back earlier than me.

How could I hide it from him? I don't know. I wasn't in any mental state to think clearly then. Besides, my parents were so darn keen on this match with Rishabh. Had I mentioned Aman to him at that point, who knows perhaps the marriage might have never happened. His parents *are* very conservative. In fact, we have visited them just once, when we stayed with them at their huge home in Hubli. I had to wear only saris the entire duration as his relatives would keep dropping in, to 'see the bride'. I had hated it but had 'adjusted' as it was only for a few days.

And now a new thought strikes me. His parents are going to get a shock when they see me in skirts and trousers as I wear only western formals to work. I wear saris only for formal occasions like weddings. Well, too bad. I am not going to change the way I dress, just because they are visiting. They can get used to a 'modern' daughter in-law. Also, Rishabh hasn't mentioned anything about it to me and I am glad about that.

His parents arrive and Rishabh, I discover, has taken a day off from work to pick them up from the airport and bring them home. He is a little miffed that I haven't taken the day off as well to welcome them. But we have an important event in office today and my presence there is needed as I am co-ordinating all the arrangements, including accompanying the chief guest (who insisted that someone from the company has to meet her, to escort her to the venue) and so there is no way that I can oblige.

When I get back from work I find the three of them sitting in the drawing room and watching television.

I greet them and I ask them how their journey was.

My mother-in-law says that it was fine. Then she says that I have lost a lot of weight. She doesn't comment on the clothes I am wearing (a short Van Huesen formal skirt and a fitted shirt) and I am happy about that. My father-in-law asks about my work and I tell him how my day went. They are sweet and pleasant and probably I had just been worrying about nothing.

I have had a hard day at work. I have been standing most of the time, and I even had to accompany the chief guest back. I am desperate for a shower and am hungry too. So I excuse myself and when I emerge, I see that the table has already been laid and a hot meal of *chappatis* and *dal* is waiting for me.

'Ma, you cooked. That is so sweet of you,' I exclaim.

'Yeah, if the woman of the house has no time, it doesn't mean others have to starve,' comes her immediate reply and she sighs dramatically and wipes her forehead with her sari *pallu* to emphasize how hard it was.

I grit my teeth and force myself to keep quiet. I badly want to say that the man of the house was at home that day and could have easily cooked the meal. The house rules are that we share the task of cooking and on working days, whoever gets home earlier, cooks. But I know that will only alienate Rishabh more.

We all eat together and I see that Rishabh is happy. I feel good to see him genuinely happy after very long.

Who knows, maybe after his parents leave, things will be fine between Rishabh and me. I make up my mind to be extra-nice and sweet to his parents, no matter what the provocation. Maybe that will please him and he will forgive me.

But I have no idea what lies in store for me and how even the best of intentions can go wrong.

Chapter 18

Aman

My third 'date' with Anjali turns out to be one on a weekend, where we go house-hunting. I have side-stepped going with Dipika by responding to Vikram's mail diplomatically. I replied to him saying that it is kind of Dipika to offer but I will manage. Then I promptly texted the company broker who has lined up about eight apartments for me to view.

Shukla has again lent me the bike. Right now, the company guesthouse is within walking distance of my office. But once I move, I would definitely need a car. At my level I am eligible for a car-loan and I have already set the papers in process and made the booking for a brand new Hyundai i-20. It isn't available in the colour that I want (I have chosen a fiery red) and I have to wait for around three weeks for delivery of the vehicle which suits me fine. I am in no hurry.

Anjali arrives dot on time (and that is another thing that I like about her: she is always punctual) and when I see her I catch my breath. She looks even more attractive today than she did the last time. She has tied up her hair in a pony-tail. She is wearing large over-sized sun-glasses, a bandana like hairband, a smartly fitted canary yellow tee and light blue denims and white heels. She is also carrying a denim bag and she looks like she has just stepped out of the 'style' pages of the magazine she writes for.

'Wow! You look good, mademoiselle,' I tell her as I greet her.

'Thank you and you ain't looking bad yerself,' she says in an exaggerated American accent.

'I love those heels. Killer ones,' I say and smile.

'What about the sun-glasses? And the tee? And the bandana? And the bag? And, oh yes, you missed out the watch too—it's a Giordano,' she says and laughs.

I join in her laughter and obvious delight at my compliments. She makes me feel so light, this girl. I am always laughing or smiling when I am with her.

The company broker Mr Ramalingam, arrives about fifteen minutes later than the time that we agreed upon. Anjali and I wait inside the guesthouse and this time Shukla is around, all spruced up as I had mentioned earlier to him that Anjali would be coming.

I introduce Anjali to him and I can see his obviously approving stare. He is checking her out, in what he presumes is a discreet way but I can easily see it and I can see he finds her hot. Anjali is oblivious to it and says a polite hello.

'I have read your column in *Tiara,'* declares Shukla.

That gets Anjali's interest immediately.

'Oh! Don't you mind admitting that you read women's magazines?' she teases.

'Well, I don't read them, my sister does and she loves your column. She showed it to me and made me read it. Great to meet you face-to-face,' he says and I can see that he is enamoured by her.

'Thank you,' says Anjali. I guess she is used to people telling her that they read her, I don't know. I can see that Shukla is dying to impress her, but he is desperately looking for something to talk about that will hold her interest.

'So what are your future plans?' he blurts out.

Anjali looks puzzled. 'Eh? Future plans? As in marriage and stuff like that?' she asks.

'Oh, no, no. What I meant is what are you writing about next?' he asks.

It is funny how I feel protective about Anjali all of a sudden because of Shukla who is questioning her.

'Oh, she is working on several things,' I tell him and Anjali looks at me and smiles. She doesn't miss how I have jumped in for her.

Fortunately we are spared of further conversation as Ramalingam makes an entry wiping his brow.

'Sorry, *saar*, got a little bit late as I had to drop off my son. He missed the school bus,' he says.

'No problem. So shall we leave?' I ask.

'How do you want to go, *saar*? Shall we go in my car?' he asks.

'No we will follow you on the bike,' I say and Anjali nods.

'But we will be going to seven-eight areas. Bike will be very hot, no?' he asks.

I look at Anjali.

'Oh! I so wanted a bike ride,' she says.

'You can keep the bike and go later also. No problem at all,' pitches in Shukla. Anjali looks at me for an answer. I tell her that once the house is finalised we can go out on the bike and she is happy.

The first four houses that Ramalingam shows us are not suitable. Either the approach to the house isn't good or the house is too dark with no natural light or the layout isn't great. To be honest, I am quite okay with all the houses he has shown so far, but Anjali's discerning eye picks out relevant points. She examines each and every room in the house, taking in the wardrobes, the windows, the natural light and several other such things, which would not even have occurred to me. I guess this is where one needs a woman's touch. They have a natural eye for such stuff. I am now doubly glad that she is with me. Apart from the pleasure of her company, the inputs she gives me in the choice of a home are indeed great. One of the houses he has shown is right next to a sewage treatment plant and Anjali straightaway rejects it.

Ramalingam has probably presumed that she is my wife as he now addresses only her, leaving me out completely. I am amused and at the same time happy to see Anjali take charge. We finally get lucky with the fifth house. The location is perfect as it is just about four kilometres from office. It is in a huge enclosed community that has several multi-storeyed buildings with spacious well-designed landscaped gardens, nice pathways to walk on, lawn, park, club, gym and swimming pool. I instantly like it, especially the gym which is very well-equipped. Anjali too approves and we tell Ramalingam to go ahead and finalise it. It is a two-bedroom apartment on the eleventh floor that faces the pool. It is also furnished very tastefully with wicker furniture, a low coffee table and lovely lampshades and curtains. Both bedrooms have beds and the house also has a microwave, a fridge, a cooking range and everything else needed for a home. I just have to move in with my clothes.

'This is nice!' says Anjali.

'It is,' I admit.

'I am glad madam liked it,' says Ramalingam.

'I am also glad,' I say and Anjali and I smile at each other.

Our company has leased several of these fully furnished houses and many employees like me who are single prefer these, as opposed to ones where you have to buy all the furniture. Ramalingam has showed us a couple of those too, but this option (where the house comes with all the fittings and furniture) makes more sense in my case.

Ramalingam asks us when we would like to shift and I tell him I want to move as soon as possible. He says I can even move in immediately.

'Well, not today. But I don't mind shifting tomorrow,' I say and he confirms that it is okay as the house has already been leased by the company for three years and was lying vacant for the past two months, as the previous tenant had moved to the UK.

Ramalingam's phone rings and he excuses himself and goes to the balcony to take the call.

'Good thing your company takes care of all this. We don't get anything like this,' says Anjali clearly impressed with Ramalingam's efficiency in finalising such a lovely house, so quickly.

'Well, you don't have to move countries on work like we do. If they didn't take care of all this, I think we would have a high rate of attrition. You know *Business World* did a survey last year of the best companies to work for and ours was in the top five,' I say with some pride.

'Ask them if they need a writer for their in-house magazine. Do you have one?' asks Anjali. I take her request at face value and tell her that I will check.

'But then again, no thanks. I will probably have to write boring corporate articles if I took that up. I am not interested in all that. So drab,' she says and pulls a face.

'What do you want to write on the most?' I ask her, amused at her antics and her candidness.

'Love! Is there anything else worth living for?' she asks as she strikes a pose, throwing both her hands up in the air.

I want to tell her that love can also hurt and wound. It can make you ache. It can make you long for a person long after they are gone. It can leave you with a feeling so incomplete that you wonder if you will ever be whole again. It can shatter you, break you and make you a different person from what you were.

But I say nothing.

'Why are you suddenly looking so pensive?' she asks.

'Nothing,' I tell her.

'Leave it, don't think about the past. Let go, it wasn't meant to be,' she says and I am taken aback at how much Anjali understands me without my saying anything at all.

Once we finish finalising the house, we go back to the guesthouse. It is already four-thirty pm by the time we reach and the staff at the guesthouse serves us some cool fresh-lime soda. Shukla thankfully is nowhere to be seen. I didn't want him grilling Anjali again.

'You can get used to this lifestyle. These people pamper you so much!' exclaims Anjali as she sips her drink.

'Yes, if I had my way I would never vacate the guesthouse. Who wants to give up all this where you are served a delicious hot meal with a smile, no matter what time you get back from work,' I say as I sink into the sofa.

'So what about my payment?' asks Anjali. Her eyes are shining with mischief.

'What payment?' I smile.

'To help you shortlist the house. These services don't come free of cost, you know,' she says.

'Name your price,' I smile.

'A bike ride for now and rest I will tell you later,' she giggles.

'As long as it is nothing illegal, I am okay,' I smile. I wonder what she has in mind. I am not sure if she means it or is joking. With Anjali, it is sometimes hard to tell.

'You know what they say. Everything you love is illegal, immoral or fattening,' she says.

And now it is my turn to laugh.

'Come, let's go for a ride,' she says and I am happy to oblige and she gets on the bike.

'Where to?' she asks.

'I don't know. I am just riding, let's see where the bike takes us,' I reply.

Anajli clings to me and I notice that she is very comfortable with me now. She holds me tight, hugging me close. I quite enjoy it. There isn't much traffic on the roads today and I am glad as I take the flyover and go onto the inner ring road. That is a nice stretch for a drive.

Before I realise it we are at Koramangala and even before we realise it we are at Ibulur, zooming through the army cantonment area, lined with large shady trees, making crisscross patterns on the road. It looks pretty and picturesque. The one thing about Bangalore that I love is the greenery. I continue riding and Anjali continues clinging to me.

'This is lovely!' she exclaims.

I just smile as I ride. I love this machine. It is an amazing feeling to be riding this. Being on a two-wheeler brings back so many memories of the time I was in engineering college.

'Hey. We are now very close to Dipika and Vikram's place, let's drop in and say hi. It must be just three kilometres from here,' says Anjali suddenly.

I definitely do not want to go to their place and face Dipika again. But I don't know how to tell Anjali that.

'No, let's do that another day. They may be busy,' I say.

'No, no, I know they are likely to be home. Don't you want to see Ria and Reema? Such dolls they are!' she says.

I do want to see the girls. I find them sweet and they are insanely fond of me. But I don't want to face Dipika.

But before I can protest, Anjali has already whipped out her mobile and she shouts now over the din of the bike.

'Yeah, yeah... We're just five minutes away... Sure? Okay—we will drop in,' I hear her say.

Then she hangs up and tells me, 'They are cool with it. Let's go and see them.'

I don't have a choice anymore. Very reluctantly I rev the bike. We make our way to Vikram and Dipika's place, with a sinking feeling in the pit of my stomach.

Chapter 19

Shruti

Being nice to his parents involves a lot more than I anticipated. It is getting harder with each passing day. The work pressure at office has increased tremendously. I am assisting in organising the campus recruitment drives. Our organisation has decided to recruit from the lesser-known engineering colleges in south India and I now have the additional responsibility of co-ordination with the placement cells of each of these colleges. I have too much on my plate already and this added load is making me a bit grumpy. And the worst part is my boss cross-checking each day, as to how many colleges have been done. Soon I will have to travel to all these places too. The only silver lining is that I will get to spend at least ten days in Bangalore, as we are doing a couple of colleges there, which means that I can get to stay with my parents for at least ten days. I desperately need that break.

As I take the bus home from work, I reflect about how much my life has changed in just over a month. Earlier, before Rishabh's parents visited, I would look forward to coming home and sharing the details of my day with Rishabh. Talking to him always made me feel better. But, ever since that fateful day that he discovered the e-mails between Aman and me, that has come to a grinding halt. (How much more does the guy want to punish me? This has gone on enough. I do wish Rishabh would forgive. But then again, I guess he must be deeply hurt. I so want him to forget all that happened, but it is a decision he has to make for himself.)

In addition to his not being communicative, his mother is fuelling the already burning fire. I do not know if she does it on purpose or whether it is inadvertent. Whatever it is, it is further straining the relations between Rishabh and me. When I ask Rishabh how long they are going to stay, he gives me a cold look and asks if there is any problem.

I do have a problem. Not one. Several. But I think they will seem inconsequential to Rishabh if I bring them up. After I come back from work, I usually shower and change into more comfortable clothes. But these days, even to take my undergarments from my own wardrobe, I have to knock on the door, as my father-in-law has a habit of locking the door while he rests. I find it bloody annoying when he does that and I have to knock and wait to enter my own room.

Then of course, there is my mother-in-law. Each day that I return, the meals are all cooked. I try telling her that there is no need to cook and one of us will do it when we get home. She says that her husband needs his dinner before seven-thirty pm as he is not only a BP patient but also a diabetic and it is imperative that he eats on time.

I don't know how to solve that problem. I leave for work very early in the morning and these days I am able to return only by eight pm. By then, dinner is already waiting.

Rishabh brings it up with me when we retire to bed that night.

'You know, this visit is becoming a strain for my mother. She is doing the cooking for all of us. She doesn't complain but I can see how stretched she is. It just isn't right. After all they are on a holiday here,' he says.

It is becoming a strain for me too but I don't think you notice that anymore.

'What do we do, Rishabh? I feel bad too. I have so much work these days. My travel is going to start too as the recruitment drives are happening. How about us employing a cook? Then she won't have to cook, right?'

My mother-in-law kicks up a fuss and turns down the suggestion as though it is the most preposterous thing she has ever heard.

'In the thirty-four years that I have been married, I have cooked each and every meal for my family. I have never employed a cook and nor will I like the food that the cook makes. It is okay. I am at home the whole day. I will cook,' she says in a tone of finality signifying that it is the end of the matter.

Our bedroom (or rather, the room which used to be our bedroom) is completely taken over by their possessions now. I try not to wince when I see my father-in-law's *kurta-pyjamas* strewn all over the pale cream faux leather two-seater that I have in the bedroom. I try to look calm when I see their suitcase lying open and their stuff spilling out. I have to fight my urge to tidy their bed which is rumpled and unmade. And as though that wasn't enough, my father-in-law is a smoker. Though he doesn't smoke inside the house (thankfully) he does smoke on the balcony of our bedroom and the stench permeates indoors and hangs around the air. I detest what my home is turning into. Their possessions have even begun spilling over into the living room.

When I ask my father-in-law if his *kurtas* need to be washed, he tells me to leave them alone, as he has worn them just once and he will put them in the wash when he wants to. I also offer to make the bed but my mother-in-law sees this as interference and she mentions this to Rishabh. She says that it isn't as though I actually do any house-work. All I do is dress up in 'modern clothes' and leave for office. What right do I then have to tell my father-in-law to put his *kurtas* in the wash? All this is narrated to me by Rishabh who is irritated that I dare speak to his father that way. I want to explain to Rishabh what exactly happened but he is in no mood to listen.

'Can't you just let it be? Does it bother you that much?' he asks and I beat a hasty retreat and tell him it is okay. Actually it isn't. But I do not want to argue with this new snappy, curt, to-the-point Rishabh.

When I mention all this to Asha, she says, 'Yeah, you are lucky. At least they will go back. Imagine my plight. I am stuck with my mother-in-law all the time. And Gaurav won't hear even a word against her. Why do you think I work late every day?' she smiles.

I nod. I can now completely relate to what she must be going through on a daily basis. No wonder she feels happy speaking to her ex. I am now beginning to understand her.

'Actually, that is a good solution, Asha. I never thought of it. I will stay back extra-hours till they leave,' I tell her.

'No babes—if you want to win Rishabh over, don't do that. Go early. Take them out somewhere. Be nice to them. Then he won't grudge you. My case is different as she is living with us permanently. But with you, it is only a few days. Do whatever it takes, no matter how much you dislike it. Buy peace,' she advises.

I think about what she has said. She is right as usual, of course. Yes, that is exactly what I will do.

So I ask my colleague (the one who has come back from her leave) whether she will pitch in for me. She agrees readily as she knows I have been doing more than my fair share while she was on leave. I tell her the urgent things that have to be done and I decide to surprise my in-laws.

On my way home, I feel benevolent at my gesture. I decide that I will take them to Siddhi-Vinayak temple. They will probably like that. And then I can take them to the Worli sea-face. We could probably have a meal outside. I text Rishabh about my plans and he texts back saying, `That is sweet of you. Thank you!`

Yes! I think I am making some leeway in thawing my frozen husband. I mentally thank Asha for the suggestion and I am in a good mood, all the way home.

I do not ring the bell and I let myself in as I want it to be a complete surprise. I don't see either my father-in-law or my mother-in-law in the living room. So I walk towards the bedroom and what I see shocks me.

My father-in-law is lying on the bed and reading the newspaper. My mother-in-law is coolly going through the contents of my bedside drawer. She now has the birth control pills that I use in her hands. She reads the label on it and then tells him, 'Look at this. No wonder they don't have kids yet. And when I ask Rishabh he says they are trying. I bet that girl hasn't told him about this,' she tells my father-in-law waving the pills at him.

'I can't understand these present-day girls. Isn't our son earning enough? What is the need for her to work ? We should have made all this clear when we were finalising the match,' he replies.

'Yes, we should have, but it was Rishabh who was in such a tearing hurry to get married to her. She trapped him with her charms and looks and our poor idiot fell for it. See, he even has to cook for her, when he comes. Madam is busy roaming around in short skirts,' she says.

I am shell-shocked and enraged by what I have just seen and heard. How dare she thinks it is perfectly acceptable to go through the contents of *my* drawer? I am seething in anger. This is the limit. What right does she have to make those comments? What business is it of hers whether I work or laze around? It is between Rishabh and me, and as long as we have no issues, she should stay out of our personal lives.

I am tempted to tell her I have heard her and give her a piece of my mind. But that will back-fire badly and Rishabh will be furious if I ever spoke to his parents like that. So I grit my teeth and take a deep breath and force myself to be calm.

Then I step back quietly and then plonk my hand-bag down heavily on the dining table to make a noise, so that they are alerted to my presence. I hear the drawer in the bedroom being shut and I see my mother-in-law emerge from my bedroom.

'Oh! When did you come?' she asks and there is no sign of guilt or remorse on her face. I would have thought she might have felt ashamed or at least been aghast that I might have overheard her conversation, but if she is, she gives absolutely no indication of it and she has hidden it well. Or perhaps it is that she thinks she has done nothing wrong by rummaging in my drawers.

'I just entered. Rishabh wanted me to take you all out. I was thinking of taking you to Siddhi-Vinayak temple,' I say, forcing myself to talk politely and sweetly even though I am fuming inside.

'Oh. Yes, we have heard a lot about this temple. It will be nice to see it,' she says.

She doesn't ask how I got away from work early or whether I have had lunch. I can see that she has cooked lunch for both of them, judging by the mountain of unwashed vessels in the sink. I make a mental note to pay the house-help a little extra this month, else she is sure to grumble, run away and find another job.

I do not know why I am doing this—making this huge effort with his parents, when all I want to do is for them to leave. Is it to save my marriage? Is it to get some brownie points from Rishabh so that he will talk to me normally again? Whatever it is, it is too late now and I kind of feel sorry for them, as they have both quickly changed and emerged.

My father-in-law asks how far it is and how we will be going. We will have to take a cab from our place in Andheri and depending on traffic it would take a good forty minutes (at least) to get there. We manage to get a cab almost immediately and my father-in-law gets into the front and I get into the back of the cab along with my mother-in-law. They discover that they detest the Mumbai traffic which crawls at a snail's pace. I am quite used to it by now but I can see that they are restless in the cab. The cab does not have air-conditioning and they are clearly very uncomfortable. My father-in-law has sweat dripping from his forehead and he keeps mopping his forehead. My mother-in-law fans herself continuously with her sari *pallu*. When we stop at a signal some eunuchs emerge, clapping and asking them for money. My mother-in-law looks terrified. I quickly take out a twenty rupee note so that they will leave us alone.

We finally arrive at Siddhi-Vinayak temple. The serpentine queues to get in almost make my in-laws faint. When I see how uncomfortable they are, I tell my mother-in-law that we need not go inside but we can just pray from outside.

'No, no, you should never do that. You cannot turn your back once you enter a temple,' she says. There are tons of people and I now realise that bringing them here was perhaps a bad idea. My father-in-law looks increasingly uncomfortable but he stands in the queue quietly as it inches forward slowly like a giant millipede. We finally emerge from the temple an hour and ten minutes later.

They are very content at having got a wonderful darshan of Lord Ganesh.

'It is worth seeing. The energy inside the temple is amazing,' says my mother-in-law.

'Yes, no wonder so many throng to it,' admits my father-in-law.

They seem happy and content. I am glad that all that effort has been worth it.

After that, I take them to Worli sea-face and they enjoy watching the waves lash against the rocks. They gaze at the sea of humanity that makes its way here in the evenings. There are young lovers, old people, students probably taking a break from college, hawkers selling all kinds of stuff, the fitness freaks who are running, families who are visiting, tourists who come in groups to see Mumbai, and people walking their dogs. They marvel at the tall multi-storeyed buildings lining the sea-face. I also tell them about the Bandra-Worli sea link and explain how it has cut down commute time drastically. They aren't too impressed by that, but they nod agreeably, nevertheless. Unless one has lived in Mumbai, I don't think one would get the importance of it, as one wouldn't know how long it used to take earlier.

They look at everything in fascination like two excited children. Watching them, I feel happy that I made the effort today. I am secretly hoping my mother-in-law will mention how sweet I was to Rishabh and all this redeems me in Rishabh's eyes.

I stand there watching the waves lash about, along with my in-laws, and think what a strange turn my life has taken. Two years back I was certain I wouldn't have a life without Aman. I think about how sweet Aman's mother was to me. I think about how it would be if she was my mother-in-law. I am certain we could have been friends—she was that kind of a woman. And now here I am bending backwards, trying to please Rishabh's parents though deep down I don't even like them.

Suddenly my mother-in-law gives out a cry. I turn around and for a few seconds what is happening does not register.

Then I gasp as I see my father-in-law collapsing on the pavement.

Chapter 20

Anjali

Maybe it was a huge mistake dragging Aman to Dipika and Vikram's place, on a whim like that. Whatever was I thinking? I don't know. All I know is it is exactly seven days, eight hours, twenty-four minutes and eight seconds since I got the last message from Aman. (Okay, did not actually count it. I used an app on my smart phone which is a time calculator that shows you the time elapsed from the last message to now.) I am miserable. I feel like a student who has written a very long and elaborate answer to a question and has then discovered that the answer is completely wrong and irrelevant.

I thought Aman and I had a good thing going. I thought I had done all the right things and the 'date' (the house-hunting trip really) had been fabulous. Until the motorcycle ride which ended in the visit to Dipika and Vikram's house. I have replayed that scene so many times over in my head, to see if I did anything 'wrong'. I can't think of anything other than the fact that I insisted we go there. Ria and Reema were delighted to see us. I smile thinking of how Ria gave a huge hug to Aman and how she brought out the doll that Aman had gifted her and explained to him the entire feeding schedule, the daytime activities and bathing schedule down to the last detail, and how Aman had listened patiently and asked all the right questions. He was interested! I found that so endearing. I noticed that during the entire duration of the visit, he did not even look at Dipika, and once or twice when she asked him something about whether he had found a house, he answered in monosyllables. I had felt obliged to provide details and gone into great depth about the houses we had seen.

'Oh, you both went house-hunting together?' Dipika had asked and I had nodded happily. Looking back now, perhaps I should have kept mum about the whole thing. I shouldn't have:

1. Insisted we go to their house.
2. Blurted out details of the houses we saw.
3. Acted like his girlfriend (maybe I did, but I swear I didn't mean to).

I don't know what it is, but I sure feel lousy waiting like this to hear from him. Men are always complaining about how difficult it is to understand women but I think it is the other way round. Men clam up and do not express what they feel. Then they suddenly stop all communication with you and vanish. And all you can do is wait. I wish men came with instruction manuals. Or rather Aman came with an instruction manual.

I fret about it and I call for an urgent 'conference' with Sriram and Latika, to discuss in depth, to help me decode 'guy-behaviour'. I text them and ask them if they can meet me at Coffee and Conversations on MG Road. All our offices are within a five kilometre radius of each other, and I know that Latika can easily get away, as she is 'on the bench' now and hardly has any work. Sriram too has a pretty flexible work-schedule and I know it isn't too hard for him to get away either. Besides, it has been a while since the three of us met.

When I reach the coffee shop, Sriram and Latika are already

waiting. Turns out Sriram went and picked up Latika and they arrived together.

I feel delighted to see both of them. The very sight of them, sends a 'tring' to my heart and I feel better already.

'Oh my God—what have you done to yourself? Look at the dark circles under your eyes. Haven't you been sleeping at all?' asks Latika.

I haven't. As soon as I wake up (which is around three or four in the morning) I check my phone to see if there is a message from Aman. I have checked at least a thousand times till now. If there was an app in the phone to tell you how many times I checked it would probably give you an accurate figure. Who knows, maybe it is two thousand times. It has become a kind of habit now—every few seconds I check to see if Aman's name pops up in my phone. But I don't want to seem so desperate in front of Sriram and Latika.

But they know me inside out. We haven't been together since class six for nothing. Sriram has it all figured out from my desperate call for a conference and from the way I look.

'Ho-Ho-Ho, I can't believe this,' Sriram says.

'What?' I ask.

'The great Anjali Prabhu, the turn-downer of six rejected-dejected men, is finally chasing a guy and he is turning her down. Ha, ha, ha, see the irony?' he laughs.

'What? Is that the reason that you are looking like this?' Latika looks shocked.

I take a moment to answer. Then I draw in a deep breath and say, 'Firstly there is no word like turn-downer. Get your language right, Mr Surve. Secondly I am not chasing him and I am just asking you, my closest buddies, what I should do.'

(Okay, I am chasing him but I am not going to admit that to Sriram.) I try to sound as casual and nonchalant as possible. Like I don't care. But of course, I fool no one.

For once, Sriram doesn't reply immediately and instead stirs his coffee. Latika is quiet too as she sips her iced-tea. I have asked for a double-shot espresso and I grimace as I taste it and then add four sachets of sugar. I feel so low, I need an extension ladder to get out of this one. The espresso is supposed to help, coffee being a mood-elevator and all that.

'Hmmm, if you ask me there is nothing much you can do. Other than wait for him to get back,' says Sriram finally.

'I could bump into him, you know. I know where his office is,' I say and as soon as I say it I don't believe I have said it.

'God, no! Don't even think about it,' Latika pounces on me.

'But what I am wondering is why the hell he hasn't messaged back and why he has suddenly gone cold. Why do guys do that Sriram?' I ask.

'Yeah, really. Why do they? I too have had my fair share, before I married Manish, of course. One moment you think you have got a great thing going. Two, three dates and then wham. The guy has vanished and then there is no trace of him. The least you owe a woman is an explanation,' Latika is vociferous in her disapproval.

Sriram, for once is speechless instead of the usual smart-alecky sexist jokes that he comes up with. I think he has figured out that this one means a great deal to me. Latika and I are looking at him like whatever he is going to say is Gospel.

'Hmm, why a guy doesn't get back? I think there can be several reasons,' he says and Latika and I wait for him to go on as he leans back and sinks a little lower into the chair and stretches out his legs.

'Such as?' I prod, impatient now to know what could be the possible reason for Aman to have suddenly clammed up.

'See, I think he could genuinely be busy and neck-deep

in work or maybe his phone is acting up and messages aren't going through, or maybe he is fighting his feelings for you and is deciding what next course of action is to be taken and he wants to be sure.'

'Or maybe he just isn't interested in me anymore,' I shrug and even to my own ears my voice sounds laden with glumness and despair, as hard as I try to make it sound like I am okay about it.

'Yeah, I don't buy that "neck-deep in work" excuse. How long does it take anyway to reply to a message? Fifteen seconds? And he can tell her that he is busy, right?' says Latika and I nod in agreement.

'See, when a guy focuses on work, he cannot think of anything else. Trust me, guys are wired differently. I know that I don't even look at my phone for hours together when I am busy,' Sriram says.

'Yes, but once you get back from work, you surely do?' I am still sceptical.

'Of course. Usually I do but if I have had a tough day, I usually unwind by watching a game on TV or some movie. I don't want to text someone.'

But Aman isn't like that. He always responds. No matter how busy he is. I had sent him a couple of messages on the IM of my phone, telling him that I had a great time and asking if he had shifted to the new house and whether he was settling in. He hadn't read it for a long time. Then when finally he had (the notification in the chat app shows me when my message has been delivered and read), there was no response. After waiting for a few hours, I thought that perhaps the messages weren't going out from his end (I have faced that a couple of times). So I had copy-pasted it and resent it as a text. He could have texted back, but he didn't. I waited for a day and then texted a casual, `Hey, how are you doing? All good?`

`Settled in?` and there was no response to that too. Then I waited for another day and finally, when I wasn't able to contain myself, I had texted him asking, `Are you getting my messages?` After a few minutes, I had got his reply, `Yes, I am.` Just that and nothing else. Couldn't the guy explain? Why was he so curt? Why hasn't he messaged after that? I feel like I will go insane if I don't get the answers soon.

'Leave him alone. There is nothing you can do unless he decides to get back to you,' Sriram finally says and what he has said is true.

'Yeah, let us change the topic and talk about something else,' I say.

Latika and I quiz Sriram about his love life. He had been on a couple of dates with a German girl who Latika and I instantly hated. But he hasn't mentioned her for long now. He is shifty and evasive when we quiz him about her. But we worm it out of him. (She dumped him and went back to Germany.)

'Now don't you both say, "I told you so",' says Sriram.

'We told you so, we told you so,' Latika and I chant in a sing-song voice like we used to at school, and suddenly three of us are laughing again without the slightest care in the world, just like we used to at school, whenever we had got into some mischief and there was no way out. There is something so darn comforting about old friendships.

And then finally, when we stop laughing Latika springs a surprise on us. She announces that she is expecting.

'OH MY GOD. OH MY GOD,' I scream and nearly trip over myself as I jump up to hug her. She leans forward and we hug each other for a while and then we are aware that the others are staring at us.

Sriram squeezes her hand and says, 'Congratulations, that is amazing,' and he is staring at her in a new light now. Somehow being pregnant automatically elevates you and makes you special.

'And why didn't you tell us immediately? Why did you let me go on and on about a guy who doesn't bother to return messages?' I ask her.

'Because you are so madly in love with him, babes, and you so desperately want to hear from him. My news… I have known now for a while. So…' she trails off leaving her sentence unfinished.

I lean over and kiss her on the cheek and she looks embarrassed at my sudden display of affection.

I know she is right.

Right now I am craving for a message from Aman much like a junkie craving for the next fix. But there is nothing I can do. We finally part and I reluctantly trudge back to my office. I have to submit my column.

Most of the staff has left early today as there is an IPL match on TV and the Bangalore team is playing. Some of them are also going to the stadium to watch. The office feels eerily empty but it matches my mood. That is exactly how I am feeling inside.

I sit at my desk for a while, thinking about my next column.

Finally I begin to write:

Five Things You Should (Or Should Not) Do If The Guy Doesn't Get Back To You

By Anjali Prabhu

So, you are into this guy and you think you have something going. Why even up to last week, the communication between both of you was great. But suddenly he has clammed up.

He hasn't got back to you even after a couple of texts from your side or worse still, his replies have become monosyllabic, brief and to the point.

What can you do now?

Here is what you can and should be doing.

1. **Do not stalk him online**: Do not keep checking his Facebook profile to see what he is up to. It can be very tempting, but you are only setting yourself up for more punishment. It will certainly cause you heartburn to see that he has plenty of time to play football, or party with friends, but none to text you. Leave his FB profile alone. Disable your account for a while, delete it, do anything, but stay away from his profile.
2. **Exhibit supreme patience**: The only way to do this would probably be to retire to the Himalayas and become an ascetic. If that is not an option, then distract yourself like crazy. Bury yourself in work so you do not obsess over why he hasn't texted back. Go join an exercise class, go meet your old buddies, catch up on movies, restart an old hobby. Patience is the name of the game. Master it.
3. **Leave him alone**: You cannot *make* a guy text you back. He has your phone number (no, he didn't lose it). If a guy wants to get in touch with you, he will find a way. Do not make excuses for him and do not fool yourself.

4. **Talk to your buddies:** Talk to one or two close, trusted friends, who have been in a similar situation. If you have no close friends whom you can talk to or confide in, join an online forum. Talking about it may not make the problem go away, but it definitely helps you cope, especially when you see that there are many others who have gone though this. It also makes you feel lighter.
5. **TTYL or vanish:** If he does wake up (whether after three days, a week, a month or whatever time period) and texts you out of the blue, act cool. Yes, we know you are elated, excited and supremely happy that he texted you. But do not show your excitement. If you allow him to think it is okay to treat you as he has just done, you are setting a precedent for repeat cycles. Wait at least a day or two or more (yes, that long—depending on how long he has taken to get back to you) and then text back a short polite text, saying you are busy.

If you follow the above methods, chances are he will get back to you soon. And if he doesn't, you have to rethink whether you want a guy who can treat you so casually.

Good luck girls!

I read what I have written thrice. I correct the typos and the small grammatical errors that have crept in, and then hit the 'send' key to Jeena.

I get her reply just as I am about to leave work.

```
Anjali,
The piece you sent—it is good. You have captured it spot-on.
I think it will help thousands of women out there who wait to hear from the bastards who text back only when it suits them or when they want something.
Jeena
P S: It helped me too.
```

Praise from Jeena is like winning a grand-slam title when you are seeded 2000 in the world. It is next to impossible. I feel inordinately pleased with myself.

And yet, I cannot stop myself from checking my phone for the millionth time to see if there is a message from him.

There isn't. I am very tempted to call him and ask him if he is all right, and what has caused this silence, but I force myself not to. It is so darn hard to follow your own advice sometimes. If he wants to get back to me, of course he will.

And for now, there is nothing I can do except cross my fingers and wait.

Chapter 21

Shruti

There are passersby rushing towards him and my mother-in-law and I join them. He has hit his head on a cement block and blood is gushing out like water from a tap. I am shell-shocked, terrified. I frantically take out my mobile and try hard to remember the ambulance number. What is it? 1001? 1002? I have no clue.

A small crowd has gathered around and my mother-in-law is now sitting next to my father-in-law whose eyes are shut. Someone has produced a bottle of water and he asks my mother-in-law to sprinkle some water on his face.

'No, don't do that. Move back please, give him room to breathe. Move back, move back,' says a voice and I see a middle-aged man taking charge. The crowd listens to him and he whips out his mobile and calls a hospital.

'There is a hospital just three minutes away. The ambulance will arrive in less than five minutes. Do not panic please,' he says to me.

It is then that I notice him. He is tall and lanky and very fit. His t-shirt is covered in sweat and he wears Nike shoes, sports arm bands and knee pads. There is some sort of a strap on his arm in which he probably carries his phone and he must have been on his evening jog. His hair is peppered with grey and his eyes look kind. There is something very strangely familiar about him. Have I met him before? I am not able to place him immediately as I am too taken aback, scared and fighting hard to control my panic and take charge of the situation.

'Thank you so much,' I mutter, not able to think of what to say.

My mother-in-law has gone pale and she doesn't know what to do. She is fanning my father-in-law frantically with her sari *pallu.*

Then we hear the ambulance arrive and I heave a sigh of relief.

The paramedics rush out and check his breathing and pulse. They transfer my father-in-law to a stretcher and carry him in.

They ask if any of us want to be in the vehicle with them or whether we will follow them. I tell them that I will ride with them and the stranger who has dialled the ambulance says that he can follow the ambulance and bring my mother-in-law over. I gratefully agree. I don't think my mother-in-law would have been able to ride in the ambulance.

Inside the ambulance, I realise that this is the scariest ride I have ever had in my life. I frantically dial Rishabh's number, but he does not answer. I text him and all I say is, `Call me ASAP`. I don't want to tell him in a text message that his father is in an ambulance on the way to the hospital.

The paramedics have now attached an oxygen mask to my father-in-law's face. They clean up the blood, but it is still gushing out. I say a silent prayer begging the Gods to save my father-in-law. I have an inherent fear of everything to do with hospitals after frequenting them for my mother's treatment and I try to calm myself by gazing out of the ambulance window. The stranger who helped us, is following us in his car. I can see my mother-in-law next to him but they are too far to make out her expression.

When we arrive at the hospital, my father-in-law is rushed to emergency care and I am asked to fill up some forms. My mother-in-law too arrives and is taken to the emergency room.

As I am completing the paperwork I become aware of the kind stranger who came to our rescue. I realise that I haven't even asked his name and thanked him properly.

I go up to him.'Thank you so much for your kindness, I am Shruti,' I say as I extend my hand. I have to fight the urge to address him as 'Sir'. Somehow his persona is one that commands respect and awe. But I resist the temptation as it feels odd to address someone I don't even know as 'Sir'. It would be ridiculous.

His handshake is firm and he says, 'Sanjeev.'

I don't know what else to say. He has been so kind, this man.

'Your parents?' he asks.

'No, my in-laws. I am trying to reach my husband,' I say.

'Where is he right now? In India or abroad?'

'He is very much here in Mumbai, but he is probably in a meeting. I have texted him and he should be calling back soon.'

'I can stick around till he gets here,' says Sanjeev. That is kind of him. I mean, getting us to the hospital here is one thing. But sticking around till Rishabh gets here—that is the kind of thing a friend would do. He has a manner that is easy and reassuring. And somehow very familiar.

On the one hand I want to accept his offer but on the other I do not want to take advantage of his kindness. I am terrified and having this guy around would be a relief rather than waiting outside the emergency with just my mother-in law for company who is as panic-stricken as I am.

'That would be very kind of you indeed but I hope I am not holding you up,' I say.

'Don't worry about it. I have nothing to do anyway,' he says and his eyes twinkle.

It is then that I recognise him. It is an 'Oh-my-God' moment for me. I just can't believe it. He can't be—or is he? I look at him once more and I am certain now of who he is. I am not making a mistake. He *is* Sanjeev Adani, the founder of Sneha Kutir and a few more organisations which are involved in the betterment of society, improving the quality of life, empowering street children, helping destitute women and many such things. He is extremely well known, respected and has even won a Padmashri Award for his services to society. I had met him many years back, while still at college under different circumstances. No wonder he seemed so familiar! No wonder I had this crazy urge to address him as 'Sir'. It all makes sense now.

'Oh my God—sir. We have met a long time back, a few years back. In Bangalore,' I blurt out, unable to contain myself and now that I have recognised him, unable to address him as anything but 'sir'.

His eyebrows knit in furrowed concentration as he tries to remember.

'You were the key speaker for the entrepreneurial summit organised at STC college. I was the corporate interface of my college. and had come to escort you from Oberoi to my college,' I say, the words slipping out in a rush in my excitement, now that I know who he is.

He breaks into laughter, 'Yes, I remember, Shruti Srinivasan, corporate interface—and your friend Aman and the spinach sandwich too,' he adds.

I am surprised he remembers the occasion and even

our names. Those were days when Aman and I had been inseparable. When I had been nominated from my college to escort Mr Adani, Aman and I had found the perfect opportunity to bunk college and hang out together. I had left college at eleven in the morning, ostensibly to be with Mr Adani. I had contacted him from the hotel lobby and said that I was around if he needed anything and that a car was waiting and available at his disposal in case he wanted to go around anywhere in Bangalore. Mr Adani had arrived from Mumbai just for this event at our college, and to get him to speak for our summit had been a huge feather in the cap for us. He had replied that he was fine and that he had some business meetings scheduled and we would leave by five-thirty pm, as the talk was scheduled for six-thirty pm. That suited Aman and me perfectly. It was one of the best times we had had. We had gone to Ulsoor Lake for a while and hung around there, sitting on a bench, gazing at the calm serene water and I had leaned on his shoulder as he put his arm around me. We had talked a lot that day. He had told me about his mother, her passion for gardening and how much he admired the sacrifices that she had made in raising him and how she had never remarried. We had talked about how both of us were the only children. I had confessed that I longed for a sibling and he had said that every now and then, while growing up, he had felt that way too. Then, after a while, we had eaten lunch at a nearby roadside joint and then hung around in Cubbon Park till it was time to go and escort Mr Adani. I had met him at the hotel lobby. Aman and I had earlier agreed that I would ride in the car with Mr Adani and Aman would follow at a safe distance, on his motorbike. Aman had hung around inconspicuously (or so we thought) so that he could follow us, but Mr Adani was sharp. He had spotted Aman in a jiffy and I had been forced to confess that he was my 'friend' and I had to introduce Aman to him.

Mr Adani had been a good sport about it and had insisted that Aman ride in the car with us. Both of us had been too embarrassed to say no and that Aman had a motorbike. So Aman had got into the front seat and I at the back with Mr Adani. Aman had said that he would have to get off much before we reached college. 'Yes, yes, you don't want to get caught in your girlfriend's official car. We too have done all this in our college days. Don't worry,' he had said.

On the way Mr Adani said that he hadn't had lunch and was hungry. He had wanted a sandwich and Aman had told the driver to pull over at Hot Bread and Bagels. Aman had recommended the spinach sandwich which was the speciality of that place and Mr Adani had loved it. He was easy to talk to, unassuming and very down-to-earth. He behaved more like a lovable college professor than a renowned personality who had founded so many institutions. Aman and I had warmed up to him instantly. Mr Adani had quizzed us about our relationship and we found ourselves telling him about how we planned to get married soon as we finished college and got a job, how we felt lucky to have found each other and how good it felt to be in love. He had laughed and agreed and wished us the very best and after that Aman had got off.

Much later, Aman and I had laughed about the whole episode as Aman had to take an auto and go all the way back to the hotel to fetch his motorbike. Aman had told me that the reason Mr Adani had spotted him in the lobby was because I kept darting love-filled glances in his direction and I had 'given him away'. I am stunned how easily all these memories come flooding back. I am able to remember it all so clearly like it happened yesterday. A single meeting with someone from what seems like another lifetime has actually catapulted me right back into that very time.

A much happier and simpler time. A time which was one of the happiest times of my life.

My time with Aman.

'Yes sir, the same Shruti. Guilty as charged. I am just so amazed that you even remember our names and even more amazed that I ran into you here,' I finally manage to say.

'I have an excellent memory for details my dear girl and as for running into me here, I always go for my jog along Worli sea-face around this time. Today in fact, I was a little earlier than usual. Maybe our paths were destined to cross again,' he says.

I have no idea whether he is teasing me or not as the twinkle is back in his eye. Whatever it is, I am grateful for his help and I tell him so.

'It is fine. You can repay me when Aman arrives and then you both can buy me coffee,' he says.

For a moment I don't get what he is saying. Then I understand. Mr Adani has presumed that Aman and I have got married. I wince.

'Umm...Things changed, sir. I married someone else,' I say. I feel so strange standing in a hospital corridor and blurting out personal details of my life to someone as eminent as Mr Adani. It feels surreal. Like I am in a dream.

'Oh,' he says. 'If you pardon my asking, what happened? You guys were so sure of each other.'

'It is a long story, sir. Circumstances changed.' I don't know how else to explain what happened.

'You sure are making me curious, but now isn't the time for stories. I would love to know though. Come, let's first figure out how your father-in-law is doing,' he says as he accompanies me to the emergency section.

'My mother-in-law is panicking, the poor lady. I wish Rishabh would get here soon,' I say.

Mr Adani asks me to stay calm. He visits this hospital often as there are eight volunteers from his organisation working here. They do not have a medical background but they help and guide patients fill up forms, assist the elderly who are alone and soothe the anxious with a kind smile and take care of all their needs. They also volunteer in the cafeteria and the non-medical administrative work that keeps the hospital functioning smoothly. Mr Adani offers to assign a volunteer to my mother-in-law, just in case she needs anything. But I tell him that I will take care of her.

After a while, Mr Adani takes leave of me. Before going, he hands me his visiting card and tells me to let him know of my father-in-law's progress.

Mr Adani has a heart of gold. I remember reading somewhere that his foundation has set up twenty-three public secondary schools in association with the Uttar Pradesh government. Here the underprivileged have access to world-class education and amenities. His venture has been very successful and he wants to extend it to other states.

But more than anything, I am thoroughly impressed by how down to earth he is despite all his success. Moreover, I am astonished at his sharp memory. I also recall reading that one thing common in most successful people is their eye for details, a sharp memory, and a genuine interest in people. He seems to have the right combination, for sure. He tells me that he has now retired and the organisations he has founded have able people who run it well. He visits Sneha Kutir regularly, however, as he is a trained counsellor and enjoys counselling people on life-skills and emotional problems. He also nurtures and motivates over 200 volunteers to give free service in about twenty hospitals all over Mumbai.

As soon as he leaves, I call Rishabh once again and this time he picks up my call. He is just out of a meeting and he hasn't seen any of my messages nor has he heard my previous calls as his phone has been on silent mode. As soon as he hears what happened he says that he will come right over. He sounds frantic with worry. I tell him that it is all under control and not to panic and that I am taking care of everything.

But deep down I am just as terrified as him. I fervently hope that my father-in-law is going to be okay. I tell my mother-in-law not to worry and that Rishabh is on his way in my best 'all-is-well' voice. Then I sit down on the waiting chair with her, outside the emergency room, and close my eyes and pray silently.

By the time Rishabh arrives, the doctor has already told me that my father-in-law is fine and the wound on his head was just external and he has fully recovered his consciousness. The doctor says that the fainting was most likely caused because of a combination of diabetes and severe dehydration. But he says that he wants to rule out the possibility of a cardiac syncope and so it is better to keep him under observation for twenty-four hours and do a few tests to rule out the possibility. He will be shifted to a private room from the emergency and Rishabh and I complete the formalities. We are informed by the hospital staff that 'one attendant is allowed to stay with the patient'. Rishabh says that he will stay overnight in the hospital and his mother insists that she will. They have an argument over that and in the end my mother-in-law wins.

So Rishabh and I drive back together. He is quiet the entire duration of the drive. I try to assure him that his father will be fine.

'Yeah, like you are the doctor and you know better than them. And frankly all this wouldn't have happened if you hadn't decided to drag them all over Mumbai. They aren't used to it,' he snaps at me.

I cannot believe he just said that. Tears sting my eyes at his tone. He is being so darn unfair now. When I texted him that I was taking his parents out he seemed happy. But now he is implying that his father fainting is somehow my fault? This is ridiculous. But I am too emotionally exhausted to fight. I have been through this entire episode of hospital, emergency and riding in the ambulance. All I want is to get home and collapse. So I do not retort or reply to him. I just keep quiet and stare out of the window. A few moments later he realises I am hurt and says, 'Sorry. I didn't mean to snap at you. I am just very stressed.'

I still don't bother to reply back. If anyone is stressed it should be me. I have bent over backwards and made an effort to be nice to his parents. I have even taken time off from work and gone all around Mumbai for them. I have done my best and I am tired now.

I turn up the music in the car and we complete the rest of the journey in silence. Rishabh has to introspect and figure out whatever it is about me that is bothering him. I have now given it all that I can. It is up to him now to decide whether he wants to keep this cold war going or whether he wants to forget about the past and move on. I am done trying.

After we reach home, Rishabh calls up his mother to check on her. A few tests are scheduled for early the next day and his mother says she is managing fine. There is a cafeteria attached to the hospital, she says, and she will eat there. She assures Rishabh that she will be okay.

I want Rishabh to talk to me. I want to tell him about Mr Adani and how helpful he was. But that would mean bringing up Aman's name again. I contemplate lying and leaving out the part where Aman was involved. But then I remember that Rishabh might have read the mails in which Aman and I discussed Mr Adani, so I don't bother.

The day's events have caught up with me now. I ask Rishabh if he will have anything to drink and when he refuses, I pour myself a large glass of wine. Wine always relaxes me and today I need it. My nerves are taut.

I sit on the balcony sipping my wine and look at the city lights and headlights of the traffic zooming by. They look like co-ordinated fireflies, moving in a line. By the time I finish my wine, I feel light-headed and relaxed. All the stress and hurt has vanished. Rishabh hasn't budged from in front of the television nor has he spoken a word to me. I am in no mood to make an effort at a conversation with him either. I have been trying to talk to him for so many days, but this husband of mine seems to have turned into a stone wall.

I fix a quick meal of some readymade *rotis* which just have to be heated on a pan and served. There is some vegetable left over from the previous day that my mother-in-law had cooked. We eat our meal in silence and then Rishabh goes back to the television. I so wish he would switch off the damn thing and at least thank me for reaching his dad to the hospital on time. I wish he would just put his arms around me like the old times. I wish he would joke and laugh.

But I know these are simply empty wishes. The time when we used to joke and laugh, like a normal couple, now seems so far away.

So I go back to the guest room (which is now our bedroom) and switch on my laptop. I am in a daze, the wine having hit me. I now want to get to the root of all my problems. I want to know what the hell Rishabh has read in my mails that has caused him to be so hostile to me. I want to know how long it has been since Aman and I exchanged a mail. Then I want to confront Rishabh with all of this. I want to shake him up and tell him to stop behaving like this.

I log into my mail account and type 'Aman' in the search box.

There *are* thousands. God—seeing them all together like this has taken even me by surprise, even though I *knew*. I can now imagine what a massive shock it must have been to Rishabh. The last one was exchanged about three months before I got married. I open a mail which he has written asking me to change my mind. It begs me to come back. It declares his undying love for me. He says he will do anything that I ask of him and not to walk away. He says he will be shattered without me. Each word in that mail still feels like a stab in my heart. Before I realise it tears are flowing down my face and I am sobbing.

I read the mail before that, and the one before and the one before. They are all identical. Aman has begged me to stay and that things will be fine. That he is still waiting for me. I remember how I used to not read any of his mails.

I remember how I used to open them and then log out of my account as I couldn't bear to read whatever it is that he had to say. I simply did not want to know. I had stopped reading his mails when I had decided to break up with him. I used to merely skim through them and not read the contents as it was hard for me. My parents had been so happy that I had agreed to let go of Aman and marry Rishabh. My mother was still under medical supervision. The endless rounds of hospitals and check-ups had left us all weary and battered. I couldn't have pulled another shocker on them saying that I want to go back to Aman. So, as hard as it had been, I had felt that this was for the best. The wedding dates had been finalised and I didn't have the courage to tell my parents that I cannot go ahead. The best way forward was to not acknowledge Aman's mails. Just like how I had not answered his phone calls. I wince now at the memories. I had felt guilty about doing this to Aman and I had hoped and prayed he would move on.

But now when I read his mails, I realise that it is me, who hasn't moved on. Even after nearly two years of marriage, I crave for Aman. I have tried hard to get over him.

And I have failed.

I wonder how he is now. In his final mail he has said that if he can't have me as his life-partner, he definitely wants a friendship for life. He says no matter what happens he will be there for me and for him, our relationship is for a lifetime.

And today, after a gap of more than two years, I read his words over and over. They seem to be leaping out at me now, taunting me, prodding me, pushing me, questioning me, begging me. They seem to have a strange power of their own.

Finally I cannot resist it anymore.

I *have* to write to Aman. I just have to contact him again.

So I compose a new message and I begin to type.

Chapter 22

Aman

Work has been all consuming, crazy, hectic in a world-will-end-if-I-don't-do-this-now way. I have hardly any time even for a meal. Earlier I would eat leisurely (okay, somewhat leisurely) at the company cafeteria located on the top floor. But these days I don't even realise when the lunch hour comes and goes. Often, when I look up from work, it is already three-thirty pm and I hurriedly order a sandwich because my stomach feels empty and hollow. I have never been this involved in work. I thoroughly enjoy the challenge even though it is gruelling. It is a field completely new to us and we cannot afford to make any mistakes. The days mostly begin with meetings and the updates and what is expected is laid out by Vikram. It is more like a commando-drill brief and work then proceeds on a war-footing.

In fact, it has been so darn hectic that when the car dealer called me and told me that my car had arrived, I had told him to deliver it to my office address. He had been so surprised. He said that usually people come to the showroom and take delivery. They also do a small *puja* and there is a formal ceremony of 'handing over the keys'. I had asked him if it was a problem to deliver and he had hastily assured me that it wasn't and of course they would do what I preferred. The sales-in-charge had driven the car to my office and I had instructed the security to let him in. Then I had asked him to park it and bring the keys up. Later, long past midnight, when I was finally ready to leave, I had gone downstairs to the basement and seen that they had decorated the car with a huge bow and a ribbon around it—gift-wrapped it for me. No wonder the sales guy had been so surprised when I had not even come downstairs to see it. In most people's lives taking delivery of their first car is a big moment. I guess it was in mine too, but I had been too busy to notice.

The car sure feels good and I feel on top of the world driving it.

It is during one of the morning meetings that my mother calls. I put the phone on silent and I mean to call her back. But I remember that she called only after two days. I feel terribly guilty as I look at my phone (which is always on silent these days) and see two missed calls from her. What if it was an emergency? What if she had been calling me for something urgent? I decide that though this pace of work is excellent for me career-wise, I should make time for my mother. I call her back immediately. After I have dialled her number I realise it is already ten pm and she must be fast asleep. But before I can hang up, she answers and she sounds like I have woken her up from sleep.

'Ma, I am so sorry, work has been hectic,' I say as soon as I hear her voice. Then I ask her if she had been asleep and I apologise for waking her up.

'*Arey* no, it is okay *beta*. You can call me anytime, you know that,' she says graciously.

This is the thing about motherhood—the unconditional love and acceptance, even though I have barely had time for her. (I haven't even had time for myself). When I hear her voice I realise how much I miss her. I decide then and there that I will fly her down to Bangalore. After all, she hasn't even seen my new place.

'How are you? Are you taking care of yourself? How is your new place?' she asks.

'The new place is nice, but it has been so hectic that I hardly get time for myself these days,' I say.

'That's good, *beta*. Hard work never killed anyone,' replies my mother. She has worked hard all her life and doesn't know any other way to be.

'Ma, you should come and visit me. For the next fifteen days, things will be crazy. That is when it all finally takes off. After that, I will have some breathing time.'

'I am coming tomorrow. I had called to tell you that,' she says and I can picture her smiling.

'What?! Tomorrow? Oh my God. Why didn't you tell me? Are your tickets booked?' I ask totally taken by surprise.

'I did try to tell you,' she says and now she is laughing, delighted at my astonishment. 'I am one of the few who got selected for this course in Bangalore on organic terrace-garden farming at the Agricultural College there,' she says.

'Oh, Ma, That is wonderful news indeed! But how did all this happen?' I ask.

'There was an advertisement in the newspaper some months back from the local horticultural association here, asking for applications as they want to encourage organic farming. When I called them up and expressed my interest, they came over and had a look at my garden. When they saw it they were convinced and nominated me for the course. Once I complete this course, they will provide me with all the material needed to start an organic terrace garden, all the supplies, fertilisers, soil and all that. Later, they will buy my produce too. It is an excellent scheme for those interested,' she says.

I am very happy for my mother.

'That is fantastic, Ma. I am so proud of you. And, Ma, you will like my new place,' I say.

Now that I know she is arriving so soon, I am happy and excited. It would be wonderful to have her over.

'And I am happy about it too but I won't be staying with you. It is a two-week residential course and I will stay at their campus. It is far-off from the city,' she says.

'Oh, but I guess weekends will be off?' I ask hopefully. It will be wonderful to have her around.

'Yes, I will see you on the weekends. In any case you will be busy on weekdays so it all works out perfectly, doesn't it?' she says and of course she is right as usual.

I ask her how she will commute from the airport to the college and she replies that they have made all the arrangements. With a chuckle, she reminds me that when I was in college that was a question she would ask me, and now it's the other way round.

'Yeah, Ma, what to do? You and I, we are together and we have to watch out for each other,' I say repeating her phrase which she used to tell me in my growing up years. She used to say it in Hindi, in a sing-song voice, and I do the same now.

She laughs and I feel happy to hear the sound of her laughter. It's funny how even though I am all grown up I am so childishly excited at the prospect of having my mother over. I am also glad that she is doing this course. My mother has kept herself busy after her retirement. She is an example for retired folks on how to live a productive life.

I decide to have a beer and sit in the balcony for a while. The balcony is fairly large and I like lying on the large wooden swing and gazing at the stars. Some days I fall asleep here and awake around midnght and stumble to my bedroom.

Today, just as I am settling down, my phone buzzes and I check it. It is a text message from Anjali.

`Hey—not sure if you are getting my instant messages or whether you are avoiding me! All well? Either ways let me know.`

I read it and wince.

Poor girl does not deserve this. She is sweet, effervescent and bubbly. I just am not ready for the relationship she wants. I remember reading somewhere that the person who cares less has more power in the relationship. As sad as it is, it is true. Right now, I care less. So I have more power. I don't want to hurt her. Yet, I don't want to lead her on. In my last relationship, I have been burnt so badly that I still hurt. I think a part of me still aches for Shruti. I do not want to get *that* involved with a woman anymore, and Anjali is breaking down my defences and my excuses.

I don't know if avoiding Anjali is cowardly or insensitive of me. Probably it is both. I am hiding from her and it isn't right. Yet I continue to do it. She has stopped instant-messaging or mailing now. I do not know whether to be relieved or whether to feel ashamed. One part of me does feel relieved that the flood of messages has stopped and yet the other kind of misses it. I know I owe her some kind of explanation. Besides, she does have a right to know.

So I pick up the phone and call her.

She sounds surprised and so very happy to hear from me that I feel like an asshole to have called.

'Hey, How have you been?' I say.

'Hey! Aman! I am good. How *are* you?'

There is so much happiness in her voice—she hasn't even asked where I have been all these days. There is no accusatory tone at all. And, for some strange reason, her happy tone makes me feel awkward. It makes me want to grovel and explain why I suddenly went quiet, even though she hasn't asked.

'I am so sorry to have dropped out of the radar like that,' I begin.

'Hey, that's okay. I know you are a busy guy,' she says simply.

'Still, I should have replied to your messages. The thing is, it has been hectic,' I say and that is of course true.

'That's fine, I have been busy myself,' she says.

'Oh. Okay. What have you been busy with?' I ask. Somehow her being busy with her own life hadn't even occurred to me and now I want to know the details.

'Well, this and that. Meeting some people, hanging out with my friends, writing my pieces,' she says.

'Oooh! And who have you been meeting? Anyone interesting?' I ask.

'We're doing this feature where we're shooting some nice-looking guys who support animals. So the shoot is happening where all these guys pose holding a cute puppy. All the women in my office are going ga-ga over the idea and the shoot is so much fun. Jeena has put a strict cap though on the number of women who can go to the location,' she says.

'Interesting. Who are these guys?' I ask.

What I want to ask is if any of the guys have been hitting on her. It's funny, how a moment ago I didn't want to be involved with her and now that she is mentioning some guys I want to know details.

'Oh some model types. Mostly dumb if you ask me. I prefer brain over brawn. These guys can't even hold a conversation. Such narcissists and a self-obsessed bunch they are,' she says.

I smile. This is why I like her so much. She makes me feel so good.

She asks me what is new and I tell her about my mother's visit. She is happy to hear about it. She asks me details about my work and I find myself talking to her and telling her in detail all that I have been doing. I had forgotten how easy Anjali is to talk to and now it is all coming back. She asks me how my house is and whether I have settled down and whether I got the delivery of my car.

I tell her that I have and she asks me how it is and when would I give her a ride in my new car.

And I find myself saying, 'Now, if you are game?'

I don't know why I say it.

'Oh Aman, that will be lovely!' she says.

And before I realise what I am doing, I find myself loading the car with a portable drinks' case and folding chairs (all a part of the set I picked up in the UK, which I haven't used up to now) and am driving to Anjali's place.

Chapter 23

Anjali

I know what I have done is blatant violation of point number five of my last article. I know I am supposed to act cool and busy and tell Aman that I will get back to him in three-four days. But I just am not able to do that. I am elated that he has actually called in response to my text. (I just couldn't resist texting him one last time. I was dying and I just had to know where we stood. I had expected no reply and had thought that if he didn't bother to reply, I would most definitely consider it a closed chapter and move on. But now not only has he replied, he is even on his way to see me. Gosh. This guy should get a Nobel Prize for sending confusing signals. What does he want?)

There is hardly any time to think. He is on his way and I am in my sleeveless top, my oldest polka dotted purple pyjamas which even have a tiny hole that I have been too lazy to mend. I am not wearing a bra and I have no make-up on either. If he sees me like this, it would be a disaster and have the same impact as an earthquake of 7.5 on the Richter scale.

I rush to my wardrobe and quickly put on my bra and contemplate what to wear. I have to look 'casual' and not too dressed. I am not able to decide. Finally I settle for a pair of shorts and a smart fitted tee. Then I quickly slip on a pair of earrings and dab on some lip-gloss. There. That looks casual enough. Like I was lounging around in shorts when he called.

I don't want my landlord to peep out and see me disappear with Aman in the car. He might give me a lecture on moral values and how it is unsafe for a woman my age to be out at this time of the night. So I call Aman and ask him where he has reached. He says he is taking the turn into the road that leads to my home and he will be here in two minutes. I tell him to park right there and that I will come out of the house and walk to where he is parked.

'Oh! But why do you have to sneak out like that? Are your parents visiting or something?' he asks.

'Oh no. I have a landlord who acts like my father. In fact, my father probably won't ask as many questions as he does. But this guy gives reports about my movements to my father. He is a distant relative and my self-appointed local guardian. I will explain when I see you,' I say as I make my way outside as silently as possible, hoping that Mr Joshi is safely in bed. I hear the blast of television and am relieved as it means that he is totally engrossed and isn't likely to keep a track on my movements.

When I spot Aman, I am so happy, I feel like doing a little cheerleader dance. My heart is already doing that and I am glad he can't look inside my head. I am insanely happy. He is wearing a light blue checked shirt and looks so attractive behind the wheel of his red car. He leaps out and comes to my side and opens the door for me. He is chivalrous and such a gentleman, this guy. I laugh in delight and I kiss him on the cheek and say, 'Hey! So good to see you.' He has the grace to blush and I find that adorable. I have to stop myself from leaning into his neck and nuzzling him. That is exactly what I feel like doing. God. Maybe Latika is right. Maybe I *am* madly in love with this guy. Or maybe it is just attraction because he is the first decent guy I have dated in ages. Who knows.

'So when did you get the car?' I ask as I slip into the passenger's seat.

'A week back and you know what I didn't even have time to collect it. I had them deliver it to my office, like it was a Chinese takeaway, can you believe?' he says.

'Oh my God, has it been that bad then?'

'I wouldn't say *bad*, as I am so darn engrossed. I guess that it is good when your work interests you so much. I don't even feel I am working. There just isn't time,' he says.

'Drowning oneself in work is the best remedy for getting over heartbreak, you know,' I say immediately and then instantly realise that I probably shouldn't have brought it up now. Maybe he doesn't want to be reminded of his past relationships. I should stop being an 'advice-dispensing-ms know-it-all'. At this rate, instead of my regular column, Jeena would probably ask me to do an agony aunt column.

But Aman is nodding in agreement.

'Yes, that is so true. In fact, that is what took me to the UK where I drowned myself in work. My work is what keeps me going,' he nods gravely and there is a sad and melancholy look in his eyes as he looks straight ahead and drives.

I put my right hand over his left hand which is resting on the gear.

'Only work keeps you going?' I ask softly.

He smiles in response.

'Tell me!' I persist.

And he smiles even wider. I squeeze his hand and he makes no effort to move it away. He is wearing a watch with a steel strap and I caress his forearm and make small circles up and down. It is a shiatsu massage technique which one of the girls in the hostel had taught me.

'Mmmm, that feels good. Keep doing that,' he says and I smile in contentment.

'So where are we going?' I ask him.

'I don't know. I never had a plan. Shall we just drive around? A bit away from the city?'

I nod. I don't care where we go, as long as I am with him. This is lovely and I am enjoying every bit of it. Suddenly I have an idea.

'How about we go to Nandi Hills?' I say.

'I don't mind. Let's go,' he says and I look up the route on my phone's GPRS and in no time we are zooming on to the highway towards Nandi Hills. Aman is playing some contemporary music and Rihanna's 'Diamonds in the Sky' floods the car. It is the perfect song, the perfect ambience, the perfect mood and all so romantic.

Suddenly we see a police car parked on the side and they are stopping all the cars and checking for drunk driving. I don't know what it is about a police vehicle that sends a kind of fear inside me. Maybe it is because I have heard stories about couples being harassed by cops. Maybe it is because the Indian police aren't the friendliest of people. Or maybe it is because in my previous birth I was a fugitive hiding from the cops. Whatever it is my hands go ice-cold as I grip Aman's hand tightly.

He realises it and asks, 'Hey, are you okay? Relax. They are checking for drunk driving I guess and I haven't had anything to drink, except maybe a beer, much within permissible limits.'

Aman pulls over and rolls down his windows. The police officer is now bending down and he asks Aman, 'Where to?'

Aman says that we are driving to Mysore.

'Girlfriend? Staying where in Mysore? In hotel, eh?' The cop leers at me, staring at my breasts.

I have never felt this vulnerable or exposed or frightened.

'She is my wife and my father-in-law is Jagadish Chettiar. I can call him right now and you can clear all your doubts,' says Aman confidently as he whips out his mobile and opens the contact directory in his phone.

The cop's demeanour, attitude and entire body-language changes instantly.

'Oooh, no need, *saar*. Simply checking. Lot of people doing drunk driving. Lot of boys and girls doing immoral activity. We are just doing our duty. You can proceed, *saar*,' he says and steps back and waves us away.

We pull away and I am speechless, half with relief, half with surprise and totally flabbergasted at how Aman had handled it.

'Hey relax. It is okay. Don't be so frightened, ' says Aman and it is only then I realise that I have dug into his hand with my fingernails in fright and there are red marks on his skin now.

I exhale deeply and let go of his arm.

Then I laugh in relief.

'Aman, I am so sorry about clutching you like that. I don't know why but I have this deep paranoia about cops. You know how it is in these parts of India, the moral policing. For a few minutes, I had visions of us being yanked out of the car and God knows what would have happened then,' I shudder.

'I know,' says Aman quietly and this time he puts his hand on mine.

'And who is Jagadish Chettiar?' I ask.

'To be honest, even I don't know! The Jagadish Chettiar I have in my phone is the society plumber whose number I had saved two days ago,' says Aman and both of us burst out laughing.

'You know, I don't want to go to Nandi Hills now. God knows there might be more check posts on the way and I don't want to keep getting stopped,' I say. Somehow this episode with the cops has spoilt my mood.

'You are right. There might be more checks on the way. The only option is to turn back,' says Aman.

On the one hand I don't want this impromptu date to end, but the prospect of being stopped again terrifies me. My heart is still thudding from the previous encounter.

'Yes. Let us. I am sorry about my irrational fear. I can't help it.' I feel apologetic about spoiling what could have probably been a great outing.

'Oh no, please don't say sorry. In fact I owe you an apology,' says Aman.

'For what?' I ask.

He is silent and he doesn't know what to say.

'Hmmm… For… you know…' he trails off.

'Hey, it's okay. I understand,' I say.

But actually I don't. Aman has sent me totally confusing signals in the last few days. I wish I could get into his head and figure out what is going on. But the one thing I have learnt is never to push a guy. I have seen enough of my friends getting pushy, whiny and clingy if the guy doesn't get back to them and sure as hell, nine times out of ten he has disappeared. I don't want the same happening with Aman and me. I want to hold on to him. I have to be patient and it is bloody hard.

'You know I had planned a surprise,' says Aman.

'Is it? What?' I ask.

'I will have to show you. I thought we would find a nice spot and park for a while? Then I will,' he says.

'Hmm… let's not stop on the highway again, Aman. I have

had enough adventures for today,' I say. Even though I want to know what the 'surprise' is, I don't have the stomach to be stopped by cops again.

'I agree. See this is what I hate about India. All this moral policing. It isn't like it was any of his business what our relationship was. Somehow in India the mindset of the society is still stuck in some archaic times,' he looks angry now.

'Yes, you're right. You know what cops do? They frighten young couples hanging out in Cubbon Park, by pointing a camera at them and pretending to take their pictures. The couples bolt like frightened rabbits. One of my friends who works in *Bangalore Mirror*, did a story on it.'

Aman frowns. 'Okay. That I must say doesn't sound too encouraging for the surprise I planned. I shall save it for another day then.'

What is this surprise he is talking about? I am dying of curiosity. I debate on forcing him to tell me. But before I can ask, we have again come to the same place where the cops had stopped us and the same guy is still there. But as Aman slows down, he gives a big grin and gestures that we can pass through.

'The small advantages of having Jagadish Chettiar on your contact list,' laughs Aman and I chuckle with him.

The moment is lost and we listen to music. I stare at Aman and he looks so handsome, his chiselled features, his short hair framing his face, his sharp nose. He looks lost in thought and he seems a million miles away.

'A penny for your thoughts,' I say.

He smiles and replies that pennies are no longer in circulation.

I tell him that I will substitute it for a hundred bucks then.

He laughs and says he always thought his thoughts were worthless but now that I have put a price-tag on them how can he refuse. He then tells me that his mother is visiting as is Mark who is coming over to stay. Mark has finished a week of white water rafting in Rishikesh and he finds India 'simply incredible'.

'Oh. So you will have a full house then,' I say.

'Oh no, my mom is not staying with me. She is staying at the Agricultural College where she is doing a course,' clarifies Aman. He then proceeds to tell me about his mother's course and how she has been chosen. There is a gleam of pride as he says it. I can sense the strong bond between his mother and him, and how much he loves her.

'You're so lucky to have this connection with her, she sounds like a wonderful lady,' I say.

'Yeah, she is incredible. After my dad's death, she has stood like a pillar of strength and has always been there for me,' says Aman.

I wonder what it is like to be that close to a parent. I have been out of my home for a while now and I haven't bonded much with either my father or mother. In fact, during the annual trips that I make to Muscat, I start getting restless on the second day itself. I get bored out of my skull, especially with the forced visit I have to make to the homes of some folks from the Indian community, with whom I have absolutely nothing in common to converse about. By the end of a week, I think my parents are happy to see me leave.

Aman drops me back home and I make him park a little away from the house. I remind him about my prying landlord. It amuses Aman no end. To be honest, I want to invite him in. Instead I assure him that I am better off walking up to the house alone.

'I guess I will say bye bye and goodnight here then,' he says. I lean forward and kiss him on the lips. He is taken by surprise. But he quickly recovers and grabs my head towards his. I kiss him harder, hungrily, my tongue exploring his mouth. This is electric. I am unable to stop myself and feel giddy. I am completely lost. It seems like we are interlocked for hours. Aman's hand has slipped beneath my T-shirt and he is fiddling with the straps of my bra, breathing harder.

Then suddenly he stops and pulls away, much to my puzzlement.

'Want to come inside?' I ask, barely recognising my own voice laden with desire.

'I would love to, Anjali, but not today,' he says.

'Why, for God's sake why?' I want to scream. I want this man. How did I ever become so brazen? So shameless? So bold? I don't know. All I know is that I have never felt this way before.

But I don't ask him why. I just look at him questioningly.

'Let's both be certain of where we want to go with this thing before we venture further,' he says and then looks away. Then he turns back towards me and then kisses me on my cheek. Like a consolation prize. Or an apology. He is looking straight into my eyes and it is a look I fail to understand. What is he trying to do? I don't know. I have no idea.

He squeezes my hand and smiles.

I can only nod.

My legs feel so weak and my mind is all dizzy, and I am unable to think. I somehow make my way back home. Aman waits till I am safely inside and once I am inside my living room I watch him drive away.

'Damn, an opportunity missed!' I think.

I don't know what Aman thinks. I don't know what he meant by wanting to be sure.

But I know what I want. I have never been more certain of anything in my life.

I decide that whatever it is, I will have a heart-to-heart talk with him. Tell him what he means to me. Confess my love for him.

It would take all my courage. But I know I have to do it. This on-now off-now thing that Aman is doing is killing me.

I get a text from Aman the next morning.

`Hey. Thanks for a wonderful evening. I had a great time.`

I smile when I read it. I guess he expected me to text him last night and when I didn't, he decided to. Whatever it is, a text from him early in the morning means that he is thinking of me. That by itself makes me happy.

`We could have made it amazing, you know!` I reply and add a wink.

`I know. Patience pays,` he writes back and there is a smiley and a wink.

`Patience used to be a nun back at my college. Sister Patience.` I type back, enjoying this.

`Ha ha ha...Was she patient or impatient?` he replies.

`That doesn't matter but if you keep this going I will become a patient,` I write.

`What ails you? What troubles you? Confide in Dr Aman?` He types.

`Patience. All in good time!` I reply and I add two smileys.

Pat comes his reply, `Ha ha ha... Touche,` he says.

There is a spring in my step as I leave for work. There is no greater recharge than having a guy you like (okay possibly the one you are in love with, I admit) flirt with you over text messages.

I decide that I won't bring up our 'relationship' just yet. Maybe it is far too early and I am terrified of scaring him off. Besides, he has texted me now on his own, hasn't he? My rules for getting a guy you want, seem to be working. Now all that I have to do is follow them to a T. I hate myself for being so indecisive about where I am going with this. One day I want to pour out my heart to him, and the next day, I want to play it cool. I do not know how to handle this Aman-thing and so I turn to my work.

I am mid-way through a small filler piece that I am working on (a boring piece about tips for single girls living on their own for which I am supposed to speak to at least four girls and get their views), when I am interrupted by a phone call from Dipika.

'Hey there, how are you?' she says.

I am surprised as she hasn't called me ever since I dropped in at their place with Aman. I had left a couple of offline messages for her, but she hadn't replied. I had assumed that she was busy.

'Hi Dipika. I am good. How goes everything? Long time,' I say and stretch as I grab my coffee which has gone cold by now and I take a sip.

'Yes, it has been a while. I did get your offliners but sorry I couldn't respond. Vikram has been travelling and you know how busy the kids keep me. I have to be on high alert all the time,' she says.

'Hmmm, I know. That's okay. How are things now?'

'Vikram is babysitting today. He got back this morning and is heavily jet-lagged. I was wondering if you want to meet? Also I have some news for you. A surprise,' she says.

'Oh! What is the surprise? Tell me!'

'Not now. In person. So do we meet or not?'

'Of course! It has been so long since we caught up. Let's

do it. I have a couple of interviews and will be done by three. Shall we meet at Phoenix Mall? Usual place?' I ask.

'Yes, perfect. Vikram would have finished his nap by then and he can handle the girls along with the maid. I desperately need to get away. If I stay in the house for any more time I will explode.'

'Ha ha, I feel the same way about office sometimes. See you at three then,' I say.

I reach the mall and walk to Café Monde where we usually hang out, much before Dipika. I call her and she says she is just outside and will be there in a few minutes. I see her walking in and I gaze at her in admiration. She is wearing black knee length shorts, a loose flowing white embroidered top, flat sandals, oversized sun-glasses and is carrying a tote bag. She can easily pass off for a woman in her early twenties, rather than a mother of two. She is very attractive and I can spot at least three guys that she passes checking her out and they are far younger than her. Dipika exudes sexuality and confidence. When I am her age, I would love to be like her.

She breaks into a smile when she sees me and gives me a hug.

'My God, Anjali, it has been so long, Time just flies,' she says.

'Yes,' I admit.

'So what have you been up to?' she asks as she settles down on the sofa next to mine. This café has nice lounge-like seating. We used to meet a lot more often here, while I was in college, but after I started working the meetings have become far less frequent.

'Oh this and that. Nothing important,' I say as I scan the menu.

The waiter appears and I order a cappuccino after

dismissing almost all the exotic items like Cuban café, Irish café, Iced Frapuccino and Devil's Own. When it comes to coffee, I am content with something that gives me my dose of caffeine. Dipika on the other hand likes to experiment and asks for a Black Currant Blast.

'Hmmm. A little bird told us that someone dropped you home the other day and something is going on between you two. Who is this someone?' she asks.

I realise that Mr Joshi must have spied upon me and passed on the information to my parents, who in turn must have called up Dipika. My mum must have asked her to 'see what I am up to' and report back to her. I make a mental note to have a chat with my mom about this. And that Mr Joshi—it seems like he has no other work other than spying on me.

'It is not a little bird. It is an ugly old vulture,' I scowl.

'So it's true then,' Dipika smiles.

'Come on. They can't keep tabs on me like that! I am grown up, an adult, and if I want, I can sleep with anyone I like. I don't think I owe anybody any explanations! Please. This is ridiculous,' I protest.

'Anjali, they are your parents. They will be concerned about you. It is not as though they stop you for anything. So are things serious between you and this mystery guy?'

'It was no mystery guy, Dipika. It was Aman who dropped me home. We had gone on a drive,' I say.

'Oh,' she says and goes very quiet.

'It isn't like we are in a relationship or anything. I mean I do like him, but it's early days yet,' I find myself explaining.

She is silent again.

'You know Aman isn't what he appears on the outside. He made a pass at me,' she finally says.

I am shocked. I can't for the life of me imagine Aman making a pass at Dipika. He respects them far too much. Or at least that is the impression he has given me. Then again Dipika is so attractive, you never know. Maybe he was tempted?

But the thought of Aman making a pass at her leaves me sick to the pit of my stomach. But yet, like a scab which you cannot stop picking, I want to know more. I want to know the details.

'What do you mean, made a pass?' I ask.

'Made a pass, Anjali. Wanted to have sex with me. A no-strings-attached kind of a thing. Of course, I refused. Then I had to ask him to leave. Why do you think he moved to the guesthouse? I had to ask him to leave,' she says.

She looks uncomfortable as she says it. I have interviewed so many people in the course of writing my articles, that I can always sense when something seems odd. Something isn't quite right here. But what it is, I am not able to immediately tell.

'He never struck me as that kind of a guy,' I find myself defending him.

She gives a little laugh, 'Yeah, me too,' she says. 'In any case if you aren't serious about him, I guess it's fine. And it's best to discover these things in the beginning rather than after getting involved. That would be messy,' she says. I notice that she doesn't meet my eye as she says it.

I shrug. 'Yeah I guess,' I finally say.

'Anyway, let's leave all this. I have some exciting news for you,' she says.

I am not at all interested in her 'exciting news' whatever it is. Her telling me that Aman has made a pass at her has taken the wind out of my sails. I feel sadly like a deflated balloon left propped up at a children's birthday party long after the kids have left.

'What is it?' I force myself to ask.

'Your parents are excited about this marriage proposal that

they have received for you. The guy is educated at MIT and Stanford. His name is Vipul. He is with IBM and lives in Washington DC. He is good looking and he happens to be Vikram's second cousin. Their family is keen to meet you.'

I draw a sharp breath.

'Dipika, you know how I feel about arranged marriages,' I say. 'I think it is preposterous that you get married after two or three meetings. What do you know about that person? What about feelings? What about love? I need to connect with someone and know them well, before I can even think of marriage. I do feel strongly about it. You know my views. And so do my parents.'

I have always told my parents how strongly I feel about this and my parents have always maintained that they are fine with whoever I choose. Their only condition is that I should tell them about it. Hence springing this surprise on me through Dipika has caught me offguard.

'Oh, Anjali. You have idealistic views. You think this so-called love survives marriage? Ask anyone who has been married five years or more and they will give you the true picture. Love and all that is okay in the initial years. Once the kids happen it is a complete different ball-game. After that it is just adjustments and compromises.'

'How can you say that, Dipika? Aren't you and Vikram happily married?!'

'Ha ha, Anjali. You have so much growing up to do. You know, you can either be happy or married. You can't be both. As for me, let's just say I am married. You know it is ages since Vikram has even noticed me. He is absorbed in his work all the time, and once he comes home, Ria and Reema monopolise his time. I hardly know the man I married anymore.'

Her voice is laced with bitterness and I am taken aback.

I know that every now and then Dipika has hinted in her conversations about it, but this is the first time she has spoken so openly about it.

'I had no clue it was that bad. But why don't you do something then? Ever considered getting out? A divorce or something?'

'I have thought about it. But then what grounds do I have? How can a little thing like being taken for granted or feeling unappreciated be cause for divorce? He is a good father. He does take care of the children and me. He earns well. Besides I have both sides of the family to consider. His parents would be heartbroken and so would mine. All this is just a part of married life,' she says.

I look at a couple seated a little away from us. The lady is obviously pregnant. The guy who is with her, presumably her husband, helps her out of her seat. He puts his arm around her. She whispers something in his ear and he throws back his head and laughs. They are so lost in each other.

'See that? That was Vikram and me in the early years. But things change, Anjali. Which is why I say things like love and all that, even out in the long run. You just have to make sure that the guy is a good guy, earns well and isn't a male chauvinist. In the long run, marriage is all about adjustments and compromises. Take my word on it.'

Dipika's words are draining me out completely. What she has said is completely challenging all the beliefs I have held about marriage so far. I had always felt when I married, it would be because I loved the guy and he loved me in turn, and we couldn't live without each other. But Dipika's views are making me think.

'That is why I strongly suggest that you should at least meet this guy. What do you lose anyway? Your parents will be delighted. Just my thoughts. Nobody is forcing you. If you want to meet him, I will set it up when he visits us. Let me know,' she says as she gestures to the waiter for the bill.

Then she says that we can go shoe shopping as there is a sale happening. By now, all my mood for shopping is gone. I feel dead and drained out. Like a vampire Dipika has sucked out all my energy. I trudge reluctantly behind her. She buys three pairs of shoes, all stilletoes, one of them studded with semi-precious stones and runs up a bill of Rs 23,000 which she pays with her credit card. I stifle a gasp.

I remember reading somewhere about 'revenge spending'. When the female partner is angry, feels ignored on unappreciated, she usually spends money aggressively on stuff that improves her appearance. I wonder if this is what Dipika is doing.

Later when I am back home I call up my mother. I ask her if they do want me to meet Mr Washington. My mother says that it is entirely up to me. She says I should tell them if I have someone in mind, so that they can turn down proposals straightaway. I assure her that I do not have anyone in mind, and the guy who dropped me home was just a friend.

'Then what is the harm in meeting him? Nobody is forcing you to get married and this is indeed a good match,' says my mother.

She is right, of course. How long can I hang around for Aman who is blow-hot, blow-cold? Maybe Dipika is right after all. Perhaps I am idealistic and foolish. Perhaps I am just holding on to some outdated notions of love which are not relevant when it comes to marriage.

But no matter how much I try to be excited at the prospect of meeting Mr Washington, I don't feel even the smallest bit of joy. Maybe I will feel it later. Maybe I will be dazzled when I meet him. After all, Aman hasn't even hinted that he would like a relationship.

What then am I holding on to? Some kind of vague notion of love? Some secret fantasy that Aman will declare his undying love for me? How silly and foolish is that.

Late that night I text Dipika and tell her that I have been thinking and all that she said makes sense. I tell her to set up a meeting with Vipul and as an afterthought I add that I am looking forward to it.

Chapter 24

Aman

I must be the only man on planet Earth to turn down the advances of a gorgeous woman who is practically throwing herself at me. I suppose I should have been happy about that kiss and elated that Anjali fancies me. The chemistry between us *is* sizzling too.

Ironically, that is precisely why I have to be doubly sure of what I am doing. Right now, I do not want complications. It was bloody hard for me to stop when she started kissing me. All I wanted to do was follow her to her house, push her onto the bed and make love to her right then and there. She is ravishingly attractive and does not even realise how much she sets my blood racing. I am rock hard right now. It has taken me supreme will-power to resist her offer. But somehow I know it is the right thing. Anjali is a great girl and I think we ought to be 'officially in a relationship' before I can have sex with her. I *know* that Anjali is definitely looking for a relationship. She just isn't the casual-sex-one-night-stand kind of a girl. Had she been, I guess I would have no problem taking her up on her offer. I do not want to hurt her in any way. And I definitely do not want to lead her on, by having sex with her and then deciding I don't want to be involved with her anymore. That would leave me with a burgeoning sense of guilt which I do not want to be saddled with.

Or at least this is the logic that I convince myself with. At the back of my mind is a niggling doubt about what I want. Are these the real reasons? Or is it because the way she kissed me brought back a thousand memories of Shruti? I do not know. All I know is that I couldn't have gone further.

I look at my wrist where her fingernails dug into mine. There are five red welts. I smile and think about how Shruti had once grabbed me the same way in a house of horror we had visited at an amusement park. To be honest, I too had been startled as people dressed as mummies and monsters leapt out at you suddenly in the darkness, but I had pretended to be cool and teased her a bit. Once outside, Shruti had laughed at the experience and averred never to go in there again even if someone paid her a million bucks to do so. With a sigh I force myself to push thoughts of Shruti out of my head. I have just had a great time with Anjali and I should stop thinking about Shruti at least now.

When I check my mails I find one from Mark who says he is arriving on Sunday. He also says he has booked himself at a hotel and would love to meet up.

I reply immediately telling him to cancel his hotel booking as he is most welcome to use the spare bedroom at my place.

Mark replies back almost instantly. He says it is kind of me and he would be happy to accept. He says that he has already made arrangements to travel to Bandipur and hence would be staying with me just for a night.

Then I remember that tomorrow is when my mother

arrives too. I pick up the phone to call her, but when I look at the time, I realise that she must be fast asleep. So I just text her, asking her to call me the moment she arrives in Bangalore.

My mother texts me as soon as she lands the next day. But I see it only two hours later, as we have been in meetings the whole morning. We are in the final stages of implementation and things seem to be in control now. Rao isn't on my case as much as he used to be earlier and Vikram is mighty pleased with how our whole team has handled the entire project. My guess is that the pressure that all of us have been under will ease a bit from the next week onwards.

I call my mother and ask her about her journey and her staying arrangements at the university. She sounds happy and excited. She says they have just arrived and have an orientation class in the evening. They have a session the next morning and then they are free for half a day on Saturday and the whole of Sunday. The sessions resume early on Monday morning. I tell her that is fantastic and that I will pick her up on Saturday afternoon. She could stay over and I will drop her back Monday morning. I tell her that Mark too would be visiting. She asks if that would be a problem.

'Oh no, Ma, not a problem at all. The house has two large, fully furnished bedrooms. You and I can share my bedroom and we will give Mark the other one,' I say. This house that I am currently living in is probably one of the nicest I have ever stayed in. It is even nicer than the place that I had in Norwich, which my mother has never seen.

I now recall how my mother had come with me to see my hostel when I had got admission for my engineering. I have come such a long way since I want to show her my house as well as my new car. My mother had sold off our car after my father died and we have never owned a car since.

She says that she will text me her address and asks if I know the place.

'Don't worry, Ma, I will find it,' I say.

My mother loves my new car and it is an emotional moment for her, though I hadn't thought of it that way.

'I wish your dad had lived to see this day. He would have been so proud of you,' she says as she blinks back her tears. My memories of my dad are few and faded. But I know it means a great deal to my mother and hence I nod.

She is even more delighted about the apartment.

'It is so well maintained, Aman,' she says.

I know what is coming next and of course I am right.

'Now, you just have to find a nice girl and that will complete the picture,' she says.

'What picture? Dirty picture?' I grin.

'Shameless! Talking to your mother like that,' she says as she playfully pretends to twist my ear and I chuckle.

'So is there anyone special?' she persists.

'Hmmm. I am not sure, Ma,' I reply truthfully.

'You aren't sure if there is anyone or you aren't sure if she is the one?' My mother isn't one to let go so easily.

'I am not sure that she is the one,' I say.

'And why aren't you sure? What is wrong with her?'

'Maaa, there is nothing wrong! Stop it please,' I beg her.

'If there was nothing wrong, you should have got married by now,' she says simply.

There exist some things that give Indian parents great joy. One is the supreme happiness that they derive out of getting their adult children married. The other great joy for Indian parents is feeding their children, stuffing them with food, even when they say they are full. The third is of course sending them for tuitions and telling them to study at every given opportunity. Thankfully I can escape the third, and the second I do not mind. But there is no respite from the first one. I sincerely believe, if Indian parents were asked to list their hobbies, these three things are what would figure most, whether they admit it or not.

'Marriage isn't high on my priority list right now and you know that,' I tell my mother.

She sighs. 'So will you introduce her to me or no? When do I get to meet her?'

'Ma, there isn't anything like that.'

'Okay, invite her over, Aman. I would like to meet your friends, get to know them,' she insists.

I know that my mother will not let this go easily. I know that what my mother wants she usually gets. And right now she seems to be on a 'let-me-check-out-this-girl-my-son-is-not-so-sure-of' mode.

'Fine, I will,' I say and I text Anjali, asking her if she wants to join us for dinner tomorrow, and that Mark and my mother would be there. She replies saying she would love to.

I tell my mother that Anjali will be joining us and I warn her not to talk about marriage at all.

'Okay, okay,' she says and makes an action of zipping up her mouth. I laugh and put my arm around her. Over the years my mother has become more my friend than a parent. Many people grow crabby when they grow old, but my mother has kept herself fit, active and her only 'flaw' if it can be called that is pestering me to get married. That I can live with, I think to myself as she ruffles my hair fondly, just like she used to do all those years ago.

My mother says she will cook dinner.

'That will be awesome, Ma. Actually I was just planning to order food, assuming you'd be tired or not in the mood.'

'No, I am not that old to be tired and exhausted that I can't cook. Especially when a potential daughter-in-law is visiting,' she teases.

'Maaaa, please. We are not even in a relationship,' I protest.

'Since when has that become a requirement for marriage? Your father and I, we were not in a relationship at all,' she grins, knowing that she is infuriating me further.

I throw up my hands and roll my eyes and she chuckles and calls me her marriage-phobic-*baccha* and tells me that marriage isn't such a bad thing. Strangely it makes me feel all warm inside. Then she asks if Mark is okay with Indian food. Mark loves Indian food. When we were in the UK, he and I have gone to places that claim to serve Indian food. They are mostly run by Bangladeshis and Pakistanis. Sometimes the food is good, but mostly it is nowhere close to the authentic stuff. I explain all this to my mother and she says she will ensure that Mark has an awesome authentic Indian meal.

Mark is delighted to hear that when I message him. He says he looks forward to meeting us. I tell him that a friend will be joining us.

Mark arrives before Anjali. He has become even fitter than the last time that I saw him. He is slightly tanned now and with his naturally tall frame, he is an embodiment of an alpha-male. Plus of course he is articulate, pleasant, well-mannered, well-dressed and charming. No wonder, he is so effortlessly able to attract women, I muse. He is carrying a huge bouquet of flowers and a bottle of wine. He hands it over to my mother and shakes hands with her, as I introduce them.

'Very pleased to meet you Mrs Mathur. I have heard so much about you from Aman. Here are some flowers for a beautiful lady. I now know where Aman gets his looks from,' he says as he hands over the bouquet to her.

I can see my mother is amused but pleased. The Mark-charm seems to be working on her as well. I smile and tell him to come inside and I drag his suitcase in and put it in the second bedroom. Mark too, like my mother, is very impressed with my apartment.

'You must be so proud of him, Mrs Mathur,' says Mark. He pronounces it as Mat-uhrrr and my mother smiles. She asks him about his family. He says that his father left them when he was five and he has two older sisters. His mother raised them as a single parent and he has studied in boarding school, right from the age of eleven. He says that his mother now lives with his step-father. My mother asks him whether it is his first visit to India and what he likes about the place, and in no time they are chatting away like old buddies.

My mother has made *chhole bhature*, one of her signature dishes and the aroma wafts across the apartment. Mark says that it smells divine. He says that the Indian food in India definitely tastes better than the curries they serve in the UK in the name of Indian food.

Anjali arrives and I rush to answer the door. When I open it I stare at her for a few seconds. She looks so stunning I have to catch my breath. She has worn a completely white well-fitted salwar kameez with a multi-coloured dupatta. Her hair is loose and she wears some kind of dangling earrings. Her eyes are lined with kohl and she has a long bindi on. This is the first time I am seeing Anjali in an Indian outfit and I am gobsmacked at her transformation.

Shyly she asks, 'Am I looking nice?', her voice barely a whisper.

I am blown away completely, and am unable to articulate

the range of emotions passing through me at that precise moment—one part horniness, one part excitement, one part pure surprise and one part sheer fascination at the magical transformation from 'Anjali-the-modern-girl' to 'Anjali-the-well-raised-traditional-Indian-girl-fit-to-be-the-perfect daughter-in-law'.

'Oh my God. You look stunning. Come in,' I finally manage to say.

I introduce her to my mother and Anjali bends over and touches her feet. I am floored. I have never seen this very Indian avatar of Anjali before. I can picture my mother holding a neon sign over Anjali's head proclaiming to me, 'Marry her, NOW'. In my mother's head, the choice has already been made. I know my mother too well.

Even the normally charming and effervescent Mark is a little in awe now when I introduce her. I can see that he doesn't know how to greet her, whether to shake her hand or just say a hi. Anjali extends her hand and puts him out of his misery. He is fascinated when he learns that she is a writer. I can see that Anjali is curious about Mark. Just like with my mother, he seems to have struck a chord with Anjali too, as she is asking him a lot of questions about living in the UK, what is different, and I find Mark laying on an extra layer of charm. It is funny how I feel like asking him to stay away from Anjali and how I feel like grabbing Anjali and steering her away from Mark. But they are both laughing about something now and Anjali seems so pleased.

I ask them what they would like to drink. Anjali says she would like anything non-alcoholic and I raise my eyebrows at that and smile.

'Since when did you become a teetotaller?' I ask.

She gestures with her eyes towards my mother, who is now in the kitchen, frying some *bhajjas* for starters. I tell her that my mother is okay and I ask if she would like some vodka, whereupon she says she will have it with Sprite, so that at least it won't look like alcohol. I laugh at how she is so bothered about what my mother will think. I want to tell her that she has totally got the seal of approval from my mother, but I don't. Instead I hand her the drink.

Mark opts for a single malt neat, with just ice. I am glad that I have stocked up on the whisky, knowing Mark's fondness for it. I am not much of a drinker and buy alcohol only if I am having company, which is the first time since I got back from the UK.

Mark loves the *bhajjas* and by the time they get over, he is already four drinks down, while Anjali is still nursing her vodka-laced Sprite. One thing that I had forgotten was how Mark has no control over his tongue once he is a few whiskys down. I should have realised that before I offered him the drink, but it is too late now.

Mark is now in excellent spirits and Anjali is throwing her head back and laughing at the jokes he is cracking with a completely straight face.

'I love the English sense of humour,' says Anjali.

'And I love Indian women. They are so different from Western women,' says Mark.

'How so?' asks Anjali.

'They seem more intelligent, prettier and definitely nicer,' says Mark, not taking his eyes off Anjali. He is looking into her eyes and narrows his eyes and smiles when he says this.

God—this is his signature move. I have heard him use this line many times on various women at the pubs in the UK. I have heard him tell countless English girls about how she is the most intelligent, prettiest and smartest girl he has ever met. I can't believe women fall for this crap.

I expect Anjali to call his bluff and see through him. But to my horror she seems to be enjoying it. She is actually blushing and she asks him how he knows.

'You are a perfect example. Permit me to say, your eyes are mesmerising. And I love your attire,' he continues smoothly. Anjali is now eating out of his hands.

I can't bear it anymore.

'Hey, Anjali, I need to show you something,' I say.

'Oh,' she says and looks as though someone has just brought her out of a trance.

'Can you step in here a minute?' I ask as I march towards my bedroom, all the time furiously thinking about what to show her.

'Sure,' she says. As she rises, she tells Mark, 'Excuse me, I'll just be back.'

She is walking towards my bedroom now.

Think, think, think... I furiously work my brain but am not able to come up with anything. I look around in desperation and spot my mother's bag. It is half open and there is a brochure of the Agricultural College. I grab that and wave it at her.

'Anjali—see this prospectus. What do you think of it?' I ask.

She gives me a strange look. She is genuinely puzzled.

'Hmmm, it's nice. Anything in particular you want me to see?' she asks as she darts a glance in Mark's direction.

'See this, Anjali. I was thinking that you can perhaps write a piece on this course?' I am improvising wildly and realise I am blabbering.

'On an agricultural course? Aman, are you drunk?' she asks.

'No, no, I was just thinking that not many women would know of this scheme that the government offers. And you know what, many women would benefit from this ...This mushroom-growing course which they offer. See—you can grow mushrooms in your home. They give you all the equipment, teach you and it is very lucrative,' I finish, all the time reading fast about what is described about the course in the prospectus.

For a moment Anjali is distracted. I know that for her, when it comes to work, she is undeterrable and focused. She so loves her job.

'Mmmm, that's not a bad idea actually. Maybe I can write about it or maybe I can pass it on to the features department,' she says.

'Ummm…and hey Anjali, one more thing,' I say.

I just have to do it. Warn her about Mark and his ways.

'You know Mark is quite the ladies man. He has a way with women. Everyone, you know, kind of falls for him,' I say lamely, not able to articulate exactly what I have in mind. I want to tell her that once Mark sleeps with a women, that will be the last that she will hear from him. Till he gets them into bed, he is all charm. Mark is one of those guys who is thrilled about the chase and once the conquest happens, he drops them like a hot potato. For him, it is a game. But I am not able to explain all this to Anjali in detail. I don't even know what to 'warn her about' without appearing like an old-fashioned, silly boor. Besides, we are not even in a relationship. If she wants to get into bed with him, I do not have any say in the matter. Also, isn't that stretching things a bit too far? Maybe Anjali is just flirting with him, enjoying his company. I do not even know why I called her away in the first place. It was a silly idea.

She is looking at me curiously now. Then she chuckles.

'Yeah, I can imagine!' she says and with that she walks out.

I have no choice but to follow her.

'So Mark, Aman tells me you're quite the ladies man, eh?' she says.

'Oh Aman isn't bad himself. In fact, he had an amazing time on that last night that he left for India, didn't you, Aman? You know she went ballistic the next day. She turned up outside our office and tried to gain entry. When she couldn't, she waited till Andrew and I came out for a smoke. Then she cornered us and asked for your number. She didn't believe us when we said you had left for India. She threw a huge tantrum for your contact details, and finally the security had to intervene,' says Mark.

Anjali looks at me questioningly as though to ask if this is true. I turn around and I see my mother too standing there.

I do not think that any situation I have faced so far in life has prepared me for the kind of embarrassment and total awkwardness I face now. I want to strangle Mark for saying what he did. But then a sane part of me tells me that in the world he comes from, one-night stands are truly no big deal. Of course I am certain that even there, one wouldn't normally blurt out one's escapades in front of parents. Or maybe they do. I don't know.

'Ummm, nothing like that. Mark's just exaggerating,' I say and I try to fix him with a glare. But in the inebriated state that he is in, he finds it hilarious and roars with laughter.

'Ooopsies, have I put you in a spot mate? I am sorry. I think I have just broken the bro-code,' he says and laughs again. I don't think he even realises that he is the only one laughing.

What I actually want to do is break his face and make him shut up.

Instead what I do is just play along and try my best to hide his gaffe and my embarrassment as much as I can.

Chapter 25

Shruti

Dearest Aman,

I don't even know where to begin and yet I must begin somewhere. I don't even know what to say, yet I want to say a lot. So let me start in the way the usual mails start, although I am aware this mail is far from the 'usual' mails you get.

How are you, Aman?

I know you probably hate me and will not even read this mail and I don't blame you. But tonight is one of those nights when I just have to write to you.

Trust me, I have thought of you a million times in these last two years. I have wondered if you are happy, if you are okay. I have replayed the events that led to our separation a hundred times in my head. I still believe that I probably couldn't have done anything different at that point in time. It meant a lot to my parents for me to get married into Rishabh's family, which is one of the most well-known families in our community. I guess from their point of view it was a 'match made in heaven' and the fact that they had approached my parents and wanted no dowry, and a whole lot of other things made a world of a difference. I don't know, Aman. But please believe me when I say that I was powerless. All I wanted was my mother's cancer to go away, for her to get well again, and I did not want to be the cause of any more stress to my parents.

Rishabh is a nice guy, Aman. I get along well with him. There is nothing for me to 'be discontent'. And yet the heart has its ways. In these two years, I have thought of you, longed for you, many times. I have tried to move on. Make a new life with Rishabh. I have tried my best to put the past behind me. Let sleeping dogs lie kind of a thing.

But Rishabh happened to read all the mails that we exchanged. I never anticipated that. I am cringing as I type these words. He accused me of still seeing you. I have denied it till I am blue in the face, but I think he doesn't trust me anymore. Or perhaps he feels betrayed and cheated. His behaviour in the past few months has undergone a 180 degree change. I do not recognise the man I married anymore.

One of the basic things in a relationship is trust. You just have to have faith. If you are going to view everything through coloured glasses, everything you see is going to be submerged in those shades that you choose to see it with.

On my part, I have tried my best to tell him, to make him understand that it is all history. I still haven't succeeded. It's been at least three months now. I don't know what to do anymore. I am beginning to give up.

And hey, guess what happened? I ran into Mr Adani. He still remembers us. I was very surprised to run into him and it took me down memory lane. We have some wonderful memories, Aman, and I shall cherish the time spent with you all my life. They were indeed one of the happiest times that I have ever known.

You had mentioned once that no matter what happens, you would like to be there for me and we could be friends.

Does that offer still hold good?

Or do you hate me too much?

Please write back, Aman. I hope that isn't asking too much.

Love

Shruti

I have poured out my feelings and thoughts in that mail. That is all I can do at this moment. I take a deep breath. For a few seconds I contemplate whether or not it would be wise to contact him. Then memories of the past come calling and they possess me entirely. The time I had with Aman flashes before my eyes—Aman smiling, Aman on his motorbike, Aman telling me that I look great in black. Aman and I laughing together, the plans that we had made for our future, the hopes that we had, and above all, it is the promise of undying friendship that lures me into hitting the 'send' button before I can change my mind. The mail is gone. I panic for a few seconds after I send it. But now I have taken that step. I have initiated contact. All I can do is wait to hear from him.

My eyes are drooping now and I am not able to stay awake anymore. I shut the laptop and I curl up in bed. I can still hear the din of the television when I fall asleep. My last thoughts as my eyes shut are that never have I, since getting married, felt so confused, so unsure, and so scared.

Early next morning Rishabh announces that he will be taking leave for the entire week to look after his parents. He says he has some urgent issues to sort out at work and will be done by noon. He requests me to go to the hospital in the morning and go to office after that. I readily agree as I am secretly relieved that I don't have to take any more time off from work. I don't have any meetings scheduled in the morning and so am able to swing it without too much of a hassle. The recruitment drives are starting soon and we begin with Bangalore. We are doing two colleges in Bangalore and I am travelling with the HR team, taking care of all the arrangements, publicity, co-ordinating with placement cells and ensuring that the whole process goes smoothly. This time we also have a visitor from overseas and hence have to be extra careful to ensure that everything goes like clockwork.

Rishabh calls his mother to check on her and tells her that I am on my way and that he will be there by noon. I take a cab to the hospital and on the seat find a copy of *Tiara* someone must has left behind. Idly I flip through the pages and a piece titled 'How To Get Over The One You Cannot Have' catches my eye. I read it and the words leap out at me.

If you are in your mid-twenties or older, chances are you have definitely been in a relationship before. Perhaps two or three or maybe even several. They have ended for whatever reasons, but sometimes, there is that one person, no matter how hard one tries, that one cannot get over.

Oh my God. The article seems to be speaking to me. I read all the points it mentions and realise that I have not followed a single one. No wonder I cannot get over Aman. Perhaps this would have helped had I read it two years ago. It is too late now. Aman is like a constant ache I have learnt to live with. Except that I have now initiated contact. I don't know if it was wise. I don't even know if he has moved on. But something tells me that he still has a place for me in his heart. You cannot erase four years of memories just like that.

No matter how much you try, no matter how much you want to love somebody else, no matter how much you convince yourself that you have moved on, deep down you know the truth. If you are deliriously happy when you think about someone and a smile creeps up on you, even when you are in the worst of moods, if even a mere thought of that person has a power to send a jolt of energy through your weary body, then it is nothing but love. You can try to squish it, pretend that it does not exist, ignore it, try to make it go away, but it never entirely does.

It always finds a way back.

The cab driver announces that we have reached, and it is only then that I even realise that I have been so lost in my thoughts. At the hospital my mother-in-law looks relieved to see me. The duty doctor is making his rounds soon and once he examines my father-in-law, we will get an update on his condition and when he can be discharged. My father-in-law seems perfectly fine now, save for the stitches he has on his forehead to seal the gash.

The duty doctor is a pleasant lady perhaps in her early forties. She looks at all the charts and says that a few more reports have to come in, and if they are clear, he can be discharged today itself. She tells us to keep his diabetes in check and to take care of his diet.

After the medical team leaves there isn't anything much for me or my mother-in-law to do. The mail I sent out last evening to Aman is playing on my mind. I am dying to know if he has replied. So I log in on my phone and check my messages. There is no reply from his end.

I am a bit disappointed. Maybe he hasn't seen my message yet, I tell myself. But my inner voice tells me, '*You haven't contacted him in two years and you write to him and expect an instant reply? You have some nerve!*'

Then I remember that I haven't even contacted Mr Adani and thanked him properly for all his help. I call him instantly and update him. He is on his way to the hospital as he has a meeting with his volunteer team. I tell my mother-in-law that I am going to the canteen and ask her if she would like something to eat or drink, and whether she is comfortable. My mother-in-law waves me away and says that she will probably nap for a while.

Mr Adani arrives almost immediately.

'Good morning, my dear girl. How are you today?' he greets me like an old pal. He sounds positive and upbeat. It is in total contrast to my current mood. I feel so dead inside.

But I force myself to smile and I return his greeting.

Mr Adani speaks to the volunteer team for a few minutes. He has something or the other to enquire of each one. I can see that he is closely involved in all his projects, and is the kind of person who is genuinely interested in people and their welfare. No wonder he is so successful in life.

Once he is done with them, he turns to me.

'Sorry to have kept you waiting,' he says.

'Oh no, not at all. You have indeed been very kind,' I say.

He asks about my father-in-law. I tell him that he is likely to be discharged by evening and that I am filling in for Rishabh who will arrive in the afternoon. He is observing me intently now and his sharp eyes do not miss a thing. Maybe it is the sadness in my voice or the resigned dispiritedness to my current situation that I find hard to shake off, that he picks on. He asks me if everything is okay.

It is not. I am confused, tired, stressed and stretched. But I do not want to impose my troubles on him. Besides, it is not like he can help anyway. It seems as though he can read my mind.

'I think it will do you good to have a cup of coffee. Want to join me?' he asks and there is no reason for me to not accept. I have some time to kill till Rishabh makes his appearance.

We go to the hospital cafeteria which is more like a posh fast-food eatery than a canteen attached to a hospital. Mr Adani goes to get the coffees. While I wait for him, I look around. It is crowded, noisy and there are delicious aromas wafting across. Most people are relishing their food. Human nature surprises me. One would almost never believe that in the floors upstairs are other people—some dying, some fighting for their lives and some getting better. But the hospital canteen has nothing to indicate that. Here people are celebrating life, enjoying food, chatting away animatedly. Just one or two diners look sad and worried. For the rest it is business as usual. The irony strikes me hard.

Mr Adani returns with two cups and takes me away to

a less crowded place, a room which is like a lounge meant for hospital staff. There are fewer people here compared to the cafeteria. I find myself asking him about how he started all this, and how he founded so many philanthropic organisations. He says that there were a few turning points in his life that prompted him to start an institution for counselling for emotional problems (which he says was a pioneer institute in India, as in the early eighties when he established his, it was unheard of in this country). I am curious now. I want to know more.

'It's a long story, Shruti, and it is all past. But every event that happens in our life, every trauma we go through, it is for the better. I am not sure if you even want to hear about it.'

'I do, sir, and would be honoured if you shared it with me.'

'Dispense with the formalities,' he smiles 'We're out of college now. You can call me Sanjeev.'

But in my head I find it hard to address him as anything but 'sir'.

'Sure...er...Sanjeev. I would love to hear your story.'

'Many years back, I underwent treatment for depression. I had to undergo counselling for more than two years. I was based in Australia then. In those days, the counselling facilities in India were woefully inadequate. I returned to India and I spoke to a friend who is a doctor. Together we founded the counselling centre, the first of its kind in the country. It was very successful and we expanded from there.'

I am surprised to hear that a person like him who is the epitome of positivity actually underwent treatment for depression.

'I didn't think I would either, till my wife eloped with my best friend. I lost two people who meant the most to me.' He states it without a trace of emotion in his voice.

I am stupefied by what he has just revealed.

'Didn't you…you know…ever try to…?' I am unable to complete the sentence.

'What could I do? She had made her choice. And so had he. This love, it is a funny thing. It can elevate you to the highest peak and plunge you to a bottomless pit. I thought I had found all the happiness in the world when I got married. How wrong I was. The path we plan for ourselves meanders in ways we can never imagine. Life never ceases to throw us googlies. It is how we handle them that makes all the difference. Sometimes you have to take control of it and, at other times, it is best to let go. And the wisest of persons is the one who knows which option to choose.'

I can only nod. His words are gentle and full of wisdom. They feel like a balm to my battered soul.

'I have shared my story. It is your turn now,' he says and the twinkle is back in his eyes. How in the world does he manage to stay so upbeat *all* the time? He must be twice my age and yet I do not have half the energy that he does.

'There isn't much of a story. I myself wonder what went wrong. Right now I feel stuck in my marriage, to the extent that, I am even contemplating divorce,' I state simply. Somehow it feels like a relief to have said it to him. It has been playing so long in my head, and the only person I have discussed it with so far has been Asha.

'Hmmm,' he nods thoughtfully. 'So you were forced into this marriage?' he asks.

I find myself explaining about my mother's cancer, I tell him about how Aman and I were inseparable and how I finally was forced to split up with him.

'I mean, I did it out of my own free will, or at least that is what I felt. The thing is I wanted my parents to be happy. I didn't want to stress out my mother and Aman wasn't being the most understanding person at that time. Also, after the scene that my father created when his mother came to visit, I don't think there was any point after that. Any potential relations were broken right then and there.'

'Hmm...' he says absorbing all that I have said. 'Shruti, the thing about life is that its very nature is change. People change, circumstances change. People act differently in different circumstances. That does not mean it is permanent. Things change all the time. And if some thing is meant to happen, it will. What is your reason for considering a divorce? Do you want to get back with Aman?'

I am quiet for a while. Do I want to? In my heart of hearts I do. But what leg do I have to stand on? It was I who broke up with him. It was I who did not read his mails.

And now, after two years, I don't know if he has moved on. I don't know anything about him, what he feels, whether *he* wants to get back.

'There is only one way to find out,' says Mr Adani. 'Ask him.'

'I did,' I find myself admitting in a small voice.

'And?'

'I haven't yet heard from him.'

'How long has it been since you asked? Did you call him?'

'No, I mailed him.'

'How long back?'

'Last night.'

'Oh, it is too early then. You don't expect him to make such a decision overnight, do you? Give him some time.'

That is just what I will do. I will wait for him to respond. There is nothing much I can do anyway.

I thank Mr Adani for his time.

'Not at all, girl. Feel free to call me if you want to talk about it,' he says and I thank him once again.

Aman, please reply. Please write back. Any word from you. Please tell me I am forgiven and that I still matter. I just need one chance, Aman. Please.

It keeps going round and round in my head. I should stop obsessing about his reply. I should focus on other things.

But try as I might, I am unable to. I somehow feel that if I get back with him, I can make a new beginning. I can put all this behind me.

I feel as though I am at the bottom of a long cavernous well, looking up at the light coming from high above. I need to climb out towards that light.

All I need is a rope.

And the only person who can toss it to me is Aman.

Chapter 26

Aman

If my mother is mortified about my amorous adventures, she pretends not to show it. Anjali on the other hand, I know is miffed and has a strange unfathomable expression.

'I guess I better get going. It is quite late and tomorrow is a working day,' announces Anjali as she stands up, bringing an abrupt end to our little party. Mark says that he too has to leave early the next morning and he would like to call it a night.

Then he walks over to Anjali and takes her hand in his, kisses it and looks into her eyes while saying, 'It was wonderful meeting you, lovely Anjali. I hope to keep in touch.'

I have never seen him do this before. It must be the corniest of moves he has ever pulled, but I find Anjali smiling and nodding. I stand there watching.

My mother asks Anjali how she would be going home as it is late.

'Oh, don't worry about me, Aunty, I will take an auto. I am sure I will find many outside,' she says.

'Of course not, Aman will drop you home, won't you, Aman?' says my mother.

'Yes, of course. It isn't the wisest of things to take an auto alone at this time of the night, Anjali. I will drop you home,' I say and I jump up and grab the car keys before she has a chance to protest.

As we walk to the door, we hear Mark thanking my mother for a wonderful evening and great food. He is charm personified. I have to hand it to the guy. Then he insists on helping my mother clear up, something that hadn't struck either me or Anjali.

In the car, Anjali is quiet for a very long time. I am too embarrassed to even attempt any conversation and sit in silence. I play some music to cover up the totally awkward situation that I find myself in.

We have driven for about fifteen minutes when Anjali says, 'Aman, there is something I have to talk to you about.'

Uh-oh. The last time a woman said that to me, she broke up with me. When a woman says, 'There is something we have to talk about' you have only two options:

1. Tuck your tail between your legs and run as fast as you can.
2. Arm yourself with enough ammunition to defuse the bomb that she is going to detonate you with, shield yourself and hope like crazy that you will survive.

Since the first option isn't available to me, as we are stuck in a car, I am left only with option two. I prepare myself to tell her about the one-night stand—how meaningless it was and how sex is so darn casual there and how it doesn't mean a thing.

But what she asks is something I had never anticipated, expected or even foreseen even in my wildest dreams.

'Did you make a pass at Dipika and did you tell her you want to sleep with her, no strings attached?' she asks and I can feel her looking at me steadily.

I can't believe this. I am so taken aback that I am not able to respond immediately. I pull over to the side of the road. There are some small cart-stalls on the side of the road selling hot noodles, momos, tea and coffee. As soon as I pull over, the guy from one of the stalls approaches us.

'What will you take, sir?' he asks.

I look at Anjali and ask if she would like to have something. She wants a cup of black coffee. I order the same.

'No milk?' he asks, surprised.

'No. Black,' I say and he scuttles off.

Then I turn towards Anjali.

'Anjali, that is so totally false and untrue. I am shocked that she has told you this. It wasn't like that at all,' I finally say.

'It wasn't like that,' repeats Anjali slowly. 'Which means there was something, isn't it, Aman? I wasn't going to ask you this, but after what Mark said, I have to know. I met Dipika the other day. And we spoke about a lot of things. She said the reason why you moved out of their place to the company guesthouse was because she asked you to leave.'

'Oh my God, Anjali. That is not true at all. I can't believe that is the story she gave you,' I say.

'Then what is the truth, Aman? What is your version? If you can have a one-night stand in the UK, perhaps you can have a one-night stand with Dipika too. And trust me, I am entirely okay with the idea of a one-night stand. It isn't a big deal—it is just sex. I have many friends who do it. But what I cannot stand is someone lying to me. Deceit is something which I cannot forgive. So be honest, please.'

She has a confused, pained look in her eyes and I feel miserable to see her like that. I swallow and then take her hands in mine.

'Anjali, trust me I will never lie to you. Yes, I did have a one-night stand in Norwich and that was just sex and nothing else. I was drunk and one thing led to another. But I have never had one night stands before that nor do I intend to have them ever again, even if I get the opportunity. When I arrived in India, it was Dipika who made a pass at me. I was shell-shocked and I scooted. Do you remember that day when I had changed my plans to meet you? It was to escape her advances. I can't just sleep with anybody like that, Anjali. It...it just isn't worth it.'

The guy comes back with our coffees and I hand Anjali her cup.

She is silent as she sips it.

Then she places her right hand over mine and squeezes it. She hasn't uttered a word but I know she believes me and has understood. I feel strangely intimate with her now, having clarified things. We sit in silence sipping the coffee.

Finally she says, 'You know, I did feel that. She is very unhappy in her marriage. She feels trapped. Maybe that is why she did it.'

'Maybe, but I have no idea why she lied to you about me.'

'I think it was because she wants me to meet Vikram's cousin. She sensed that there might be something between us. Of course, I told her there is nothing and it's all in the nascent stages and it is not a relationship at all,' she adds hastily. She looks so cute I want to lean over and kiss her right there. But I let her continue.

'Who is this Vikram's cousin? Where did he come into the picture from?' I ask.

'Oh, he is Mr Washington. He is from MIT, apparently very good-looking and smart and all that. Dipika and my parents want me to meet him.'

'Mr Washington? That is a strange name.'

She bursts out into delighted peals of laughter. 'That is not his real name, silly. That is what I have nicknamed him as he lives there. His name is Vipul.'

'Oh, okay,' I say and then I pay the guy who brought us coffee and we continue our drive to Anjali's home.

'So are you meeting him then?' I ask.

'I might. I don't lose anything in meeting him, right? You never know who is destined for whom when it comes to things like marriages,' she shrugs.

She asks me to stop the car in the same place that we did the last time. She says that her parents came to know about my dropping her, as her landlord called up her dad and told him.

'Oh my God. Did you get into trouble then?' I ask.

'No no. My parents are cool with anyone I choose. They are very open-minded like that. It didn't get me into trouble, but it sure bagged me a date with Mr Washington.' she says and then she studies my face carefully, as though watching for a reaction.

I don't miss it at all.

Then she grabs my face and kisses me real hard. She is aggressive and I cannot help but respond.

Then she pulls away and says, 'God…you silly man. You still don't get it, do you? I love you, you fool.'

I am speechless. I am so taken aback by her directness and her candid confession.

'Bye, Aman,' she says laughing at me.

And then she gets down and walks away without once turning back.

I am so dumbstruck that all I can do is stare.

When I get back home, my mother is waiting up for me.

I was hoping that she would be asleep by the time I returned. I am in no mood for any conversation with her. The thunderstorm that is Anjali has hit me with full fury and I am still reeling in the aftermath.

'I think she is perfect. Such a sweet girl. She even took the trouble to wear a *salwar kameez* just to meet me. And she didn't drink in front of me either. I think she comes from a very good family,' my mother declares without any preamble.

'Ma, please, how do you know how she dresses otherwise? And is it so necessary to have this conversation now?' I say. I half want to add that the drink she had was laced with vodka, but I do nothing of that sort.

'It is not necessary, but it is needed. And I don't have this grey hair for nothing,' says my mother firmly.

I groan.

'Aman, it has been two years now. Each time I bring up this topic, you shove it aside as if it is of no importance. I think it is high time you took a call instead of burying yourself in your career. There is more to life than just work, *beta.* Why, in our times, we knew how to have fun. We worked hard, yes, but we did not kill ourselves like this. And I cannot understand your generation. What is there to think so much? I can see that she likes you, dotes on you, even. And you are refusing to acknowledge even to yourself how you feel?'

'Ma, I don't feel anything okay? She is just a friend,' I insist but the words sound hollow even to my own ears.

'Oh is that so? Why did you whirl her away when Mark was talking to her? I have seen more of this world than you, *beta.* Don't think your mother is an old fool. I didn't miss a thing,' she says.

I am caught out now. I cannot deny that.

'I never even think of you that way, Ma. In fact, you are one of the coolest, hippest mothers I know and I am proud of you,' I say as I give her a hug.

'You know what, you are just like your dad. So afraid to make a commitment. So afraid to acknowledge and commit to a woman. Had I left things to your dad, we would have never got married and you wouldn't have been born,' she says.

My mother, over the years, has told me a lot of stories about my father, about how studious he was, how he loved to read and how handsome he was. He was her senior in college and he had stood first in the university. He was naturally shy and my mother was bold and unabashed. She had cornered him after college one day and declared her love for him. He had bolted like a rabbit. My mother was not one to give up. He tried his best to avoid her, but my mother had her ways. Soon after college, he had got a job. My mother used to go to his office, after college and wait outside. As soon as he emerged, she would inveigle him into a conversation and he did not know how to refuse. The word soon reached my mother's father who was one of the well-known people in Gwalior as he held a position of repute at the local bank. My mother declared to him, when he spoke to her about it, that if she got married, it would be only to my dad and no one else. My grandfather then approached my dad's father and asked for his son's hand in marriage for his daughter, and that was how they had got married. I can see the happiness on my mother's face as she narrates this story once more. Whenever she does, she is overwhelmed with emotions. These are her cherished memories. Her refuge. I don't mind hearing her repeat them, over and over. It makes her so happy to recall them.

'Yes, Ma, I know,' I say and I hug her.

'See, in my times, we were so sure of what we wanted. Not like you all, the confused generation which has no certainty about anything. And let me tell you, the years I had with him, they were the happiest years of my life. Fate snatched him away from me. But oh, the time that we had. You are missing out so much, Aman. Let go, and just live.'

I want to point out to my mother that she was lucky. My father did not walk out on her and marry someone else. My father responded to her. Hers was a 'happily-ever-after' story while mine is a 'happily-has-been'. There is a huge difference in the two.

But the earnestness with which my mother is talking to me, trying to convince me about Anjali, the joy in her eyes as she talks about my father, all of it makes me just keep quiet and nod.

'Look, *beta*, if you want, I can speak to her parents. I am certain that she loves you and if you ask her to marry you, she isn't going to say no. It is up to you now.'

'I know, Ma, I know. Let me speak to her first. Then I will let you know,' I say.

'That is my son,' says my mother and she kisses me on the forehead and ruffles my hair. The joy on her face is unmistakable. She is content with my words and it shows.

I watch her for a long time after she goes to bed. Over the years she has become frail. I remember how smooth her hands used to be—they are covered with slight wrinkles now. There is more grey than black in her hair and it is thin, barely covering her scalp. Her face still looks young though, and she sleeps like a child, curled up on her side.

I think about how hard she has worked, over the years, after my father passed away. I recall how she has been strong and never shed a tear, at least not in front of me. I remember how she has struggled at her job, trying to give me as many comforts as she could. I am filled with a tenderness that is indescribable.

All she wants for me is to get married.

Mark is leaving very early the next day. He is sheepish and he hopes he hasn't caused any trouble for me.

'I am sorry, mate. For me, it is just the thrill of the chase and I think I got a little carried away last night. She is, errm… you know…quite lovely.' He looks embarrassed.

I just laugh.

'Yes, she is,' I say.

Mark might have unwittingly done me the biggest favour of my life. But for him, I don't think I would have actually figured out with certainty, my feelings for Anjali. I still wince at the word 'feelings'. Did I just think *feelings*?

My mother too has to be dropped to her college and we leave home fairly early, so that she makes it on time.

Once I drop her off, I drive back to work. I am early and there is nobody around. I am glad about that. I settle down at my cubicle and take out my phone and open the Instant Messenger. Then I take a deep breath and start a chat with Anjali.

Me: Hey there, madam.

She responds almost instantly, as though she was anticipating this.

Anjali: Hello, sir.

Me: I have something to tell you. A confession actually.

Anjali: What? Don't tell me you have the hots for Dipika and you lied about making a pass at her?

Me: Ha, ha. No, I am not going to tell you that.

God—she is making it very hard for me.

Anjali: Then what are you going to tell me?

This is my perfect chance. I am not going to miss it now.

Me: Please don't meet Mr Washington.

Anjali: Why not?

Me: Because, I love you. And I think we will be good together.

Anjali: What? I didn't get that. Please say it again.

Me: Scroll up and read it. You are the second woman I am saying these words to in my life.

Fuck...I shouldn't have typed that but it is too late now. Even in my confession of love for Anjali, there is Shruti looming in the background, as the woman I first fell in love with. Why the hell did I type that she was 'the second'. I could have done away with that little detail.

But Anjali doesn't seem to mind.

Anjali: Aman Mathur. Finally! I think we should celebrate!

Me: Yes. Friday night?

Anjali: Four days twelve hours and fourteen minutes.

Me: Amazing! You actually calculated so fast?

Anjali: Of course. Can't wait!

Later I call my mother and tell her that I have spoken to Anjali.

'Great! Did you get her parents' phone numbers? Let me not delay. I will call them straight away,' she says.

'Slow down, Ma. All in good time,' I say and as I hang up I find myself smiling and actually looking forward to Friday night.

It is on a Wednesday morning (when there are two days six hours and twenty-four minutes left to meet Anjali, which she never fails to remind me, each time we chat) that I see a mail from Shruti in my inbox. I can't believe it. It is a bolt from the blue. I blink for a few seconds.

Shruti has written me a mail? Now? After two whole years?

I find myself holding my breath as I quickly open it. There are a hundred emotions running through me as I read it. On the one hand is a strange sense of revenge, a satisfaction that she has finally written to me. She has admitted that she has not got over me. I feel vindicated to see that. I have struggled the same way for so long now that it has almost become a part of my persona. On the other hand, I feel a huge sense of sadness mingled with pain because she is unhappy. And I recognise that mixed with all this are still fond feelings for her. And the most surprising part is that I can still relate to her. Each and every word that she has said resonates with me.

I am not angry with her or even bitter.

I think for a long time whether to reply to her or not. I am not able to focus on my work. I am not able to concentrate on anything. I see two message notifications from Anjali and for the first time, ever since I confessed that I love her, I find myself unable to open her message and read it.

One mail from Shruti has caused such tumult inside my head. I was so sure until now.

I hate myself for being this way. I hate myself for still letting Shruti affect me this much.

I think for a long time on what to do.

And finally I hit delete. Then I go to the trash can and delete it from there.

'Are you sure you want to delete these items permanently?' pops up a message.

I hit yes. I am sure.

Almost.

But there is no option for that.

Chapter 27

Shruti

It is more than thirty-six hours since I mailed Aman and there is no reply from him. Maybe he hasn't seen the mail? Maybe it went into spam? There could be a chance of that. I keep checking my mail every few minutes, on my phone, till I reach office.

When I finally reach, it is already lunch time. Asha is waiting for me.

'Hey, how is your father-in-law now?' she asks.

'Looks like he will be discharged today. Rishabh is taking over from today. He is off for a week. Huge relief for me.'

'Good thing too. I think you have done more than your fair share here. Actually I feel guilty, Shruti, as it was I who suggested you take them out that day.'

'Don't be silly. I hadn't even thought of it like that. Besides, whoever anticipated his landing in the hospital.'

'True. I was just thinking Rishabh should have been pleased that you are making an effort with his parents.'

'Yes, he was too, till the hospital thing happened. After that, it has been so hectic there hasn't been time for anything. And you know what, I met someone I know at the hospital. You might have heard of him—Sanjeev Adani.'

'Oh! You know Sanjeev Adani personally? How?' Asha is impressed.

So I tell her all the details.

'Wow, you have led such an interesting life, Shruti. What fun you must have had at college.'

'Yes, it was good,' I admit. 'Maybe that is why I am having such a hard time adjusting to being a married woman now.'

'What rubbish. You were doing fine till Rishabh started this nonsense of not talking to you.'

I think about that. She does have a point, but she does not know the whole truth. On the outside, I was fine. Our married life wasn't very exciting, but I had nothing to complain about either. Rishabh was a pleasant enough guy. But deep down, I know I longed for Aman's vivacity, his ability to make me laugh and more than anything, the way he worshipped me and made me feel like a goddess. I missed that. Life with Rishabh was ordinary, mundane, boring. And it wasn't his fault.

When I get home that evening, Rishabh is already home and so are my in-laws.

My father-in-law seems more or less okay now, except for the bandage on his head. He is able to move about very easily. I feel quite sorry for them now. In Hubli, they have so many people around them and my father-in-law is like a feudal lord. Here he is helpless and totally dependent on Rishabh or me.

I feel bad that their first visit to their son's house has ended in hospitalisation.

Rishabh announces that they have decided to cut short their visit and go back early. He has already spoken to the doctors and they have said he is fit enough for air-travel.

'I am so sorry,' I tell my mother-in-law.

'For what?' she asks.

'Had we not gone on that visit that day, all this wouldn't have happened,' I say.

'What is destined, is bound to happen. We cannot control everything. We should be happy that nothing worse happened and he is okay. And honestly we enjoyed ourselves that day,' she says.

I feel a surge of relief hearing this from her. They don't hold me responsible at all. I like the pragmatic approach that my mother-in-law has taken to the whole situation. I hope that Rishabh has heard her. I look around to see if he has, but he is on the balcony busy on the phone.

Once my in-laws leave, the emptiness that existed between Rishabh and me, becomes even more pronounced. There is hardly any time left for me to travel to Bangalore and there is a lot to be organised for the recruitment drives. I come home late and Rishabh is conveniently parked in front of the television. He does not even bother to greet me or make any conversation.

The wall between us has been steadily growing and if I do not do anything about it, it will turn into a permanent one.

'Rishabh, I think we should just talk,' I say.

'There is nothing to talk about,' he replies.

'We can't go on like this.'

'We are, aren't we?'

'Come on, Rishabh, you know what I mean. Why are you punishing me for something I had no control over? For something that happened *before* I got married to you?'

'I wish I had known, Shruti. I was a fool. You lied to me

saying there was nobody. How can I trust you anymore? Almost two years with you, it feels like a sham now.'

'Rishabh, we keep going around in circles about this. You keep repeating yourself over and over again. Don't you think we should find a solution?'

'What solution? Don't you think I have a right to be angry?'

'Yes Rishabh, you do and I am sorry. I have begged you for forgiveness. What more can I do? I made a mistake and I am sorry, okay?' I don't realise that my voice has automatically increased in volume. I am mad at Rishabh for being so stubborn about this.

'Don't raise your voice, Shruti.'

'Don't tell me what I can and can't do.'

'Suit yourself then. I am not here to take any nonsense that you dish out. I will speak to you when you are calmer,' he says and he walks into our bedroom and opens a book.

I am fuming with anger. I want to shake him now. Make him see sense. I follow him to the bedroom.

'See, Rishabh, we have a good thing going. Let us put the past behind us. Let us make a new start,' I appeal to him, pushing aside my anger. If I stay calm, maybe he will be more receptive.

He does not even reply. He turns off the light and goes to bed.

I feel like I have been slapped. I slip out of bed and sit on the balcony, staring at the stars for a long time. I think about my marriage with Rishabh. I think about all that has happened.

And finally when I come to bed, I know what I have to do. It is not going to be easy, but I have to do it. There is no other way.

I have made up my mind.

Chapter 28

Aman

The sound of the doorbell seems to be coming from somewhere far-away. I struggle to open my eyes. I lie still for a few moments, groggy with sleep, trying to listen for another sound. But there is none. I only hear the comforting buzz of the fan. Then I think that perhaps I imagined it and I go back to sleep. Just as I settle down comfortably, it rings again. This time there is no mistaking it. I mutter a curse under my breath. Who the hell is it? I am in my boxers and I cannot be bothered to wear a shirt. It is probably some hired help who is ringing the wrong doorbell.

I walk to the door and open it a little bit so that I can peep out. I struggle to open my eyes because there is bright sunlight streaming in and all I can make out is that it is a woman.

'Yes?' I say not bothering to look at her, still trying to keep the sun out of my face.

'Aman. It's me,' she says.

The voice sends an electric jolt through my body drugged with sleep.

For a few seconds I think that maybe I am hallucinating. And then it registers. Slowly.

I am shell-shocked. My throat has gone bone dry. My

heartbeats have increased. In a jiffy, my sleep has vanished and I am instantly awake. This time I look at her in the eye. Just to convince myself that I am not hallucinating and this isn't some dream. She gazes back at me unflinchingly.

I almost stop breathing.

Standing before me is Shruti. She has haunted me even in my dreams, stolen my sleep, given me such a lot and yet taken away so much from my life. And now here she is, standing before me now.

'Fuck,' is all I can say.

She smiles. A smile of familiarity. A smile that says a million things without saying a word. A smile that understands. A smile that can come only from years of shared intimacy and closeness. It is as though she was expecting me to say just that.

'You look good, Aman. Can I come in?' she asks as I step aside and she walks in, without even waiting for my answer.

She wears the same perfume. God, I can recognise it anywhere. Eternity by Calvin Klein. There are a thousand emotions running though me right now. Hurt. Confusion, Excitement. Disbelief. More confusion.

I realise that I am still staring at her, like she is unreal. She has walked into my living room and made herself comfortable now.

'I am so sorry to barge in like this. There was no other way you would see me,' she says simply.

I am still gaping and somewhere at the back of my mind I am aware that I am still in my boxers.

'And yes, you look even sexier than you did the last time we met,' she says as her eyes roam all over my body and smiles.

'Excuse me, I'll just be back,' I say and I rush to the bedroom. I wear a pair of shorts and pull on a T-shirt that is lying around. Then I quickly wash my face and hurriedly brush my teeth, all the time thinking that this is so surreal.

Shruti is sitting just a few feet away in my house, in my drawing room. How the hell did she find me? How did she know my address? Why has she turned up here like this? What does she want? Does her husband know she is here? What has happened?

I hurry back outside and she is in the balcony now, staring out at the pool.

'Nice place, Aman,' she says.

I just nod and I am unable to talk.

'Do you hate me so much that you don't even want to talk to me?' she asks

I am unable to speak. Now I know what it means when people say they are tongue-tied. For the first three months after she left me, I dreamt of this scenario, every single day. I prayed for it. I hoped and hoped that she would come back to me.

And now my prayers have been answered. Except that it is two years later. Just when I was certain that I was moving on and that Shruti was a closed chapter. I would have thought that not responding to her mail would have driven the point home. Made it clear to her that I want nothing to do with her. And yet she has turned up at my doorstep and now she is asking me if I hate her.

What do I tell her? How can you hate a person who was the 'perfect one'? How can you hate four years of indelible, incredible memories, probably the happiest ones of your life? How can you hate the one you have tried so hard to get over and who yet haunts you in every single relationship that you have had since? How can you hate someone whom you compare every woman you meet to?

What Shruti and I had was pure magic. There was no

other way to describe it. But she was the one who had walked away. She was the one who hadn't answered at least hundreds of my mails. I remember the pain, the wait, the torture that she has put me through. And now two years later she has turned up out of the blue, asking if I hate her. What do I say?

'Say something, Aman. Anything. This isn't easy for me, you know,' she says, twisting her stole around in her hands. It is only then that I even notice her clothes. She is wearing an emerald green top with a deep V-neck, casual jeans and a silk stole that she is clutching. She looks bewitching. She hasn't changed at all in these two years. Short hair makes her look even younger and make her eyes seem larger.

They are fast filling up with tears now. I panic. I don't want her to cry.

'I don't know what to say. I am sorry. Please don't cry,' I blurt out without knowing what exactly I am saying.

'Can I have some coffee please? I have come straight from the airport,' she says, and I can see that she is trying to blink away her tears, not wanting to create a scene.

God—I know her so well.

'Of course,' I say and I walk into the kitchen and switch on the electric kettle and Shruti follows me.

She stands at the kitchen doorway and stares at me while I make the coffee. She likes it strong with just a spoon of sugar. I like mine with a little more milk. I silently hand her the mug and she carries it to the dining table and pulls a chair and sits down.

It is like I have turned into a zombie on auto-mode in her presence. I follow her.

'You still remember how I like my coffee, Aman? This is perfect,' she says as she takes a sip.

It is not only the coffee but I remember every single detail about you, Shruti. About us. About the magic that we shared. About how good we were together.

And how carelessly you threw it all away.

'Yes, I remember,' I finally manage to say.

She smiles again and her smile is something that does me in. But I notice now that it is tinged with sadness. There is something in her eyes that I cannot comprehend.

We sit in silence for a few seconds sipping our coffees and I cannot bear it anymore.

'Shruti, I think you owe me some kind of an explanation. What is all this about? Where is your husband? Is everything okay? Why have you suddenly turned up like this? And how did you find me?' The questions tumble out.

'Whoa, slow down. I will explain. Let me recover,' she says.

'If anyone has to recover, it is me Shruti. You at least knew you were going to see me, but heck, I am totally unprepared for this.'

'I know. That was the plan,' she says as she looks at me over the rim of the coffee cup as her hands go around it.

I have now got over the initial shock of seeing her and I am angry now. But yet I am not able to ask her to leave. Every sane and sensible bone in my body is telling me that it is what I should do. I should just ask her to disappear just as she appeared. I can then go back to my life.

'Look, I am sorry, Aman,' she says as she reaches out and places her hand over mine. I withdraw my hand quickly, like she has touched me with burning coal.

'Do you hate me?' she asks again.

'Why do you keep asking me that? Don't tell me you caught a flight from Mumbai just for that?'

'So you knew I was in Mumbai?'

'Yes,' I admit. 'I looked you up on Facebook once. Even though you had blocked me. And changed your name.'

'Aaah… yes. I am sorry, Aman. I can now say with certainty that I was not in my senses then. You know, I so desperately wanted my marriage to work. I so badly wanted to get over you and trust me I tried. I tried hard Aman. But…' She is unable to go on.

Is she telling me that her marriage is over? Is that why she is here? God—this cannot be happening. Just when my life was beginning to fit back together. Just when I finally thought that I was over her.

'Is your marriage finished? Is that why you are here?'

'I don't know, Aman. I do not know. Nothing makes sense anymore,' she says. The earlier coolness and assured demeanour when she had just rung my doorbell and walked in, is gone now. Shruti looks so sad and vulnerable that all I want to do is to rush to her, take her in my arms and assure her that everything will be okay. I fight hard to control the urge.

'What happened, Shruti? Are you okay?' I say. I cannot bear to see her like this.

'I have never felt so uncertain in my life, Aman. Things between Rishabh and me, they aren't so good anymore. We haven't spoken properly to each other in months. I do not know what to do,' she says.

So her marriage isn't over. A part of me is sad to hear that but another part of me is hugely relieved. Had she ended her marriage and walked out, I don't think I would ever have the strength to bear it, face it or accept it.

'Do you want to talk about it?' I ask.

'I don't know where to begin,' she says.

'How about we start by you telling me how in the world you found out where I lived?'

'Hmmm. I have my ways.'

'I can see that. But who told you my address? How did you track me down?'

'It wasn't so hard, Aman. I knew you were with the same organisation from your Linked-in profile. But I wasn't sure if you were in India. So all I had to do was call up your head office and ask for you. I told them I am from your college and we were trying to gather all the alumni for the golden jubilee celebrations and hence wanted to trace you. I got to know you were in Bangalore. They told me you are in the company guesthouse and even gave me the number. I called up the guesthouse and came to know that Shukla is there. I pestered him and he had no choice but to agree. I made him promise me that he won't breathe a word to you.'

'He sure kept up his promise,' I say dryly.

Shruti's eyes are damp now. 'I feel miserable now to have walked out on you like that, Aman. I was such a fool. But at that time, what I did seemed right. My mother was too ill back then. All I wanted was for her to recover.'

I don't want her to cry. She is looking at me now, waiting for me to say something.

'Two years is a long time, Shruti. I was devastated after you left. I think I must have written a hundred mails to you? Did you even read them?'

'I did. Except that I read them a week ago. And that is why I am here,' she says.

I am stunned.

'You read my mails after two whole years? And then you decided to see me?'

'It isn't quite the way you put it, Aman. I did see the mails that you kept sending. But I was going through a very hard time then. I had made up my mind to marry Rishabh. We had broken up. Whatever we had, it was over. So I didn't read your mails in detail. I merely glanced at them, without taking in the words. We hadn't exactly parted on great terms, had we? We were so immature then, Aman. Or at least I was.'

'What made you read them now?' I ask.

'Rishabh. He read all the mails between us and he was shell-shocked to know I had been in a relationship. He feels betrayed. He hasn't been talking to me properly ever since. He feels that I have wronged him deeply.'

'You hadn't told Rishabh about us?'

'No. In retrospect, I have wished a thousand times that I had. Maybe I wouldn't have been here had I told him.'

I don't know what to say to that.

God does have a cruel sense of humour. For two years I dream, wait and hope that Shruti will come back. For two years, I struggle to get over her by burying myself in work. I suffer. I hurt. And finally when I am healing, she is here.

I think about Anjali. I think about my mother. I think about how hopeful my mother is that things between Anjali and me will work out and how much she looks forward to welcoming Anjali as her daughter-in-law.

'Aman, do you think… You and I… a second chance, Aman?'

I realise that Shruti has just said something and I haven't been listening. I have been so caught up in my turmoil of thoughts which are coming down like an avalanche now. All I have caught are the words 'second chance'.

'Sorry Shruti. I haven't been listening. What did you say?' I ask.

'Was talking about us, Aman. About how we deserve a second chance. Don't you think?' she asks.

I am quiet for a long time.

Or at least it seems like a long time to me.

I have made up my mind. Some things are just fated. They may not work out exactly like how you had wanted, but they are meant to happen so you learn to grow.

'Shruti,' I say and she looks at me with eyes so full of love that I have a hard time going on. The lump in my throat feels like a million jabbing pins. There is no way out but to end this once and for all.

'Look…' I say but I am unable to go on.

'Aman, whatever it is, be honest please,' she says and she is twisting her stole even harder now.

I take a deep breath. 'Shruti, there is someone else in my life now. I am so sorry,' I say.

I can see her face fall and I can see her wince. I hate myself for having to tell her. This is the same pain that she had inflicted on me when she had walked out two years ago. And God, I know how much it hurts. I do not want to do this to her. But prolonging it will be worse torture.

'Who?' She struggles to say it.

'Someone I met and I like,' I say. Then I find myself telling her about how I struggled to get over her, how I moved to Norwich and how the box, full of things that she had given me fell out of the attic, and how I struggled with her thoughts haunting me and how I had tracked her down on Facebook. Then I tell her about how Anjali and I started exchanging messages. I tell her about how much Anjali adores me and all that she has put up with. I tell her about how she has helped me laugh and smile once more. It was like I had gone into a zone where nothing mattered except work. I had been so numb but it was Anjali who helped me feel whole again. Who made life worth enjoying once more. It is she who has stood by my side, steadfast and loyal—a true friend. The more I talk about her, the more I realise how fond I am actually of her.

Shruti listens quietly. She doesn't say a word. And finally when I finish, all she says is, 'I understand, Aman.'

It is so hard for me to see her like this.

'Look, Shruti, make peace with Rishabh. Give him time. He will come around. Trust me, I know,' I say.

She nods.

'Shruti, I think things like marriages are predestined. No matter what you do and how much you try to avoid it, you end up with certain people. Sometimes it is people you don't even think you will end up with. But the universe spins a web and things change. And you have been married what—nearly two years now? Isn't that too short a time, Shruti? Go back and make an effort in your relationship now. Be nice to him. Accept him for who he is. And you know what? When things go wrong, just keep doing your own stuff. Sometimes it helps. I know, because that is what I did. And that is what helped me.'

I feel a strange sense of relief as I say it. I feel vindicated. Light-hearted. As though a huge burden has been lifted.

There is no doubt in my mind anymore. Shruti will always be the one I cannot have. And I am now okay with that.

There is just one thing left to do. I go to my bedroom and I take out the black suitcase, my ex-box which I had shoved into the loft when I had shifted to this house. But this time, I know exactly where it is unlike that time in Norwich, when it had fallen out and surprised me. Even though it is just a couple of months since then, it feels like a million years ago.

But never in my life have I been surer of what I am doing than now. It is amazing to feel this certain.

I return to the living room and I hand over the box to Shruti.

She looks at me questioningly.

'I have to return it to you, Shruti. I have held on too long,' I say.

She opens it and I watch her as she slowly recognises all the things in it. She shuts it and tears are flowing now.

I look away.

'I guess this is it then, Aman,' she says.

'Make it work with Rishabh, Shruti. Go back to him. The people who love us—they all deserve second chances,' I hear myself saying.

'Well, I'll try,' she says and shrugs and she stands up to leave.

I want to hug her, say a bye and wish her well. But I am unable to move and my arms feel like lead.

'Bye, Aman,' she says and she walks out with the suitcase and she pulls the door shut.

I stand for a few minutes looking at the closed door.

Then I walk to my balcony, the one that overlooks the road. I see Shruti emerge. She walks down the road with the suitcase and empties the entire content into a dustbin which is full of garbage. She leaves the suitcase open next to it on top of the heap. She walks for a bit more and hails an auto.

And that is the last sight that I have of her.

I continue sitting for a while in the balcony till I see the truck approaching to clear the garbage.

Then I get up and make my way in. I call up my mother.

'Ma, I have decided that I am finally ready to get married,' I say.

'Ooooh. Finally someone has woken up and paid heed to my words. What happened suddenly? Did the sun rise from the west this morning? ' says my mother.

'I don't know about that. It's just that the sunshine reached my heart this morning and threw light on the cobwebs. Of course, I had to brush them away then,' I retort.

And even over the telephone I can feel the warmth of my mother's joy.

Epilogue

Aman and Anjali got married to each other. Anjali's mother still cannot stop boasting about her son-in-law Aman, to all her friends in Muscat. 'Sooo good-looking, very cultured and so suitable for Anjali. They make a perfect pair,' is her constant gush. She and Aman's mother get along like a house on fire, and she has already invited Aman's mother to Muscat, who much to Aman's surpise has accepted.

Shruti went back to Mumbai, after her recruitment drive in Bangalore. Rishabh came around eventually, just like Aman predicted. Shruti finally feels ready for a baby, and she intends surprising Rishabh as well as her parents and her in-laws with 'good news' sometime soon.

Aman's mother went on to start organic terrace farming workshops in Gwalior and has provided a means of livelihood to many rural women. Aman is extra-proud of his mother.

Anjali quit *Tiara* and started her own magazine called *A Bit of Time* which publishes true stories on romance, break-up, love, dating and relationships. The magazine has broken even within just six months of its circulation.

Mark went back to the UK, completely in love with India. He wants to start a travel venture to India, where he gets groups of tourists from the UK and gives them a 'uniquely Indian experience'. He wants to tie up with Aman for the same, and Aman is considering it seriously.

Sriram is still single, ready to mingle and keeps asking Anjali to find him 'a suitable girl'.

Latika gave birth to a beautiful baby boy and according to Anjali, Latika makes the 'perfect mom'.

Asha still keeps in touch with Navin and they remain good friends. They can vouch that there will always be 'The one you cannot have' and it is fine if that is so.

Acknowledgements

Whenever I write a book, this is my favourite part. Here is where I get to gush unabashedly and thank the wonderful people in my life, who I feel blessed to have, and who inspire me to write.

A huge thank you to my readers (both blog readers as well as book readers, the two are not mutually exclusive) who shower me with so much love.

To my dad, K V J Kamath, who continues to be my biggest strength. He may not be physically with me, but his spirit is very much alive. He was a great guy and an amazing individual, my dad.

To Satish, my rock, my best friend, my support system, my first reader, my first editor and in his own words, my biggest fan. A big thanks for putting up with all my moods, whims and being an awesome partner. I couldn't have asked for more. (Okay, a bit more perhaps, but I shall tell you in person!)

To my mother, Priya Kamath, who gives me wonderful story ideas, and never gets tired when I call her up at odd times to discuss what turns the plot takes and what she thinks of it. I inherit my sense of humour and the ability to laugh at any situation, from her. She is a strong woman, my mom.

To Atul Shenoy and Purvi Shenoy, who think their mother is the coolest mom in the world and for being extremely proud of me.

To Mayank Mittal, for being a great pal, for giving me inputs about each and every chapter, for encouraging me and for being just a phone call away.

To Suresh Sanyasi, for reading the entire manuscript as soon as it was sent, and reverting promptly with feedback. Your support means a lot.

To Ramya Ramjee, for believing in the book and making me feel awesome. It feels wonderful to have a match of wavelengths. It was great to keep discussing the characters and the book with you. And your enthusiasm is infectious!

To Rathipriya, who is the sister I never had. Life would be empty if I did not have you. You understand me in ways which even I don't understand myself.

To Jayashree Chinne, my wonderful friend who is so darn proud of me. A friendship of thirty years and still counting. Your support means the world to me, Jayu!

To Shabina, who believes in me and thinks the world of me.

To Niall Young, whose discipline, talent and perseverance motivates me a great deal.

To Sachin Garg, for being a great morale booster and an awesome buddy. I enjoy the time I spend interacting with you. You cheer me up and make me believe that I am a good writer.

To Nishu Mathur, into whose home I can pop into anytime, and I know I will be greeted warmly with a cup of tea. Thank you for your encouragement and thank you for telling me that the book was wonderful.

To Dipa Padmakumar, an awesome buddy, and each time we meet we simply pick up from where we left off. It is great to always be welcomed in your home and I value our friendship, Dipa.

To Gautam Padmanabhan, one of the most grounded and

down-to-earth individuals I have ever known. Thank you for being so supportive. Also you have an amazing sense of humour and a sharp wit! You have my complete admiration and respect.

To Krishna Kumar Nair and Varsha Venugopal. It is a pleasure to work with you both, and you are the epitome of efficiency and professionalism. Varsha, I have so enjoyed discussing my characters with you, and you get me perfectly.

To Gunjan Ahlawat, for a brilliant cover. To Aradhana Bisht for being a very kind and sweet editor, Paul Vinay Kumar for bringing the book to life, to Sudha Sadanand and Deepthi Talwar for making the book better, Jayanthi for telling me that she loved my books, to Rajaram Rawool, Narayana Gururaj and Sathya Sridhar for the great support. All of you are a joy to work with, and make a marvellous team.

To Sonja Chandrachud, a great friend, a superb writer, a warm and kind-hearted individual. I so enjoy our long chats, Sonja!

To J K Bose, who I respect a great deal. But for him, I would still be an unpublished writer, with my manuscript languishing in my laptop. Thank you Mr Bose!

To Kiran Manral, Madhuri Banerjee, Ravi Subramanian, Milee Ashwarya, Vyshali Mathur, Rashmi Bansal, Shinie Antony, Vani Mahesh, Manreet Sodhi Someshwar, Manjiri Prabhu, my friends from the writing world who fill me with positivity. The discussions and interactions I have had with each one of you are enriching and I deeply value your support.

To Suma Rao, for being an awesome friend and Prathibha Rajesh (Prats) who is very encouraging towards me and supports me so much.

And as always to my darling Lostris, who teaches me to live in the moment, who gives the term loyalty a new meaning, who inspires me with her zest for life, who shows me every single day that nothing matters except love and if you love somebody, you will always forgive them, no matter what.